Set in
STONE

THE STONE SERIES: BOOK THREE

DAKOTA WILLINK

AWARD-WINNING AND INTERNATIONAL BESTSELLING AUTHOR

PRAISE FOR THE STONE SERIES

"There's a new billionaire in town! Fans of Fifty Shades and Crossfire will devour this series!"
— **After Fifty Shades Book Blog**

"It's complex. It's dirty. And I relished every single detail. This series is going to my TBR again and again!"
— **Not Your Moms Romance Blog**

"This read demanded to be heard. It screamed escape from the everyday and gave me that something extra I was looking for."
— **The Book Junkie Reads**

"Hang on to your kindles! It's a wild ride!"
— **Once Upon An Alpha**

"A definite page turner with enticing romance scenes that will make you sweat even during those cold winter nights!"
— **Redz World**

"Alexander and Krystina are an absolute must read!"
— **Tracie's Book Review**

"I would gladly hand over my heart to Alexander Stone!"
— **Crystal's Book World**

DAKOTA WILLINK, LLC

Library of Congress Cataloging-in-Publication Data
ISBN-13: 978-0-9971603-4-5
ISBN-13: 978-0-9971603-5-2
ISBN-13: 978-1-954817-12-8
Set in Stone | Copyright © 2017 by Dakota Willink | Pending

Original Cover Design by: BookCoverMasterClass.com Copyright © 2017
Editing by: Silla Webb
Formatting by: Dragonfly Ink Publishing
Cover art modifications by Dragonfly Ink Publishing Copyright © 2020

BOOKS BY DAKOTA WILLINK

The Stone Series
(Billionaire Romantic Suspense)
Heart of Stone
Stepping Stone
Set In Stone
Wishing Stone
Breaking Stone

The Fade Into You Series
Untouched (New Adult Romance)
*Defined (*Second Chance Romance)
Endurance (Sports Romance)

Take Me Trilogy
(Billionaire Romantic Suspense)
Take Me Under
Take Me Darkly
Take Me Forever

Standalone Titles

The Sound of Silence
(Dark Romantic Thriller)

Please visit www.dakotawillink.com for more information.

SET IN STONE

THE STONE SERIES: BOOK 3

DAKOTA WILLINK

DRAGONFLY INK PUBLISHING

This one is for the readers...

"A woman is the full circle. Within her is the power to create, nurture and transform." ~ Diane Mariechild

1

Krystina

As I dressed for work, I looked out at the horizon through the floor to ceiling windows in the bedroom of the penthouse. The sky looked ominous. The blackened clouds off in the distance showed a heavy snowfall was imminent. I absently wondered if it would be the last of the season. I was becoming tired of the cold winter winds and was looking forward to seeing New York come to life in the spring.

Alexander, my gorgeous and delectable fiancé, stood in front of the window and was buttoning the cuffs of his fitted Versace dress shirt. I shifted my attention from the threatening skies to admire him while he dressed. From the navy silk tie hanging untied around his neck to his perfectly tailored pants, he was dressing for business, yet he displayed the powerful virility of a man in his prime. His nearly jet-black hair was still damp from the shower, falling in soft locks that barely skimmed the top of his collar. When he casually strode over to the dresser to pocket his wallet and cell phone, his movements were confident, yet sexy as hell. I felt a stirring, my lust for him always shimmering just below the surface.

As if noticing my watchful eye, he looked up at me and flashed me one of those lopsided smiles I had come to love so much. He knew he was gorgeous and knew I loved looking at him. Sometimes it was hard to believe he was mine. All mine.

Embarrassed to be caught staring, I shifted my eyes back to the darkening skies and finished fastening the last few buttons of my blouse.

"Even with the nasty weather that's brewing, I don't think I'll ever tire of this view," I said, motioning to the Manhattan skyline. I truly loved my city, and its grandeur never ceased to amaze me.

Alexander glanced absently over his shoulder out the window before moving a few steps toward me. Wrapping both arms around my waist, he pulled me close.

"I have all the view I need right here," he said huskily before brushing his lips over mine. He hadn't buttoned his shirt yet, leaving his chest bare for my touch. I skimmed my fingertips over his abdomen, up to the honed muscle of his pectorals. His soft shiver and low moan sent my heart skipping.

I returned his gentle kiss, unable to do anything but feel the touch of his lips on mine. It was as if the earth beneath my feet melted away and time seemed to stand still. His tongue grazed over mine and set me on fire. His kiss, always so possessive and domineering, consumed me. It was his signature. His stamp. And nothing else in the world seemed to matter.

Except when it did.

I suppressed a sigh as a wave of sadness overcame me and I pulled my lips from his. I rested my head against his chest, listening to the steady beat of his heart. There were times when I felt like I could stay this way forever, but those times had been few and far between as of late.

I had once thought moving in with Alexander would be a big adjustment for the both of us. Surprisingly, we settled into an easy routine with very little friction. From our morning shower schedule to planning our meals, the stereotypical domestic life had come easily. Vivian, the housekeeper, would pick up the groceries while Alexander and I were at work. She used to prepare our evening meals daily, but I eventually chose to take it over. I enjoyed it. On the days when I was unable to cook, we would either get takeout or Alexander would make breakfast fixings for dinner, as he proved unable to make anything other than an omelet.

I smiled to myself at the memory of Alexander's mad dash for the fire extinguisher after he nearly set the penthouse kitchen on fire. He had attempted to make a dish of Italian sausage and baby portabellas but underestimated the amount of grease the sausage would produce. Grease overflowed from the shallow pan he used, making for a hard-fought battle. It was one the kitchen inevitably won. I recalled watching my fiancé, a man who dominated everything in his life, be forced into submission by an oven. It may have been one of the most comical scenes I ever witnessed. I recalled laughing until my sides ached.

We were so happy that day.

That moment in time, the laughter we shared, now seemed like eons ago. Something shifted over the past few weeks and it changed our dynamic. Our relationship had become strained, although I couldn't quite pinpoint when it all began. I only knew Alexander's controlling nature was taking over our lives. I was beginning to feel lost, like I didn't know who I was anymore.

"Where are you?" Alexander asked, breaking me away from my thoughts. I looked up at him and cocked my head to the side innocently.

"What do you mean?"

"You seem far away in thought."

I wanted to tell him what I was thinking. I knew I should tell him how I felt. He needed to know how much he was literally dictating *everything*. From the building of our new home to the discussions about our pending wedding, he wielded his full power and left me little room to express my wants or desires.

No, Krystina. Not a good idea, Krystina. Don't do that, Krystina.

While I understood his past dictated who he was, his need for order and control was becoming stifling. Something had to give. I couldn't breathe. Even still, I loved him so much it hurt. The tension between us was killing me. I wanted my Alexander back. I wanted us back. I only wished I knew when the balance had shifted so I could fix it.

Not wanting to voice my concerns and start the day with an argument, I smiled and stared deep into the sapphire eyes I adored so much.

"Not far away," I assured him. "I'm right here. Where I belong."

I moved my arms up to wrap them around his neck. The light from the nearby lamp sparkled off of my left hand and caught my attention. Tilting my head up, I held out my hand to look at the diamond and sapphire ring Alexander had placed on my finger.

It was a symbol of hope and the dream of a white picket fence. I smiled every time I looked at it. It was a sign that even two people like us, as messed up as our pasts were, could still find happiness. I knew he would give me all that and more. It was a reminder that things between us would get better. Relationships were full of ups and downs. Lately, I felt like our honeymoon phase was already over, although we hadn't even made it to the altar yet. I told myself this was just a bump in the road and nothing more.

I wrapped my arms tighter around his neck, pulling his hard body closer to mine. His hands trailed up and down my spine before coming to rest at my waist. I felt a tug and realized he was attempting to pull my blouse free from the waistband of my skirt.

"Oh, no you don't, mister! We'll never get to work on time if you start that," I joked and untangled myself from his arms.

"I kept you up late last night, angel" he said with a wink.

I laughed at the devilish gleam in his eyes.

"Yes, you did," I agreed. My cheeks began to redden as I thought about the passionate love we made the night before. As strained as things had been, sex was never an issue for us. Our passion for each other was the one thing that could erase all the problems from the day.

"So, take the morning off. Go in after lunch time."

"Mmm...now that's a novel idea," I murmured.

"Good. I'm glad you see things my way," he said, as if the matter was settled. "A morning off is just what you need."

It was then when I realized his suggestion wasn't a joke. It was a command.

"Wait. I didn't think you were serious. I can't take the morning off," I laughed, trying to keep my tone light. "I have too much to do."

He pulled away from me and frowned, worry lines spreading over his beautiful features.

"I'm sure whatever it is you have to do can wait. Besides, you can use your home office to handle anything pressing."

"I can't just show up at work whenever I please. I have a responsibility, not only to Turning Stone, but also to the people who work for me," I pointed out.

His frown deepened. He appeared to be contemplating my words, but thankfully didn't push it further. Instead, he took a step back and began to fasten the buttons of his shirt. Sadly, I knew the tender moment we shared just a second before was now over. Turning away, I moved towards the walk-in closet to retrieve a pair of heels.

"Have it your way. You've just been very tired lately. I don't want you to become run down." He paused and seemed to remember something. "Speaking of being run down, Hale has been stretched pretty thin trying to run security for the both of us. There have been too many schedule conflicts and it's making me uncomfortable. I asked Hale to line up someone else to take over your security detail and chauffeur responsibilities. He starts next Monday. Hale will bring him by your office this afternoon so the two of you can get acquainted."

I stopped on my way to the closet and turned back to him.

"Alex, I don't need a bodyguard or a driver. Do you think it's really necessary to hire someone else?"

"Absolutely. Like I said, Hale is swamped. He can't do it all alone."

"No, you're misunderstanding what I mean. I don't use public transportation because you don't want me to, which I understand even though I got along fine with it for years. The Porsche you gave me just sits in the parking garage at Cornerstone Tower because you insist on Hale driving me everywhere. I can get around on my own," I said with a shake of my head. "You worry too much about me."

"Krystina, you're failing to recognize a very important factor. You're with me now. That became public the minute we exited the car at the Stone's Hope Charity Ball together. You can't be alone. The press will eat you alive."

I laughed.

"I think I can handle a reporter or two, Alex," I assured, attempting to keep the conversation lighthearted. However, the smile faded from my lips when I saw the seriousness of his expression.

"The only reason why you haven't seen your face all over

the tabloids is because I've shielded you from it. They have learned to leave me alone, at least for the most part, because I refuse to give them anything. You, on the other hand, are fresh meat."

I shook my head sadly.

"I think you're being a little paranoid. It can't be that bad," I said gently. I placed my hand on his arm for reassurance, but he wasn't having it.

"This will not be a debate. I'm not taking any risks with your wellbeing or your safety, Krystina. Not again," he insisted firmly, casting me a knowing look.

I knew what he was referring to. He didn't need to spell it out for me.

If it wasn't for that damn car accident...

My stomach tightened as images from that awful day flashed before me. It was more than just a car accident.

Kidnapped. Locked in a trunk. Charlie and Trevor.

I shuddered, still able to hear their menacing voices in my head. I could still feel the panic. I could still smell the stale odor from the trunk and hear the crunch of metal when the car rolled. The memory raised the hair on the back of my neck and goose bumps peppered my arms.

Don't think about it.

I tried to push away the thoughts about that terrifying day, only to have them evolve to the gut-wrenching weeks that followed. I often wondered if those weeks were harder than the incident itself. I didn't like to remember how vulnerable Alexander had been. To see such a strong and utterly alpha man completely broken from worry as he sat by my hospital bedside was something I would not soon forget. I squeezed my eyes shut in an attempt to block out the horrific experience.

Trevor is dead. He can't hurt me anymore.

It was over and time to move on. However, I knew Alexander was right. While I may have thought he was overreacting about the press, Charlie was still a very big concern. If Alexander felt I needed my own personal bodyguard, so be it. It would be smart to concede this one thing.

"What's the name of the security detail who will be coming to see me?" I acquiesced, knowing I would have a bodyguard whether I agreed to it or not.

"Samuel something or another," Alexander replied absently as he shrugged into his suit coat. After knotting and straightening his tie, he glanced at his Rolex. "It's almost seven. Hale will be here shortly. Are you sure I can't convince you to take the morning off?"

"I'm sure," I told him firmly.

"Alright then. I just need to grab a few things from my home office, then we can be on our way. Oh, and one more thing," he added. "I have a stylist coming by in the morning to fit you for a dress for Matteo's grand opening."

My eyes widened in surprise.

"A stylist? Are you serious?"

He looked at me, seeming perplexed by my question.

"Of course, I'm serious. Why would I joke? I'm not sure if anything I purchased for your wardrobe is suitable," he stated matter-of-factly and motioned to the closet full of clothes he provided for me. "The restaurant is named after you, after all. You'll need to be dressed for the occasion."

I thought of the massive walk-in closet full of designer clothes, none of which I purchased for myself. In fact, the only name brand clothes I owned prior to meeting Alexander had been purchased by my mother.

"Well, yes. I suppose..." I trailed off, at a loss for words, wanting to scream.

Maybe I want to shop for a dress myself!

"Good. The stylist will be here at nine. That should give you plenty of time to choose something," he informed me, oblivious to my astonishment.

Speechless, I nodded. I could only wish there was a way for us to go back to the place we were last night. Naked, in each other's arms, as if the world and all its troubles did not exist. But that was out of my control; just as dressing myself apparently was too.

2

Alexander

After walking Krystina to her office in Cornerstone Tower, I made my way to my own office. Entering the elevator, I punched the code into the keypad that would take me up to Stone Enterprise on the fiftieth floor. As the elevator ascended, I mused over Krystina's behavior from the morning.

She was off. Very off.

I saw her bristle when I mentioned the stylist, but it was for her own good. Hitting Fifth Avenue on her own would leave her vulnerable. If I could take her shopping myself, I would. Unfortunately, my day was full. I had too many contracts to review and I couldn't rearrange any of my meetings.

Nonetheless, I thought there was something more than just the stylist that was bugging her. I could not put my finger on it, but Krystina hadn't been acting right for a few weeks. Our relationship seemed tense, her temper was shorter than normal, and she seemed visibly exhausted. I attributed all of it to the long hours she had been working. While this week might have been her first week back to Turning Stone Advertising since the accident, she had poured over client files for a solid week before hand. It was apparent the rigorous schedule had taken its toll on her and burnout was imminent.

I urged her to take it slow, but she was too damn stubborn. She went in with a full head of steam on day one. It was time I put a stop to it. I missed my angel. If it meant I had to tie her down to keep her healthy, so be it.

I envisioned Krystina being tied down. Naked. Instinctually, my cock twitched.

I haven't pulled out the ropes lately. Perhaps I should tonight.

I mused over the thought as the elevator chimed the arrival to my floor. I exited the lift and acknowledged Laura, who was already behind her desk tapping away on the keyboard of her computer.

"Morning, Laura."

"Good morning, Mr. Stone," my assistant greeted in return. "Your schedule for the day is printed and on your desk. Will you be needing me to go over any of it with you?"

"No, Laura. I looked over the emailed version of it on the ride here. If I need anything, I'll let you know."

"Very good, sir. I just forwarded you an email from The Carnegie Corporation. You're being considered for the Andrew Carnegie Medal of Philanthropy for the contributions the Stoneworks Foundation makes to the city. The winner will be announced at the Governors Charity Ball."

Fucking great. Another dinner to attend.

Being considered for the award was an honor, but I didn't need the recognition. The Stoneworks Foundation did a lot for the city, but it was not the only foundation to do good deeds. As far as I was concerned, there were many others who deserved the recognition and publicity over me.

"Send the email to Justine. She can handle it," I dismissed. "Anything else?"

"Yes. You should also know PR called. They are still fielding questions about Mr. Charles Andrews. They'd like to know if you changed your mind about making a statement."

"No, I have not. Stephen has been in touch with the DA and both agree it should wait until after the trial. We don't want a media spin to give the defense an edge."

"I'll tell them, Mr. Stone," she said and turned to pick up the phone. Leaving her alone to talk to the Stone Enterprise public relations team, I headed into my office.

Once I reached my desk, I sat down and fired up the computer. I skimmed through the slew of emails that had come since last night and went over my schedule for the day. My morning and afternoon were jam-packed, as I was still paying for taking so much time off after Krystina's accident. Resigning myself to the hefty workload, I got straight to it.

Clicking on the emails by order of priority, I shot off the responses needed to those working on building permits. Construction invoices were forwarded to Bryan, my accountant. Acquisitions were another beast entirely. Schmoozing over the owners of the potential properties I wanted to acquire required more time and finesse. I opened an email from John Benson, the owner of a derelict fifteen-story apartment building in Chicago, only to find he decided to up the list price.

Damn it! The greedy bastard is no different than Canterwell.

I shook my head. I wanted that building badly. It was a great location with a lot of potential, but not for the increased price tag. The projected renovation would be costly if I wanted it to become something worthy of the Stone Enterprise name. I fired off a quick rejection reply, knowing the stingy old man would come around eventually.

I made sure to copy Bryan in on my response, knowing my accountant would be happy I decided not to budge on my initial offer. I just had to play Benson's game for a little while longer. He would come around, and when he did, I would be ready. A few cocktails and a couple of greased palms should be all that was needed to secure the deal nicely.

The next email was from Justine. The subject line was blank. Assuming my sister was sending me something to do with The Stoneworks Foundation, I opened it. I was surprised to see it was just a short note informing me about a date change for Charlie Andrews' trial. It had been moved up. My eyes moved to the top of the email to see the recipients. She had copied in Stephen, my lawyer.

Good.

However, her email wasn't sitting right with me. I frowned. It wasn't because the trial date had been changed. These things happened. Not to mention, I had been putting pressure on Thomas Green, the District Attorney, to speed things up. What bothered me was the fact the news came from Justine in an email. She normally came to see me personally or called when it came to matters with her ex-husband. But then again, Justine had been noticeably absent as of late.

Since Krystina's car accident, it was like she fell off the grid. If it weren't for communications regarding Stoneworks, I wouldn't have heard from her at all. I often wondered if she was harboring guilt over what happened. I made a mental note to call her later in the day. At the very least, we needed to talk before the trial and make sure we were on the same page. But I knew my sister, and I also knew a phone call to her would not be a quick one. I fully expected her to be a bundle of nerves over the upcoming trial. She would be looking for a project to distract her and I just happened to have the perfect thing in mind for her.

My intercom buzzed and Laura's voice came through the line.

"Mr. Stone, your eight o'clock is here."

I glanced down at the neatly typed schedule Laura had left on my desk. Samuel Faye, the security detail Hale had uncovered, was scheduled to meet me at eight. I wanted to go over a few things with him before he met with Krystina.

"Send him in, Laura," I replied.

When Samuel Faye entered my office, I was surprised to see how different he looked in a suit. At our initial meeting, he wore frayed jeans and a tattered t-shirt. His hair was dusty, and two days' worth of stubble covered his face. Hale explained that Samuel had just come off work at a construction site, a temporary job he took on after leaving the Navy. Regardless of his unprofessional attire, Hale had given Samuel a strong reference and his military background spoke of his competence. But I recalled his handshake more than anything. It was firm. Sturdy.

Now, here he stood, dressed in a neatly pressed navy suit. Clean cut and polished. His dark hair was cut with precision and sharp intelligence marked his brown eyes. He looked younger than I remembered, a detail that shocked me somewhat since I'm normally more observant. I assessed him again and my eyes narrowed into slits. He cleaned up good. Too good, in fact. And this was the man I was going to put in charge of Krystina's wellbeing. He would be everywhere she went, mirroring her daily activities, and watching her every move.

Unease and jealousy swirled in my gut. I pressed my lips into a tight line and tried to shrug off my suspicion, as it was completely baseless. Hale was fond of Krystina and he knew me very well. He wouldn't have chosen Samuel if he couldn't be trusted.

Still, I didn't stand as he approached my desk. I stayed where I was, eying him coolly, as he stretched his hand out to me. It was an arrogant power play, but a necessary one until he learned his place.

"Mr. Stone. It's a good to see you again, sir," Samuel greeted formally.

I leaned forward and returned his handshake. It was exactly

as I remembered it. Strong. A lot could be said about a person through a handshake. I pushed the nagging worry aside and focused on that until I could get a better read on his character.

"Have a seat Samuel," I told him and motioned to one of the two chairs in front of my desk. He immediately sat, his back ramrod straight, posture assertive and perfectly correct. If I peered around the desk, I was confident his heels would be together and his toes apart. Just like Hale, Samuel Faye was a military man, through and through.

"Please, sir, call me Sam."

"Sam, I know Hale and I have already gone over the job expectations with you. However, I have a few other concerns that you should be aware of before your meeting with Krystina." I paused and took in his attentive gaze while he waited for me to elaborate. Out of pure curiosity, I switched gears and asked, "Why did you accept this job, Sam?"

"I have the utmost respect for the Commander, sir," he began, referring to Hale by his retired Navy status. "Commander Fulton expected only the best from the men who served him. I know that to be true even after he retired. When he approached me with the opportunity, it was an honor."

"That's it?"

He tossed me a knowing smile.

"Well, the money you offered was kind of hard to turn down too."

He laughed lightly after his final statement. It was true. The salary he was used to didn't even compare to what he'd be getting from me. Nonetheless, he needed to know this was not about earning a quick buck.

"Money cannot be your motivation. Krystina will not be just a paycheck to you."

Samuel sobered instantly.

"I never thought she was, sir."

"Good. You should also know she's stubborn and doesn't

think she needs you for protection. I have no doubt she'll be resistant. Don't let that deter you. It's not your job to win her over. Her safety is of the utmost importance here. Hale and I have done a good job of shielding her, but she's naïve."

"Sir?" he questioned.

"Don't misunderstand me. Krystina has a brilliant mind, but she isn't used to being in the public eye. I've already addressed social media usage with her. She no longer uses Facebook or any of the other social platforms, but you should still monitor that just in case. However, I suspect the press is going to become a problem in the very near future." I leaned back in my chair and crossed my arms. "There's a court case coming up soon, one that's sure to cause a big stir. Hale has been working to ward them off, but they're like dogs after a bone. It won't be long before they make an attempt to get to her for a story. You cannot allow the press near her. In the off chance they do get to her, 'no comment' is all you or she needs to say. Do you understand me?"

"I understand, sir."

I narrowed my gaze and leaned forward on my desk before speaking again.

"One last thing. Krystina is everything to me and she is about to become my *wife*," I warned, emphasizing the last word and allowing it to sink in. "Don't forget that."

The statement was my not so subtle way of telling him to protect Krystina at all costs, but it was hands off. His eyes widened, but only for a moment before he quickly recovered.

"I won't forget, sir," he promised with a nod.

"I'm glad we understand each other. Now, my original plan was to have you start on Monday. However, the court case I mentioned has been moved up. I'd rather have you in place sooner, allowing more time to get yourself acclimated to the position. Take the morning to get your affairs in order. Krystina is expecting you later this afternoon. Consider yourself on the clock from that point forward."

Samuel and I went through the final motions of signing paperwork to get him on the payroll. Once we finished, I sent him on his way. I had a mountain of contracts to get through and couldn't afford to spend all afternoon ensuring my message to him was clear. In the off chance I wasn't, I would make sure Hale kept a watchful eye on the young security detail.

Before long, it was nearing two o'clock. I sat back in my chair and rubbed my hands over my face. My eyes hurt from staring at the computer all morning and the early afternoon. I detested long days in the office where I did nothing but pour over buying contracts. I hated reading the fine print even more. I preferred a more hands-on approach when working on business deals, but a few time sensitive property acquisitions had not allowed that today.

My stomach growled, reminding me I'd skipped lunch. Giving my eyes a break from the glare of the computer screen, I stood to walk over to the mini-fridge to see what was available. Working lunches were a norm for me and Laura knew to keep it stocked for the occasion.

Opening the refrigerator, I perused the contents. Settling on half of a ham sandwich and an energy drink, I went back to my desk. After I was seated once more, my email pinged with a new notification. It was from Krystina.

TO: Alexander Stone
FROM: Krystina Cole
SUBJECT: Reminder

I'm sure you know, but since we never discussed it this morning, I just wanted to remind you about our appointment with Dr. Tumblin after work today. Try to be a little more open to things today. Please. For me.

Love you,
Krystina
XOXO

I scowled, a knot of dread forming in the pit of my stomach.

Like I would actually forget about the damn shrink.

A sort of restlessness began to set in as I thought about the upcoming appointment. When Krystina made the suggestion to go see a psychiatrist together, I should've known better than to agree to it so quickly. We had been seeing Dr. Tumblin for the past month and, as far as I was concerned, the appointments were nothing but a waste of time.

Tumblin wasn't telling me anything I didn't already know. Every week he dragged us through the gauntlet, insisting we discuss a past I would rather leave dead and buried. And worse, every session meant an increased risk of him learning the truth about where I came from. When he poked and prodded into those issues, my back went up.

However, Krystina felt therapy was necessary, even if it went against every fiber of my being. My privacy had always come first and foremost. I guarded it well. Keeping an open mind was a goddamn struggle, yet I tried. I had to for her, despite the fact I was failing to see any sort of positive impact. I was still experiencing frequent nightmares and Krystina seemed more withdrawn than ever.

I looked down at the sandwich that was half eaten. Suddenly, my appetite was lost, and I pushed it away before typing my response.

TO: Krystina Cole
FROM: Alexander Stone
SUBJECT: Re: Reminder

I haven't forgotten. And yes, angel. For you, I will try.

Alexander Stone
CEO, Stone Enterprise

I hit send, and my thoughts drifted back to the strained air between Krystina and me. My gut told me it was because of these damn appointments, and not because she was overworked. I just couldn't be sure. However, if it was work related, I may be able to remedy that problem.

I recalled the list of potential clients Krystina told me about over dinner last week. Acting on instinct, I buzzed Laura through the intercom.

"Laura, get Sheldon Tremaine on the line."

It was time to call in a favor.

3

Krystina

I clicked the door closed behind the brooding Samuel Faye, my newly appointed shadow. He was polite, formal. And positively boring. Sure, he was well built, fit. I'm sure he would provide ample protection against whatever it was Alexander thought I needed protection from. I just hoped he would stop referring to me as ma'am in the very near future. It made me feel old.

Nevertheless, I gave him his first job assignment. Since I had no plans of leaving the office today and I would be with Alexander all evening, I told him to take the rest of the night off. There was no sense in wasting payroll dollars. I was pleased he did as he was told without question. I think. I wasn't sure if Samuel would be taking direction from Alexander or me. More than likely, it wasn't me, but I couldn't waste time worrying about it.

It is what it is.

Returning to my desk, I went back to sorting emails. It was a slow, painful process I'd been struggling with all week. I created three folders: one for rejected proposals, a second for prospects, and a third one for projects in the works. As I clicked on the next email, I superstitiously crossed my fingers and hoped it wasn't another rejection.

"Damn it!" I swore aloud to my empty office. It was another thanks-but-no-thanks response for our services. I clicked off the email from the potential client and sent it to folder number one. I tried to shrug off the rejection.

Sometimes things just don't go as planned, Cole. Shake it off.

However, if I were being honest with myself, not much of anything had gone as planned all week. No matter how hard I tried, things just seemed to go from bad to worse. Tilting my head from side to side, I cracked my neck and tried to stifle a yawn. Fatigue was setting in and I still had a long night ahead of me. In an attempt to summon more energy, I sat up a little straighter in my chair and extended my arms in a stretch. Looking around, I surveyed the entire length of my office.

Alexander had pulled out all the stops to make sure everything was perfect for me. Not only did I have an entire floor of Cornerstone Tower at my disposal, I was able to call one of the poshest offices in the city my own. It was everything I ever dreamed of. From the floor to ceiling windows and polished hardwood desk, to the sprawling wall mural with the Maya Angelou quote, it was an impressive space. At times, it was hard to believe it was mine. The fact it was all mine only solidified my determination to fix the predicament I was in.

And it was a big one.

Focus, Cole.

I sighed to myself and spun my chair around to flip on the office stereo behind me. Using the music as motivation, I turned back to my computer, determined to stay focused on the task at hand.

My first week back to work since the car accident had been rough. When I proposed buying Turning Stone Advertising from Alexander, I had high hopes. The company held great potential and only lacked in direction. I truly felt it wasn't anything a little elbow grease couldn't fix.

However, after spending nearly three weeks in a coma, then another five weeks resting as per doctor's orders, my business affairs had been put on the back burner. My employees kept the ship afloat during my absence, as they were used to operating with little instruction before I came along. Nevertheless, they allowed seventy-five percent of the potential contracts I had lined up to fall through the cracks while I was out. They weren't the most pro-active group of individuals to say the least. As a result, the direction and progress I made when I first took over Turning Stone had to be revisited. My ideas to make the advertising company take flight were suffering from more than one major setback.

Conversely, the buyout contract I signed with Alexander was airtight. I made sure of that, and I refused to play the fiancé card. Just because I was now engaged to the sole owner and billionaire CEO of Stone Enterprise, didn't mean I could shirk my responsibilities and commitments.

I couldn't play the damsel in distress role even if I tried.

Either way, the circumstances for how and why I got into this position didn't matter. They wouldn't change the simple fact I was short on clients and one-month delinquent on my buyout payment to Stone Enterprise. I was back to square one. My only option was to keep plugging away.

Moving the computer mouse to click on the next email, I absently hummed along to "Walk" by the Foo Fighters. I smiled to myself when I realized how apropos the lyrics were to my current situation. The singer sang about finding your place and conquering challenges, which is exactly what I felt like. It was like I was learning to walk again.

As I waited for the email to load, a knock at my door interrupted me.

"Come in," I called.

Regina poked her head in.

"Sorry to interrupt, Miss Cole," my secretary apologized. "But I wanted to tell you this in person rather than just buzz your line."

My stomach dropped.

Please don't give me more bad news.

I quickly exited out of my inbox and gave Regina my full attention.

"No worries. What's up?" I asked, attempting to come off casual. Like I wasn't terrified of losing yet another client.

She flashed me a bright, if not a somewhat devious, smile and the corners of her eyes crinkled. I took it as a good sign. If she were giving her notice, she wouldn't be smiling like the cat that swallowed the canary. I tried to relax a bit.

Regina sat down in the chair across from me and smoothed out her long floral skirt.

"Mr. Tremaine called," she informed me.

I raised my eyebrows in disbelief, hoping beyond hope it was the Mr. Tremaine I wanted it to be.

"Sheldon Tremaine, the owner of Beaumont Jewelers?" I asked just to be sure.

"The one and only. He read over the proposal you sent to him on Wednesday, and he wants a meeting. I offered to schedule one with Clive, but he wants to meet with you directly."

I tried to keep my jaw from hitting the floor.

"Regina, that's great news! Did you set it up?"

"Yes, ma'am. It's already in your calendar. You are set to meet a week from today. He seemed very anxious to sit down with you, actually. He's going to come here, despite the fact I told him you would go to him."

I relaxed and leaned back, trying to absorb what she was saying. A meeting with Sheldon Tremaine of Beaumont Jewelers was a huge deal and exactly what I needed. He was one of the largest diamond distributors in the city. If I signed his jewelry business as a client, I could rest easy knowing the expenses for Turning Stone would be covered for the next year, including the buyout payments to Stone Enterprise. I couldn't afford to screw this up.

"We are going to need all hands on deck next week to get ready for this. Turning Stone needs this contract," I told Regina. "Please schedule a mandatory staff meeting for Monday morning. We'll need to prepare a full portfolio, including mockups, before I meet with Mr. Tremaine."

"Consider it done."

"Thanks, Regina," I said and beamed at her. It was a relief to finally have something positive in the works.

"It's good to see you smile, Miss Cole. I knew this would brighten your day. I know it's been a crazy first week back, but things will get better. I just don't want to see you kill yourself in the meantime." She paused and gave me a tentative smile. "Try not to do everything alone. Accepting a little help from the fiftieth floor when it's offered isn't a bad thing."

I cocked my head to the side and narrowed my eyes at her. When Alexander found out how buried I was, he offered to send his personal assistant, Laura Kaufmann, down to my floor. He thought she could help me get caught up, but I refused him. This was something I needed to do for myself. Turning Stone was my baby and it was my job to fix it. The fact Regina noticed was surprising. I didn't think she was so observant.

"Am I that obvious?" I asked her.

"When I leave for the day at five, you're still here burning the wick at both ends," she pointed out. "The time stamp on your emails tells me you've been pulling at least twelve-hour

days. I don't want to see you worn down. If there is one thing I
learned while you were out, it's that this place needs you."

"I'm a big girl, Regina."

"I know you are," she said and stood to leave. "But I'm old
and I worry."

I laughed. Regina was barely fifty.

"You're not that old!"

"I could be your mother, so I say that's old enough," she
joked back. "I'm headed out in about a half hour. Is there
anything you need before I go?"

I glanced at the clock. It was nearing four-thirty. I had to
meet Alexander in the lobby at five.

"No, I'm all set. In fact, I'll be leaving around the same time
as you are."

"Alright then. Enjoy your weekend."

"Thanks. You too, Regina," I returned and watched her exit
my office.

Feeling optimistic about my schedule for next week, I
powered down the computer and began to sort through the
piles of client folders sitting on my desk. As I put them away
into the file cabinet, I tried to switch gears and mentally
prepare for the next order of business for the day – the therapy
session with Dr. Tumblin. In an instant, my good mood
vanished. I was truly dreading the appointment, even if it was
entirely my idea.

After I finished putting away the client files, I grabbed my
coat and purse. Hitting the switch to power off the lights in my
office, I took a deep breath and tried to let go of the tension that
was already beginning to set in my shoulders.

Maybe Alex won't be so resistant today.

I tried to be hopeful, but I wasn't really feeling it. Round
four of therapy was less than an hour away, and it literally felt
like I was about to head into a boxing match. The sessions
weren't going well because Alexander had been fighting them

every step of the way. As a result, I had been snappy and short tempered with him over the past few weeks. I couldn't help it.

Bite your tongue. Don't snap at him today.

I repeated the thought to myself another three times as I closed the door to my office. Making my way down the corridor to the elevator, I steeled myself for what might lie ahead.

4

Alexander

"Laura," I said into the intercom on my desktop phone.

"Yes, Mr. Stone," she immediately responded. That was the best thing about my personal assistant – she never kept me waiting. Ever. Her incredible efficiency was one of the reasons I could power through my work days so seamlessly.

"Did Sheldon Tremaine get in touch with Turning Stone?"

"He did, sir. A meeting has been scheduled for next week Friday with Miss Cole."

I smiled, pleased everything was going according to plan.

"Excellent. And you made sure he knows to be discreet?"

"Yes, Mr. Stone. I made that very clear."

"Good. The last thing I need is for Krystina to find out I arranged the deal for her," I said with a frown as I considered the potential fallout. "She won't like it."

Laura hesitated before responding, but when she finally spoke, I could hear the amusement in her voice.

"No, I don't imagine she would be very happy."

I chuckled to myself. Laura was quickly learning Krystina's independent, if not stubborn, nature. Not happy was an understatement. Krystina would be livid if she knew I called in a favor to get her that contract, even if it was one she desperately needed. Bryan had given me the numbers. I knew she was struggling. Still, I had to admire her tenacity and determination to make it on her own. In a way, she reminded me of myself when I first established Stone Enterprise.

"Keep me apprised on the outcome of that meeting," I told Laura.

"I will, sir. Anything else?"

"Just one more thing. I'll be leaving the office in a few moments. Tell Hale I won't need him to drive us tonight. I plan on taking the Tesla."

"Yes, Mr. Stone."

I hit the end button on the intercom and spun around in my chair to look out the tall windows in my office, completely oblivious to the Manhattan skyline before me. From fifty stories up, I had a front row seat to some of the most sought-after real estate in the country. Instead of appreciating the view, my mind was on Krystina. I thought again about how tired she seemed this morning.

She's doing too much, too fast.

The last thing she needed was to end the week with the psychiatrist she had been so adamant about us seeing. I had to find a way to convince her to drop it. It was nonsense. The more I thought about it, the more I was convinced my instincts were correct. Yes, Krystina was over worked, but the tension between us began weeks before her return to Turning Stone. It all began after we started seeing Dr. Tumblin. We had been through enough. We didn't need some head-nutter to come between us.

Turning away from the windows, I stood to put on the suit coat that was slung over the back of my office chair. It was time to change strategies. If Krystina didn't want to see what this was doing to us, then it was up to me to make her see it. That was one of my strengths after all. Convincing others to see things my way was what propelled me to the top of the real estate game. I just needed to take the emotional aspect out of the situation and use that strength to my advantage.

After leaving my office, I made my way to the elevator that would take me to the lobby of my building. During the descent, I contemplated how I should finesse Krystina into my way of thinking.

I could simply refuse to go.

I frowned, knowing that wasn't the solution. The problem was, my usual patient diplomacy was failing me. I relied heavily on that patience to achieve success. Yet, with Krystina, it seemed to fail me at every turn. The woman, as much as I loved her, drove me completely insane. Nothing ever seemed to be in order whenever she was involved.

My temper was another concern. It flared more often than not during our appointments. To me, that was a very dangerous sign. The blood running through my veins was poisonous, and I couldn't afford to lose control. Not again. I already lost it once with Krystina, and I couldn't allow a repeat occurrence.

Images of her facial expressions from that emotionally exhausting day on my yacht came to the forefront of my mind. It was the day I told Krystina about my past. I practically choked on every word I uttered that night, despite knowing she needed the truth about my parents. I had been wound tight, and the anxiety caused me to snap.

"Alexander, you're hurting me!"

Her words were a constant echo in my dreams while I slept. Her eyes, horror stricken as my hands encircled her throat. Her beautiful lips, twisted into a grimace of pain. Yet, even when the sunrise came to chase away the darkness, the memory of what I had done still haunted me.

I cringed from the recollection. Even though it happened months ago, at times it felt as if it were only yesterday.

Forget it. It's in the past. There's no changing it.

I shook my head to clear it. I learned an important lesson that day, one I wouldn't soon forget. I was reminded of the many fundamental reasons why I had to maintain order and control in everything surrounding me. However, these therapy sessions almost felt like a power exchange. I needed to put an end to them. Too much was at stake.

When I reached the ground floor, I exited the elevator and walked down the corridor toward the lobby. I spotted Krystina near the main doors. Her back was to me, and she appeared to be looking down at her phone. My eyes skimmed up her legs, past the hem of her skirt, to the delicious view of her behind in the custom-tailored suit.

Perfection.

The corners of my mouth turned up in appreciation. Setting her up with my personal tailor for her business attire was a small stroke of genius on my part. While Krystina had good taste and looked stunning in everything she wore, my tailor had sculpted skirts and pantsuits that fit her flawlessly. Nevertheless, I couldn't wait to get her home where I could rip it off. I imagined pushing the hem of her skirt up to her slender waist and wrapping those lithe thighs around my hips. My balls tightened as I thought about burying my length inside her, filling her with my seed.

Oh, you'll be begging for it tonight, Miss Cole.

As I came up behind her, she must have sensed my presence because she turned to face me. Never one to ignore her beauty, I took in her face. She had the most elegant jawline, hard yet soft. Her full lips never failed to draw me in, and it was difficult not to imagine them wrapped around my dick. She looked as beautiful as always, but she was also pale and a little drawn. Faint circles shadowed the underside of her deep brown eyes.

Damn it!

Not wanting to stir up another argument about the long hours she kept this week, I suppressed a frown and threw her a casual smile instead. Wrapping an arm around her waist, I pulled her close and placed a gentle kiss on her forehead.

"Ready to go, angel?" I asked.

"Ready when you are," she said and smiled in return. However, it didn't quite meet her eyes. Krystina's emotions were often written plainly on her face and I could read her like a book. Her forced smile was obvious.

She's just as tense as I am over these damn appointments.

To me, it was just another reason we shouldn't be having them. Choosing not to voice my thoughts, I stepped back and took hold of her elbow to lead her out of Cornerstone Tower toward the parking garage. When we reached the deep metallic blue Tesla, I waited for her to properly fasten her seatbelt before pulling out of the parking space.

Once we began the short drive to Tumblin's office, I noticed she was unusually quiet. The only sound that could be heard in the car was from the radio, a sultry tune by Bishop Briggs. Another day, I may have suggested I add the song to one of the playlists I made for her a few months earlier, but today wasn't that day. Her uncharacteristic silence told me something was bothering her. This was more than just tension over the appointment.

I glanced in her direction. She was staring out the passenger window of the Tesla as I braked for a red light.

"You have that look again," I told her.

"What look?"

"Like you did this morning. Lost in thought," I remarked offhandedly.

"I was just thinking about our meeting with the builder

next week. I'm curious to see the architects plans for the property in Westchester," she commented.

I noticed her tone lacked any sort of excitement and sounded somewhat flat. I also noted how she referred to it in a very impersonal way. She spoke of it like it was just a parcel of land, as if it wasn't *our* home we were building. It was disappointing and troubling. She should have shown more enthusiasm about building our home together, but she seemed detached whenever the subject came up.

"Yes, I'm looking forward to you seeing the plans too. I think you'll like my ideas and what he's drawn up to implement them," I murmured absently, and I observed her pallor once more. "Are you feeling alright, angel?"

"I'm fine. Just a little tired. I would kill for some caffeine right about now. Do you think we have time to stop for coffee?" she asked.

"You shouldn't rely on coffee so much, Krystina. It isn't healthy for you. Besides, if we stop, we'll be late for our appointment."

She frowned and looked at the clock on the dash.

"Yeah, you're right," she agreed and turned to stare out the window again. She cleared her throat and I couldn't help but to notice she sounded slightly congested. I wondered if she was showing the beginning signs of a head cold.

The light turned green and I hit the accelerator, although I had half a mind to turn around and head for home.

She should be in bed. Resting.

"We can reschedule our appointment if you'd like? I know it's been a long week for you," I suggested tentatively, even though I already knew what her answer would be.

"No, Alex," she sharply dismissed. "This is important. We finally started making progress last week."

"Hmm," I murmured. What she called progress and what I called progress were entirely different things.

As if noticing her clipped response, she placed a hand on my knee, gave it a light squeeze, and smiled at me.

"It will be okay," she said, adapting a softer tone. "Like I said in the email, just try to keep an open mind today. In fact, both of us need to take a different approach to this. We can find a middle ground here. I know we can."

"Perhaps."

Or perhaps we scratch the whole fucking thing.

I glanced down at her hand resting on my knee. The passing street lights glinted off the diamond and sapphire ring I placed on her delicate finger nearly two months earlier, a symbol she would soon be mine. All mine.

It was strange to think about my life before meeting her. I was successful and wealthy, having never once dreamed of settling for just one woman. From clubs to subs, jumping from one woman to the next had simply been easier. It meant no emotional attachments and a hell of a lot less risk. Until death do us part was never once on my radar.

Until I met Krystina.

She made me realize how dull and mundane my life had actually been. When I proposed marriage to her, she truly shocked me by saying yes. I expected her to put me off or question it in typical Krystina-like fashion. I assumed I would have to work to get her to see my way of thinking, but she had barely put up any sort of resistance whatsoever. She simply said yes. At that moment, I was the happiest man alive.

I was still somewhat astounded by my sudden urgency to settle down, but it wasn't an unwelcomed feeling. After our chance meeting in a grocery store, she sent my world into a tailspin and she unknowingly changed me. Each day she made me feel new and unfamiliar emotions. She made me realize I didn't want to live my life in solidarity any longer. I knew on the day I met her, I wanted her. I haven't looked back since.

I cast a sideways glance at her ring again.

Mr. and Mrs. Alexander Stone.

I want that. Now.

If only she would stop dragging her feet.

While Krystina had been steadfast in her commitment to marrying me, her actions showed otherwise. It wasn't one particular thing she did or said, but more about the way she avoided discussing any sort of plan. I wanted to get married sooner rather than later. Having our relationship officially set in stone as soon as possible was my top priority. She, on the other hand, was content putting off our wedding for another year or more.

I had no intention of waiting a year and her unwillingness to go over any of my proposed plans was grating on my nerves.

"So, I talked to Justine today," I casually mentioned.

"Oh? I haven't seen her in a while. What's new with her?"

"Her nerves are shot. Did you see the email I forwarded you about the date change for Charlie's trial?"

"Yeah. I saw it was moved up."

"In my opinion, the pending trial is getting the best of her."

"I think all of us are a bit keyed up over that," she murmured. "I can't wait for it to be done so we can put this behind us."

"I couldn't agree more, angel. I couldn't agree more. But I know Justine. I think a project would be a good distraction for her right now. She doesn't handle being bored or anxious very well."

"So, you've told me," Krystina replied with chuckle. "I could talk to her about the program I'd like to launch at the women's shelter. She might be able to help me brainstorm ideas for helping the rape victims who come to Stone's Hope. That should keep her busy enough. Unless, of course, you already gave her something to do."

"Actually, I did. I told her to start researching wedding planners, locations, and florists. It's something I should've thought of sooner. Party planning is what she does best, plus it will get the ball rolling for us."

"Alex, we haven't even settled on a date yet, or the type of wedding we want."

I pursed my lips in annoyance as I stared at the traffic on the road ahead. I wanted to point out the only reason we didn't have a date was because she wouldn't set one, but then I thought better of it. I didn't want her to get riled up, so I maintained a neutral tone.

"The wedding can't be anything extravagant, Krystina," I stated firmly. "Don't overthink it. Simple is best."

"What if I want a big fancy wedding?" she asked quietly. Her tone was subdued, but I could sense the challenge in her question at the same time.

I turned to look at her, only to find her brows furrowed. I fought the urge to reach out and smooth the creases between her eyes.

"Is that what you want? A big wedding?" I asked, hoping her answer would be no. A big wedding was simply out of the question.

She frowned.

"No, not really."

I breathed a sigh of relief.

"Good, because it's not an option. Less media attention is better. I've had my fill of warding off the press as of late. They've been like vultures ever since the accident, and Charlie's trial has them chomping at the bit," I spat out loathsomely. "Justine understands that, and she'll communicate it with whomever she chooses as a wedding planner."

"Oh. So, *Justine* and *her* chosen wedding planner are going to decide on it all then?"

Her quiet tone was gone, replaced by an extremely sarcastic one. The emphasis she placed on my sister's name wasn't lost on me. When she pulled away the hand that had still been resting on my knee, I could almost hear the warning bells go off.

Careful, Stone...

"I told her to get with you on the details, angel. Don't worry," I placated.

"I see..." she trailed off, quiet and distant once more.

She was clearly upset over something I said. I pressed my lips into a thin line, trying to figure out what it was. We continued to drive in silence, the tension crackling in the air between us.

I slowed the car as we approached the building that held Tumblin's office. After maneuvering into a parking space, I overrode the automatic power down of the Tesla by pressing the emergency brake, effectively killing the ignition. I then turned to face Krystina. The lighting from the street lamps cast shadows over her face and emphasized the dark circles under her eyes.

"Are you sure about this, angel? You look really tired."

There was a lengthy pause before she responded.

"Alex, you know I'm sure. It's you who isn't."

The bitterness in her voice made me grimace. Her uncanny ability to read through me never failed to be unnerving.

"Krystina –."

"Let's just go in, Alex. We're going to be late," she interrupted. And with that, she didn't bother to wait for me to come around and open the car door for her. Instead, she opened it herself and got out.

I slammed my palms against the steering wheel.

Fuck!

Her abrupt exit from the car was infuriating. However, as I watched her make her way toward the building, my stomach felt like it had lead in it. I was reminded of the last time she exited the car without me; it was the day Krystina left me at

Club O. I thought I lost her, and it was a moment in time I never wanted to repeat.

I rubbed my hands over my face and took a deep and calming breath to rein in my mounting temper. Resigned to another round of psychological warfare, I climbed out of the car and followed her inside.

5

Krystina

"Miss Cole, can I get you anything while you wait? Tea? Coffee?"

I looked up at the pleasant and motherly face of Patricia Ward, Dr. Tumblin's attentive receptionist. She had a soft voice that was calm and soothing. I suspected that was part of the reason she was hired. A glance around the waiting room would show more of the same. Calm and soothing. As if the muted pastels were a strategic design plan to make a patient relax; to make them feel like they weren't about to go through an emotional cyclone upon entering the private office of Dr. Joseph P. Tumblin.

"Coffee would be fantastic, Patricia. Thank you," I said.

I sat back in my chair and began to tap my foot, clocking the minutes until I would be called into Dr. Tumblin's office. As we had in previous weeks, I spoke with him first, then Alexander took a turn. After we each had our private sessions, Dr. Tumblin would sit down with us together to discuss what was talked about during our one-on-ones. I wasn't sure if I liked the current arrangements, but Dr. Tumblin insisted we try it.

The receptionist came over to me with a cup a piping hot coffee. The aroma was like heaven to my nose. Handing me the cup, she pointed over to an area on her left.

"Cream and sugar are right over there on the minibar. Please, help yourself," she told me before retreating back to her desk.

I stood and walked the few steps to where Patricia had pointed. Adding a few dollops of cream and an individual package of granulated sugar, I stirred the coffee absently while thinking about how Alexander might be reacting to the things I discussed with Dr. Tumblin.

He's probably going ape-shit right about now.

I shook my head and thought back to the night when I mentioned to Alexander that he and I should go to therapy. I had no idea it would turn out to be this difficult. I thought it was a good idea. After the car crash, life seemed to come full circle and I didn't want the nightmares of our pasts to interfere with us anymore. We had our whole lives ahead of us and I wanted nothing to hold us back. He was my everything. My dark knight. He was my heart and he set my soul on fire.

However, I was starting to wonder if my insistence to attend therapy was a good one. Alexander warned me. He said he wasn't a fan of shrinks. That was the understatement of the year. I just wished he could see what I saw – a tormented man, haunted by the demons in his past. I witnessed his turmoil almost every night while he slept. I hated when he awoke from the nightmares ripping him apart. It nearly broke me. I felt it was imperative for us to work through this.

Together.

Unfortunately, Alexander was having none of it. His value for privacy took precedence. I wasn't allowed to mention certain parts of Alexander's past, making it difficult to speak freely to Dr. Tumblin. The only thing he knew was that Alexander's parents were dead. Nothing more.

I took a sip of the coffee and winced from the bitterness. It certainly was *not* anything like the coffee La Biga would've served, but at least it was caffeine.

Beggars can't be choosers.

I sighed to myself and reclaimed my chair in the waiting room. Settling in, I went over our conversation during the car ride here. It was frustrating. I tried to keep my cool but knew I had failed miserably. The minute he mentioned his sister's involvement in our wedding plans, it became a real struggle to bite my tongue. His domineering nature was taking over all aspects of my life. Of our lives. Navigating his needs with my own was a difficult balancing act. I understood Alexander's demand for control, but he was taking it to a whole new level. I just wanted to scream.

What about me? Don't I get to plan my wedding? Don't I get to have a say in the house we are going to live in together?

I looked up when I heard the door to Dr. Tumblin's office open. The psychiatrist smiled kindly at me.

"Are you ready, Krystina?" he asked.

"As I'll ever be," I joked with a slight grin, even though I wasn't really kidding.

When I walked into the office, I found Alexander pacing like a caged animal. Despite his obvious agitation, I couldn't help but to take a quick moment to admire the way he could own any room with just his mere presence. Standing over six feet, he commanded power and radiated prestige. I would never tire of watching him. Even when he was angry, he was impossibly gorgeous.

His dark waves were wild, as if he had been running his hands through them in frustration. His rumpled hair only added to his Adonis-like appearance. His sapphire eyes flashed when he saw me come in, and his lips were drawn into a grim line. Nevertheless, his apparent anger didn't stop the magnetic pull I felt whenever I was near him. He was like the other half of my soul, and at times I felt like I couldn't breathe without him.

I fought the urge to go to him, wanting nothing more than to melt into his arms and completely forget about the therapy session all together. However, the tension in the room could be cut with a knife. I hesitated, not wanting to make the wrong move and potentially make a bad situation worse. Afraid to utter a word, I quietly sat down on the plush peach colored sofa in the office and ran my hands over my skirt in an attempt to keep them from fidgeting.

"Alex, why don't you take a seat?" Dr. Tumblin suggested.

"I'd rather not," Alexander responded curtly. He wasn't even attempting to cooperate.

So much for trying to find a middle ground.

"As you wish," Dr. Tumblin said and directed his attention to me. "Krystina, Alex and I revisited the concern you mentioned last week."

"Krystina and I have already talked about this," Alexander hissed through gritted teeth. "She knows where I stand on the matter. Having further discussion about it is pointless."

Dr. Tumblin's face remained impassive. Alexander's jaw had an angry tick. I took it as a warning sign, as I knew it meant he was nearing his breaking point.

"Krystina is concerned about the increased frequency of your night terrors," Dr. Tumblin said patiently, despite Alexander's obvious agitation.

"My night terrors?" Alexander questioned mockingly, as if the term was the most ridiculous thing he'd ever heard. "Is that what we're calling them now?"

"Yes. What we haven't discussed is the content of them. The content, as well as Krystina's theory about why they might be occurring, holds merit and is worth exploring. She mentioned you used to attend a BDSM club."

Alexander's eyes flashed angrily in my direction. I winced and looked away. I knew I was going to be in major trouble for divulging that little snippet of information.

"Your point?" Alexander snapped testily.

This isn't going well at all.

I huffed out a breath from frustration. This convoluted idea of therapy was proving to be a failure, as almost all subjects were off limits. Alexander held too many secrets, making any sort progress near impossible.

"BDSM was a big part of your life. You have used it as an outlet," Dr. Tumblin calmly pointed out before turning to me. "Krystina, let's talk about your concerns a little more in depth. Shall we?"

"Well, it wasn't a huge concern. I only brought it up because I thought there might be a connection. I don't know," I said with a shrug.

I'm not the doctor. How the hell should I know?

"Why do you feel like there is a connection?" he probed.

"Because Alex's nightmares have been coming more and more frequently. Nearly every night," I added, glancing nervously in Alexander's direction. His nightmares were the touchiest subject of them all and I had to proceed with caution. "I only wondered if the frequency has anything to do with his decision to step back from the more extreme BDSM lifestyle he was used to. I worry that, without the outlet he had for so many years, his demons are possibly manifesting in other ways."

I shrugged and looked down at my hands. Despite my efforts, they were fidgeting in my lap. I clamped my palms together to still them and focused my attention on the subtle circular patterns in the office carpet. I knew I shouldn't have been nervous about the conversation taking place. After all, this was one of the reasons we were here.

"Alexander, what are your feelings about that?" Dr. Tumblin asked.

"I *feel* like I've already explained my position on this over a hundred times. But, since we are being so open all of a sudden, I will tell you what I told her. Yes, I turned to BDSM at a young age. It was an outlet for a time. I've done things, a lot of things, many would call freakish. Hell, I was a member of a sex club for Christ's sake! Fucked up, right, Doc? But it doesn't define who I am. I've told Krystina this before. I haven't...we haven't," Alexander corrected, motioning his hand back and forth between us. "We haven't given up BDSM. We are anything but vanilla, not that what I do with my fiancée is any of your business. I just dropped the club scene. It's not an outlet for me anymore because I don't need it to be, and it certainly isn't the sort of place I want Krystina to go to."

"But Alex, if it's something you need –" I stopped when he swore again.

"Jesus fucking Christ, Krystina! Is this really about what I need? Or you? The problem is, you have no goddamn clue about that world. What you saw at the club doesn't even begin to scratch the surface of what really goes on. Do you want to be a collared submissive? Caged? Do you want to be dragged around in black leather with the other submissives, on your knees and sucking off your Master? Bowing to his every whim, even if that includes sharing you with another man or woman?" He paused and narrowed his gaze on me. His sapphire eyes burned dark, almost navy in color. "Yeah, that's right. If I wanted to, I could share you and you wouldn't be allowed to question it. I'd own you. So, tell me. Do you want me to break you, Krystina? Is that what you want?"

He spat out the harsh questions like he was demanding my answers, although he already knew what I would say. I winced from his words and my cheeks flushed pink. He was speaking as if Dr. Tumblin wasn't even in the room. A shiver ran down my spine, and I shook my head.

"No," I told him quietly. "I don't want that. I didn't think you did either. You told me you weren't an extremist."

"And I'm not. That's why I was able to adjust to being with you so easily. I chose you. I knew I didn't want another random whore who spreads her legs for any man willing to dominate her."

My stomach rolled from the thought of him being with someone else. And not just a random whore, but any woman at all.

"Alex..." I trailed off, unable to find the words I needed to explain my rationale.

"Listen to me, Krystina. I was done with that life the moment I met you. Bringing you to that club, even if it was only once, was a mistake. I only want what you can give me. Nothing more. I no longer need that life to be an outlet for me. And, quite frankly, I'm not seeing how any of this connects to my nightmares."

"I'm not saying it's connected," I interjected. "It really was just a passing thought last week. I probably shouldn't have said anything."

"You're right. You shouldn't have!" Alexander snapped.

"Please, Alex. Calm down. Lashing out at Krystina isn't the answer," Dr. Tumblin placated. "Perhaps we are discussing the wrong thing here. Tell me, why BDSM? What was it an outlet for?"

"Why don't you ask Krystina? Apparently, she's been a wealth of information lately," Alexander spit out. His fury caused me to blanch again.

"Look, I'm sorry for divulging your damn secrets, okay? I

just can't figure you out lately," I said, and my voice cracked. I could feel the sting of tears from frustration in the backs of my eyes, but I refused to let them shed. "It's not only your dreams. It's everything – from the wedding, to the house, and even my wardrobe! It's like your need for control has intensified, and it feels like I'm navigating a minefield half the time. Maybe I'm way off the mark, but I'm just trying to make sense of it all. That's how I came up with the theory about you and the change in your BDSM lifestyle."

"The mind works in mysterious ways, Alex. You know this," Dr. Tumblin said softly.

Alexander abruptly stopped his rapid pacing and whipped his head around to stare at Dr. Tumblin. I stilled when I saw the set in his jaw. The temperature in the room dropped dramatically. Ice was near forming. By comparison to how heated he appeared just a moment before, Alexander suddenly looked arctic. When he finally spoke, his voice was eerily calm.

"Yes, it does. And right now, my mind is telling me our time here is up."

"Alex, we still have another thirty minutes," I pointed out, shocked he wanted to leave so soon.

He turned to look at me.

"No. It's time to go."

In the blink of an eye, the calm façade was gone, replaced by genuine anger as he hastily slipped into his navy suit coat. We were clearly done with our appointment. Alexander was, as usual, calling all the shots. Feeling awkward and embarrassed by Alexander's outburst, I stood up and began to put on my jacket.

"Perhaps we've accomplished enough here today," Dr. Tumblin said as he came around the desk he had been sitting behind. He had a worried expression on his face. "Krystina, please call if you need anything. In the meantime, Patricia will schedule the next appointment for you on your way out."

"Krystina will not be calling you and there isn't going to be another appointment," Alexander announced with an air of finality.

"Wait. What?" I asked incredulously.

"You heard me. I'm done."

6

Alexander

The entire ride back to the penthouse went by in silence. Krystina hadn't muttered a single word, which was completely fine with me. I was so revved up from the damn session with the shrink and I wasn't thinking clearly. I was too furious over the fact she told him about the club. Any discussion at this point would only end badly. We would never go back to see Dr. Tumblin again, of that I was sure. There was only one thing that would fix the state of things between Krystina and me.

When we pulled up to the front of the penthouse, I got out of the car and walked around to open the door for Krystina. Cold wind whipped around us and I held open my suit coat to shield her from the worst of it as we made our way inside to the lobby.

Jeffrey, the blithering doorman for my building, quickly stood and hurried out from behind the lobby's security desk upon our entrance. He had been staring down at his phone

the mere idea of being denied, but her resistance was also a turn on. At times, I didn't know if I wanted her to submit or to fight, but the thought of breaking her was amazingly arousing and my cock grew harder at the idea. I would have her submission and she knew it.

Her cheeks were flushed, and her eyes were like molten fire. But it wasn't from anger. That look said she comprehended what was coming. She knew we were about to settle this like adults. Naked.

I groaned and pressed my lips to the shell of her ear.

"You're fucking gorgeous when you're aroused."

"I'm not," she tried to refute. However, her labored breaths betrayed her.

"You are. I know that look in your eyes, angel. Your cheeks. Your breathing. I know you're already wet. You won't deny me."

I pressed my mouth to hers once more, fisting one hand through her lush curls while my other kept hers pinned securely behind her back. Although, she made a slight attempt to resist, I wouldn't allow it. My dominant side was coming out. Powerful and blinding. I took her fully, assaulting her with my tongue until she was like malleable putty.

I released her hands and pulled her hips tighter against mine. My cock throbbed as I pushed up against her, and a fire coursed through my veins. She had stopped fighting me, but I could also tell she didn't want to surrender. However, she knew she had to. She knew I had to win. When her arms flew around my neck and her fingers began to intertwine through my hair, I smiled inwardly. Victory never tasted so good.

There's my angel.

My message to her was clear and needed no explanation. She understood my authority. There would be no more talking and no more arguing – at least for tonight. Krystina and I required that physical connection to bring us back to where we belonged. I needed to feel her body, warm and submissive, under mine. It was the only thing that could erase the tension between us.

The elevator doors opened to the foyer of the penthouse. We both stumbled out, tearing at each other's clothes with an animal-like frenzy. She kicked off her shoes as I slid her skirt off with expert precision. When she was in nothing but her bra and thong panties, I brought my face down to her breast, biting at a taut nipple through the thin lacy material of her bra. She gasped and threw her head back, her need now just as hot as mine. Her gentle moans and bodily responses to my touch were the strongest of aphrodisiacs, driving me to the point of madness.

God, how I fucking love this woman...

I flicked my tongue up the side of her neck and stopped to nip at her ear. Her fingers fumbled with the buttons of my shirt as I loosened my tie. The rapid succession of her breath matched mine, both of us fueled with nothing but pure carnal need. Impatient, I ripped the shirt apart, causing the buttons of the cotton Versace to scatter over the tiled floor.

"Oh! Your shirt!" she said with surprise when she realized what I had done.

"Who cares? I have others," I growled, sealing my lips over hers once more.

Sliding a hand down her smooth belly, I slipped inside her panties to find her wet slit. The minute I found her pulsing nub, she sucked in a sharp gulp of air.

"Alex!" she hissed against my lips, raking her nails across my back. I slid a finger inside.

"Oh, angel. I knew it. You never disappoint me," I murmured, appreciating how ready she always was for me.

Her hips pushed up against my hand, searching in desperation for quick release. I grunted, not wanting to waste another minute. The need to be inside her was fierce. In one swift move, I bent to scoop her up from behind her knees and cradled her in my arms. Moving to the dining room, I set her down on the sprawling table and laid her back. She was trembling. Desperate.

"Oh, god..." she breathed, writhing beneath me. "Please, Alex. I need to feel you."

I loved it when she begged.

"Give me your hands," I ordered. She complied immediately as I ripped off the tie still hanging loose around my neck. Wrapping the tie around her wrists, I secured it with a tight knot. Dipping my head under, I positioned her bound hands so they were resting at the base of my neck. "Don't move, angel. This is going to be rough."

Her eyes flashed with desire, causing my cock to throb and ache, knowing I was so close to feeling her snug heat. I reached down to quickly unfasten my belt and dropped my pants to below my hips. My erection sprung free, craving the constriction of her moist walls.

Bracing one hand on the table for balance, I used the other to notch the throbbing tip to the outside of her waiting entrance. In one quick thrust, I plunged my shaft through her tight clasp until it was completely sheathed. I let out a groan of pleasure.

"Oh, yes!" Krystina cried out.

Cupping her ass, I pulled her body closer to mine and shifted my feet to get the leverage I needed to drive all the way home. And for me, when my cock was buried deep in her body, I was home. It was the place where I claimed her to be mine. I was her conqueror and I owned her. I lurched forward again, and she let out a gasp as her body worked to accommodate my girth.

"That's it, angel. Take me. All of me."

The rippling of her heat drove me wild, but I held steady as I waited for her to get there. I hissed through clenched teeth and pushed harder. By the time I felt her clench around me with her building orgasm, I was ready to explode. Invigorated by the feel of her slick walls, I increased the speed of my thrusts.

"Alex!"

"Yeah, baby. Say my name. I want to hear you scream it."

Over and over again, I impaled her. Her eyes rolled back, and her moans turned into screams. She came around my cock, her wet canal slathering me on all sides. Her cry of release was all I needed to lose myself. It was my turn.

I sunk deep and hard until my seed burst forth, filling her completely. I came with such a violent force, I was left shuddering and trembling in her arms.

7

Krystina

I lay limp in Alexander's strong arms, our rapid heartbeats slowly returning to a normal rhythm. During our crazed sex frenzy, we somehow made it to the bedroom and went at it another two times. The only time we paused was to grab a quick bite to eat in between rounds. Even then, Alexander was still touching me, caressing my breasts as he hand fed me bites of local artisan cheeses and a variation of seasonal fruits.

I lazily swirled my fingertip over his chest, feeling completely and utterly spent. I loved how he could make me forget everything in an instant. With his gorgeous face taut with desire and his expression filled with something much more tender, I wanted nothing more than to erase the turmoil between us and just feel. And do that, he did. Time and time again.

"How do you do that?" I murmured.

"Do what, angel?"

"Make everything go away. We went from wanting to rip

each other's throats out, to ripping each other's clothes off. You're awfully sneaky, Mr. Stone. Do you know that?"

"I just know how to tame that sassy mouth of yours," he laughed.

I propped up on one elbow and stared down at him.

"My sassy mouth? I believe you were the one to have a tantrum in Dr. Tumblin's office," I pointed out.

Alexander didn't say anything at first but reached up to tuck a loose tendril of hair behind my ear.

"Shh, angel. No more fighting," he said firmly and placed a finger over my mouth to silence the argument I was about to make. Cupping the back of my neck, he pulled me back down to rest my head against the side of his chest.

He's right. No more fighting.

Nevertheless, there was still a very important issue that needed to be addressed. It wasn't about today's therapy session, as that was a dead issue. Based on his reactions in the office just a few hours before, I knew we wouldn't be going back. It didn't matter. Even I was failing to see any benefit from it. There were too many secrets that needed to stay hidden, and progress would be limited because of it. However, therapy or no therapy, I couldn't ignore Alexander's overly controlling ways as of late. He had to tone it down a bit before I snapped.

I went back to tracing small circles over his pectorals and thought about how to bring it up. I really didn't want to argue, so I had to carefully choose my words so as not to sound confrontational.

"Alex, ever since I was released from the hospital, you've made all the decisions. I know it's just your nature, so I let it go for a time. But...lately, I feel like I'm starting to lose a little bit of myself," I said quietly.

"Krystina, you know why I have to be in control. It's who I am."

"Yes, and I understand that. But I worry about after we

marry. Marriage is supposed to be a partnership. Certain things should be decided together, if you know what I mean," I explained cautiously. I glanced up at his face to see his reaction. When he merely raised an eyebrow at me, I continued on. "When it comes to our house and our wedding, I want to plan them together. I don't want you to make all the decisions for us."

"Angel, I've asked for your input," he tried to counter.

I pursed my lips and tried to suppress the building agitation. He truly didn't see what he had been doing. Choosing a different way to approach the situation, I swung a leg over his hips and sat up so I could straddle him. He pushed his hips up against me, and I could feel his erection begin to harden, the head of his thick cock pressing against my entrance. How he was able to even think about round four was beyond me. His sexual appetite was insatiable. I for one wouldn't be walking straight for a few days at the very least.

"No funny business," I scolded playfully. "I'm trying to have a serious conversation here."

"Is that why you moved to sit on top of me? Is this a power play to make you feel more in control?"

"Maybe," I said with a guilty smile.

"Okay, angel. I'll give you this, but only because I'm curious about what's been bugging you. Besides, if you have something to get off your chest, I'd rather you do it when you're naked," he added with a cocky smile. A wicked gleam flashed in his sapphire eyes.

My stomach did a flip, stirring with renewed desire, and it was a real struggle to stay focused. The more he looked at me that way, the more I felt like round four was definitely imminent. I ran my hands up and over his chest, appreciating the hard lines of honed muscle. Not bothering to suppress a groan, I leaned down to kiss the side of his neck and breathe in his scent. He was intoxicating. As long as I lived, I would never get enough of this man.

"Maybe we should talk about this tomorrow," I murmured into his ear.

"Oh, no you don't, my little sex goddess. Quit paying attention to the devil on your shoulder for a minute," he told me, and I could feel the vibration of his laughter.

"Hmmm...but the devil is so much more fun," I replied, playing along with his joke about my cartoonish self-conscious that plagued me every once in a while.

I flicked my tongue around the lobe of his ear, but Alexander wouldn't be deterred. Pushing me up to a sitting position, he looked pointedly into my eyes.

"You wanted to talk. Let's just do this now and be done with it. What's bothering you?"

Knowing I shouldn't put it off, I reluctantly placed my hands on my thighs so as not to be distracted by him.

"Well, you said you asked for my input. You really haven't, Alex. The conversations were always about decisions you already made."

"Such as?"

"Take the house in Westchester for example. You and the architect worked on the plans. You've designed the layout of everything. We are almost ready to break ground, yet I haven't even seen the blueprints. There is also the wedding. You decided it should be a small intimate affair, which I'm not opposed to. However, for all you knew, maybe I wanted to fly to Las Vegas to elope."

"That's out of the question," he stated firmly. "Vegas is such a cliché. Not to mention, I think it's a foul city. We would never get married there."

His statement just further proved my point.

"Do you see what I mean?" I asked and gave him a small I-told-you-so smile.

His eyes narrowed before the comprehension dawned.

"You've got me there, angel. Well played. What do you propose we do?"

He flashed me a sexy, crooked smile. I knew then that I had gotten through to him.

"I think we should start with the basic fundamentals and take things one step at a time. I'm pretty sure we are in agreement about the size of the wedding. I really don't want to go to Vegas, and a big flashy wedding just isn't me. So, a smaller, more intimate affair is good for me if that's what you want."

"Whatever works, angel. I just want to make you Mrs. Alexander Stone. To officially claim you as mine," he said with a coy smile as he reached up to cup my breasts.

"Stay focused," I scolded and pushed his hands away. "I'm going to have to talk to my Mom about all of this too. As much as she drives me crazy, I want her to be a part of it all."

"Wow, I didn't realize you wanted me to stop touching you so badly. Bringing up your Mom? Talk about a mood killer."

I shook my head and chose to ignore him, continuing to talk since I finally had his attention about what I wanted.

"I was also thinking about the stylist who's supposed to come here tomorrow. Can I cancel the appointment?"

"Why would you want to do that?"

"Well, I thought I could text Ally. I haven't seen her in a while. If she's free, I thought maybe she and I could go shopping tomorrow for a dress for Matteo's grand opening. She probably needs to get one too. And..." I paused, suddenly feeling sheepish.

He looked at me quizzically.

"And what, angel?"

A slow grin spread across my face, the abashed feeling being replaced by unexpected excitement.

"We can't have a wedding if I don't have a dress," I explained.

"I suppose you're going to tell me I can't go with you."

"Of course, you can't go! You're not allowed to see the dress before the wedding!" I exclaimed, totally aghast at his suggestion. "I'll just be trying to get ideas anyway. Who knows? I might not even find anything I like. Then there's the issue of bridesmaids and groomsmen. If we decide to have them, I haven't really thought about a color scheme. A shopping trip might give me a starting point at the very least."

"You're rambling, Krystina," he said and began to laugh. It was a full, throaty sound that was contagious, and I found myself laughing as well.

"I'm sorry. I didn't mean to get so carried away."

"I don't mind at all, angel. Your enthusiasm is a welcomed change. But if you insist on shopping without me, I do have one condition."

The sudden wave of laughter I had a moment before came to a screeching halt and I immediately sobered. I knew what he was going to say, but I asked anyway.

"What's your condition?"

"Hale and Samuel have to accompany you."

I knew it. So much for a girls' day.

"Both of them?" I asked, genuinely surprised he would think I needed two security guards.

"Yes, both. Samuel is a little wet behind the ears. While my expectations for him are clear, shadowing Hale for a day or two will be beneficial. However, I understand having them there might seem intrusive. I'll make sure to tell them to stay out of sight. You won't even know they are there," he tried to assure.

"Hmmm...we'll see about that," I murmured. I tried to imagine how two men, as tall and broad shouldered as Hale and Samuel were, could manage to stay hidden in a dress shop. The idea was almost laughable.

"I'm happy to see you show some eagerness for the wedding, angel," he told me as he tenderly tucked a stray curl behind my ear. "Is this why you've been so distant whenever I'd bring it up? Because you want to have a say?"

"Yes," I told him with a nod, pleading with my eyes for him to understand.

He ran his hands up and down my arms softly.

"Why didn't you say anything sooner? I thought you were just trying to put me off."

I closed my eyes and released a sigh. Shifting so I could lay back down beside him, I nestled into the crook of his arm and placed my hand over his heart.

"I love you so much, Alex. I didn't mean to seem like I was putting you off. I can't wait for the day I become Mrs. Alexander Stone. But I know how you need to be in control. I just let it go too far this time. Before I knew it, I felt like I was suffocating. I'm sorry for not speaking up sooner."

"I will admit, you've been a royal ball of sass these past few weeks. At least now I know why," he said with a light laugh.

"Let's not fight anymore," I told him and snuggled in closer.

"I'm a realist, Krystina. I know with you that will never be possible."

"Maybe," I admitted with a yawn.

Alexander tucked the satin comforter around us, wrapping us together in a tight cocoon. My eyes grew heavy as I stared out the massive windows covering the far wall in the bedroom. Wispy clouds moved slowly over the quarter moon, mesmerizing me into a near dreamlike state. When Alexander reached up and began to stroke the top of my head, I sighed in contentment.

"At the risk of sounding like I'm ordering you around, I'm going to tell you to go to sleep. You've had a long week and I don't want you to be too tired for tomorrow night."

"Yes, it has been a long week," I agreed sleepily. "How do you suppose the turnout will be tomorrow?"

It was all I could do to stay awake to hear his answer.

"It's my oldest friend's restaurant and it's named after my fiancée. Curiosity over that alone will draw a large crowd. The press is inevitable, but Matteo needs the publicity. All reporters who will attend have been thoroughly vetted. Still, you should be prepared for the gossip mill, Krystina."

"People are so nosey."

I could feel his chest vibrate as he laughed lightly again, but he never stopped rubbing my head.

"Yes, they are. But don't worry about that now. Just go to sleep, angel."

Not needing any further coaxing, I closed my eyes. Exhaustion hit me like a ton of bricks. In a matter of seconds, I felt my body slip away blissfully until all conscious thoughts ceased to exist, falling into dreamless and much needed sleep.

8

Alexander

I place my hand on the knob.

Fear consumes me. I know what's on the other side.

Justine.

And him.

I don't want to open it. I know I have to because I'm the big brother. Justine needs me. The door swings open, but everything is wrong. It's not my home.

What's this? Where am I?

I see the river.

Then I see her! It's my mother!

She's standing near the water's edge. I need to run. I have to get to her.

I run as fast as I can. Left foot, right foot, left foot. With every stride I take to close the distance, that flowing ebony hair gets further and further away.

No! Don't go away! I'm almost there!

The muscles in my legs feel like they are on fire, but I need to keep going.

Almost there. Keep pushing.

I look down at my small feet, wishing the tattered running shoes would give me more traction. I couldn't wait for the day when I could make money. I could buy myself better shoes.

Clean shoes.

No more dirt.

No more holes in the toes.

But shoes don't matter right now. I only have a little further to go. Propelling myself forward, triumph surges through me when my hand makes contact with her shoulder.

Finally. I've found her. My gut churns with nervous anticipation as she slowly turns toward me.

"Alex!" a voice calls from behind me.

Krystina. It's Krystina's voice. She sounds afraid.

I turn my head around to see what's wrong, only to feel the woman within my grasp slip away from me. I reach out to her.

"Wait! Come back!" I cry out. But she continues to move away, so far that I can barely make out her silhouette.

"Alex!" Krystina calls again.

Torn over which woman I should chase after, I look down in anguish only to see a pair of bright white track shoes on my feet.

Clean shoes. Adult sized shoes.

I'm not a child anymore.

I look up again at the slowly disappearing woman. I couldn't reach her. I've lost my mother again. I have to go to Krystina instead. She's my future. I need to get to her.

I run in the other direction toward the sound of Krystina's voice. Daytime turns to night, and fog billows around me as I run. It obscures my vision and I can't see her, but I can hear her shout my name.

"Krystina!" I call. "I'm trying to find you."

"Alexander, you're hurting me!"

I look around frantically. A roaring begins in my ears, fierce like the sound of a stampede.

"No, angel. I didn't mean to! Forgive me, please! Where are you?"

"Alex, please!"

Her voice is closer now. I turn to my left. There she is, standing in a pool of crimson red, clutching her bloodstained abdomen. Tears stream down her face, but her expression is emotionless.

It seems to take forever, but I finally reach her. I'm frantic. She needs medical attention.

"Krystina, what happened? Who did this to you?"

She stares back at me, her deathlike gaze cold and vacant when she finally speaks.

"You did."

I JOLTED AWAKE, shock reverberating through my system. It took me a minute to collect my bearings. I glanced over at Krystina and saw she was sleeping peacefully. Breathing and unharmed.

Just a dream.

My heart pounded in my chest, but I was careful to keep still in the bed. I didn't want another one of my nightmares to be the reason she woke. Not again. I tried to shake off the nausea, feeling repulsed by the haunting images plaguing me.

Rolling onto my side, I watched my sleeping beauty. Her peaceful and angelic face helped to calm the roaring pulse of blood in my ears. Her lips were slightly parted, and her steady breathing created the gentle rise and fall of her breasts. I wanted nothing more than to lose myself in her, but I knew she needed sleep. The fitful dreams inundating me most of the night had woken Krystina more often than not.

My nightmares were the same as usual. They always began with the child version of myself reliving the moments before I discovered my father's dead body, evolving into the adult version of myself chasing after my mother. However, the dreams had changed recently. Krystina's face and voice were now intertwined in the web of images, causing me to wake up feeling fearful she wouldn't be there. I was afraid she wouldn't be beside me in our bed. Or worse – that I had physically harmed her in some way. While every dream ended differently, there was one constant theme. Krystina was hurt, and I had been the one to cause it.

I rolled onto my back and tried to fall back asleep. Visions from the night flashed before my eyes. I could still see my mother running, her black hair flapping behind her in the wind as she ran. I could hear Krystina calling to me as I chased shadows into the unknown. I could almost smell the blood dripping from her body. I turned my head to look at her once more, needing assurance she was okay – that it was only a dream.

She's here. Beautiful as ever, and present. Just relax.

But I still couldn't shake off the unease. I glanced at the clock. It wasn't quite five in the morning yet. I felt anxious, and my skin was covered with the sheen of a nervous sweat.

Giving up any thoughts of falling back to sleep, I rolled over and climbed out of bed. I had office work to do, but it wasn't the distraction I needed. An intense physical work out was the only thing that would clear my head after such a disturbing night. If it weren't for the fact it was barely dawn, I would have called my trainer for a cathartic sparing session.

I quickly threw on a pair of gym shorts, left Krystina alone in her peaceful slumber, and headed toward my home gym in the penthouse. Once I was there, I went to the stereo system with the hope that music would drown out the sound of Krystina's scared voice from my nightmare. I turned it on, and Bastille blared through the speakers. Startled by the loud volume, I quickly lowered it to a reasonable level.

I pressed my lips together in annoyance. I rarely played music that loud. That meant Krystina must have used the gym recently.

I'll have to remind her to turn it back down after her workouts.

How she found the time for a workout over the past week was astonishing. It was no wonder she looked so tired. I made a mental note to monitor her gym time going forward. While I appreciated her desire to stay physically fit, she was pushing herself entirely too much and everyday my concern about her health grew.

After selecting a series of songs to accompany my workout, I stepped up to the treadmill. I began my warm up to the instantly identifiable voice of Sia, her raspy voice holding just enough dark qualities to match my mood. As the belt began to pick up speed, I thought about everything that had transpired over the past few weeks.

Years of study allowed me to take a step back and analyze everything rationally. I knew why I had nightmares. They were brought on by fear and childhood trauma. As to why Krystina was now manifesting in those nightmares was most likely due to fear and trauma as well. I had almost lost her in a near fatal car crash. The images of her being found in the trunk, her lifeless body and blood-matted hair, would forever be singed into my brain.

While she was now alive and well, I was still very much afraid. I was afraid of losing her, but in a different sense. I was afraid to lose her because of something I fucked up and was subconsciously terrified my temper would get the best of me again. If that happened, I would be no better than my father. Krystina deserved so much more.

I didn't need a shrink to tell me these things.

As my feet pounded through the last mile on the treadmill, sweat began to drip down the side of my face. I grabbed a towel from the handrail, wiped away the perspiration, and slowed the treadmill to a cool down.

Satisfied my muscles were warmed up enough to go a round with the punching bag, I climbed off the treadmill and headed to the far corner of the room. As I made my way there, the ping from a cell phone notification sounded through the room. I picked up my cell that I had left sitting on the bench press and saw it was a text from Hale.

Today
5:43 AM, Hale: *A reporter got in to see Charlie yesterday.*

I felt all the blood drain from my face, before it came roaring back with a vengeance. It went from ninety-eight degrees to two hundred twelve in less than a second.

Fuck!

Without hesitation, I dialed Hales number. He picked up on the first ring.

"I thought you had this handled!" I barked.

"It was handled, Mr. Stone. However, there was a new guard on duty yesterday. He just transferred in from another prison. I wasn't made aware of him until the Correction Commissioner called me this morning to let me know Charlie had a visitor."

I slammed my fist down on the seat of the bench press.

"A visitor? It wasn't just any visitor, Hale! It was the goddamn fucking press!"

"I'm aware, sir. I was assured it won't happen again. In the meantime, I already have a call in to *The City Times*. The reporter was Mac Owens. If he has anything substantial, I'll shut it down."

I considered the source to assess how bad the situation could potentially be. Mac Owens had been trying to dig into my past for years but had little success. He was now with *The City Times*, a smaller newspaper with decent credibility. Their reporting was wide ranging, anywhere from national politics to local gossip columns. I knew I shouldn't take the threat lightly.

"Hale, we've kept Charlie quiet for months. I'll be damned if I let some rookie prison guard fuck it up. Keep me posted."

"Will do."

"I mean it. I want updates on every detail, no matter how small."

I hit the button to end the call and fought the urge to throw the phone against the wall. Instead, I tossed it back onto the bench. At that moment, I needed to beat the shit out of a bag until my fists were raw. Not bothering with boxing gloves, I stepped up to the punching bag and took a bare fisted swing.

Hitting the vinyl felt good. Almost too good. I beat at the bag, over and over again, looking for some form of cathartic release with every blow.

I need to fucking think.

A multitude of emotions pumped through my veins. Between the barrage of nightmares and the latest news about Charlie, my goddamn head was spinning. Images swirled. Krystina's voice was a constant echo I couldn't push away.

"Alexander, you're hurting me!"

I spun around and struck the bag with a forceful back fist and tried to erase the memory. I could still see the fear in her eyes, fear that mirrored my mother's when my father came after her.

I am not him.

I turned again and landed a strong roundhouse kick, forcing the visions from my past to my more immediate threat.

Charlie. The fucking leach.

Just the thought of him sent me into a rage, causing the image of his face to project onto the bag. I imagined his bones and cartilage crumbling beneath my fists as I inflicted another punch onto the cylindrical bag.

My fury toward the man came from someplace deep within me. It wasn't just about what he did to my sister, or about how he made her a victim in an endless cycle of abuse. It was also from what he put Krystina through, and from how I nearly lost her because of his greed. Just thinking about what could've happened to her, my angel, tore at my gut.

I threw another punch, even more forceful than the last, before I caught myself. I had to calm my temper and think this through rationally. I needed to regain control. I closed my eyes, took a few calming breaths, and resumed at a more measured pace.

Snap. One. Two. Three. Kick.

I counted the reps over and over again, using the tempo to simmer my boiling rage. Punches flowed freely, the snap keeping my rhythm flowing as I moved effortlessly around the bag.

Breathe. Maintain balance.

It appeared as if Charlie was back in the game again, but it wasn't anything I couldn't handle. His meeting with a reporter could only mean one thing – he was scared. Exposing the past was the only leverage he had left.

I had worried about what he might say during the upcoming trial. However, it only took a phone call to the right judge to have the trial closed to the public, as the sensitivity of Krystina's testimony easily convinced the judge to rule on closure. It never occurred to me that Charlie might seek out a reporter.

It was clear he still had the plea deal in his sights. This would be his gambling chip, making it safe to assume he planned to use the reporter to influence me to drop some of the charges against him. Attempted murder, kidnapping, extortion – the list was long, and Charlie knew I had been in touch with the District Attorney about making every single charge stick.

Perhaps I shouldn't have fought the deal Charlie wanted to make.

How much he actually knew about my past still remained to be seen, as Justine never elaborated on how much she told him. I only knew I had to shut him down. It wasn't an option. Krystina was still unaware of one major detail from my past. I'd be damned before I let him use it to tear us apart. I couldn't lose her.

Not again.

I often wondered if I should've just told her everything that night on *The Lucy*. I wasn't sure why I didn't. After all, I had given her the worst of it. The part I left out shouldn't matter. She knew of the potential monster I could be. That was more than enough.

Thirty minutes later, I was drenched in sweat and my knuckles were raw from the repeated striking on the vinyl without the proper gear. However, my mind felt clearer. While I was still searching for answers on how to handle the situation with Charlie, I no longer felt like I wanted to rip him limb from limb. I delivered a final blow to the heavy bag and reached a decision.

There was one secret I still clung tightly to. If Charlie knew it and shared his knowledge with a reporter, it wouldn't be long before it was all over the news. I couldn't allow Krystina to find out that way. She needed to hear it from me. More importantly, she deserved an explanation for why I had kept it from her.

I have to tell her before it's too late.

A glance at the clock told me she would probably wake soon. Deciding I would tell her over breakfast, I grabbed a towel to wipe the sweat off my face and neck.

I felt Krystina's presence before I saw her. Slowly turning around, my angel came into view. She was wearing one of my t-shirts and her beautiful legs were bare. My gaze traveled up the long length of them until I reached her face. Her eyes penetrated mine and raked over my features. I knew what she saw. It was what I saw in the mirror every morning – eyes haunted from a past I couldn't escape.

"Good morning, angel," I greeted lightly.

"I'm all about taking out my frustrations on a punching bag, but I think you were trying to kill it. You're up really early. Everything okay?" she asked groggily with a yawn as she came towards me.

Appearing to not care about the fact I was covered in sweat, she wrapped her arms around my waist and rested her head against my chest. I brought my hand up to stroke her hair, appreciating the soft feel of her luscious brown curls between my fingers.

"Everything is just fine," I lied. I couldn't help it. Her embrace was like heaven and I didn't want to ruin it. "Are you hungry? I can make us omelets if you'd like."

"Mmm, that sounds good," she said and looked up at me with a sleepy-eyed smile. "But you know me. I need coffee first."

I leaned down and planted a kiss on the tip of her nose.

"Why am I not surprised?" I joked and squeezed her tighter to me.

We stayed that way for another few moments, a silence settling between us. I knew she was thinking about the numerous times my dreams pulled her from her sleep throughout the night. I could tell she was worried by the way she clung to me, as if she were hanging on for dear life. I hated that I was the cause for her concern.

Because of that, I couldn't lay anything else on her today. After weeks of tension, we were finally in a good place. I just wanted to stay there for a little while longer.

Later. I'll tell her later.

9

Krystina

It was nearing four o'clock on Saturday afternoon. Allyson and I had been shopping for hours. Surprisingly, we both found dresses for the grand opening of Matteo's restaurant in record time. I settled on a floor-length dress of royal blue chiffon. My neck and collarbone would be exposed enough to show off the triskelion necklace Alexander bought for me after we first got together. I hadn't worn it in a while, and I knew he'd be pleased to see it on me. Allyson found a yellow silk dress that hugged her curves in all the right places and complimented her golden hair beautifully.

By eleven that morning, our dresses had been charged to Alexander's account at Bergdorf Goodman on Fifth. Afterward, we hit up Murphy's for an early lunch and to catch up on each other's latest gossip. By one o'clock, our appetites for both food and girl-talk had been appeased and we were on our way. We had been browsing wedding dress boutiques ever since.

"What about this one?"

I looked up to see Allyson holding out a long white satin

dress full of lace and frills. The train on the wedding gown had to be at least a mile long. Why she continued to gravitate toward flounce and extravagant beadwork was beyond me. The last thing I wanted to look like was a bedazzled cupcake. I wanted a more classic look. Plain. Simple. With a shake of my head, I pressed my lips together and frowned.

"There's too much going on. I'm looking for something simpler," I told her.

"Krys, this is about as simple as it gets!" she exasperated loudly. "You're engaged to a billionaire. I don't think simple is going to work."

"I already told you. Alex and I decided to go with a small wedding. Neither one of us wants an extravagant affair, Ally."

"What does your mother say about that?"

I rolled my eyes.

"I haven't told her yet. She's still trying to come to terms with the fact I'm engaged."

"I figured as much," Allyson laughed. "I went down to the main office for the apartment building this past Tuesday to pay the rent, only to discover Frank already paid it. I think your mom still has hopes of you moving back in with me."

I sighed.

"I'm sorry, Ally. I'll talk to my stepfather about it."

"I'm not sure if it will do much good, at least until the wedding day and you actually say the words 'until death do us part'. Speaking of which, how small of a wedding are you talking about here?"

Grateful for the opportunity to stop talking about my mother, I casually walked over to the row of bridesmaid's dresses. I tossed Allyson a small, yet knowing, smile.

"Oh, I don't know..." I innocently trailed off.

"Krys, seriously. I mean, all of New York is going to want to have a front row seat to this. You have to know that."

"Well, it won't be *that* small of a wedding." I paused and

looked meaningfully at her. My subtle grin turned into a beaming, earsplitting smile. "It will be big enough to have a maid of honor."

She looked genuinely shocked and I thought she might drop the gaudy dress that was still in her grasp.

"Me? Really?"

"Of course, you! Who else would I have asked, silly?" I laughed.

"I don't know. I just assumed Alex would want his sister," she said, still sounding shocked. I didn't understand her surprise. I would never dream of a wedding where she wasn't by my side through it all.

"Well, you know what they say about the word assume," I joked. "Honestly, Alex and I haven't even talked about it. Who I choose for a maid of honor is my decision. You're my best friend and like the sister I never had. I wouldn't have it any other way."

Allyson beamed and her eyes filled with tears of happiness. Unexpectedly, she screeched loudly from excitement. Scrambling to hang up the dress in her hands, she fumbled for a moment before eventually dropping it to the floor.

"Screw it. The dress is ugly anyway," she pronounced. She hurried over to me and threw her arms around my neck. "You're getting married! I'm going to be your maid of honor!"

She screeched again. People around us stared. The unexpected commotion drew the attention of a nearby saleswoman. She pursed her lips in disapproval when she saw the wedding gown tossed haphazardly on the floor. I was fairly certain she wasn't accustomed to having her overpriced wedding dresses trampled. Hale and Samuel, their watchful eyes never far away, peeked out from whatever corner they had been hiding in. My eyes briefly met Hale's. Once he realized everything was okay, his lips formed a subtle smile. Although he never voiced it, I knew he was happy Alexander and I were getting married too.

I returned Allyson's fierce embrace before pulling back to disentangle myself from her arms.

"Yes, I'm getting married," I said and laughed. "But I'll never get a dress if you keep tossing them on the floor. You're going to give me a bad rep and no boutique will let me through their doors."

I was only joking, but Allyson looked horrified.

"Oh my god!"

She quickly turned around to see the saleswoman replacing the wedding gown to its proper place. Allyson apologized profusely but was rudely brushed off by the stuffy woman. After the dress was once again hanging, the woman walked away. Perhaps I had a case of shop-til-you-drop syndrome setting in, but her poor attitude rubbed me the wrong way. At that moment, I decided I was done with boutiques. Alexander's tailor came to mind.

Maybe I can find a good seamstress and have a dress custom made.

That was definitely an idea to consider. I was confident Justine knew of one. I made a mental note to ask her and turned my attention back to Allyson.

"Come on Ally, we should get going. I want to make sure I have enough time to get ready for the party tonight."

"Yeah, me too. I'm really looking forward to it. You definitely need to look your best, especially since Matteo named the restaurant after you."

I narrowed my eyes. There was something off about her tone, but I couldn't place it. In fact, she always acted a little off whenever Matteo's name was mentioned.

"Does that bother you?"

"Of course not. I mean, it's not really named after you. It was named for Alexander's *undying love* for his angel," she joked, drawing out the words with exaggeration and laughed. "I think the story behind it is incredibly romantic, actually. Why do you ask if it bothers me?"

"It just seems like you and Matteo have been spending a lot of time together, that's all," I observed.

"He's a nice guy," she said offhandedly.

"Oh, come on, Ally! You're talking to me, remember?"

"Okay, okay. So, he's more than a nice guy. I am female after all," she added wryly. "I know a prime piece of eye candy when I see it."

"And?" I pressed.

"I don't know. It's hard to explain. I just get the impression he comes from a family where the women stay home and cook all day? Do you know what I mean?"

I eyed her quizzically.

"No, I don't actually."

"Let's just say I don't think his family would appreciate him being with someone like me, someone who's an active member of several women's rights organizations. His family is super old school Italian," she tried to wave off.

I arched a brow. I knew my friend and I could sense her conflict, almost as if she was second guessing her beliefs. That wasn't like her. There was more to this than just Matteo's old-fashioned family.

"His family isn't him, Ally," I pointed out nonchalantly. Allyson sighed.

"You're right. He isn't his family, but he is the forever type. Like, the settle-down-and-have-lots-of-babies kind of guy. I'm not ready for that sort of thing. Not for a long time," she paused and flashed me a devilish grin. "For now, I'm content leaving all that to you."

"I don't know about the baby part," I laughed. "Alexander and I haven't even broached the subject yet. I'm sure that's a long way off, if at all."

"You should probably have that discussion before you tie the knot. Just saying." She shrugged.

"I suppose you're right, but I'm not entirely sure what I think about having kids. I wouldn't even know how to bring it up to him. I've barely just gotten back on my feet. I have so many plans. Alexander, my career...I just can't imagine taking on anything else at the moment."

We walked toward the exit of the boutique. Samuel held open the door for us. Hale trailed behind in our wake. If I turned around, I was sure I'd find his observant gaze taking in everything around us. I envisioned them following a smaller version of Alex or myself wherever they went. School, dates, proms. No privacy. They'd be shielded and protected from the world, yet there would always be somebody watching. While I had begrudgingly grown accustomed to it, I wasn't sure if I wanted to subject my children to that.

If. If I have children.

And it was a big if.

I shivered, finding just the mere thought of being responsible for another human absolutely terrifying.

Alexander

I STARED BLANKLY at the news article on my computer screen. It was the one Hale emailed to me around noontime. I read it over at least one hundred times since receiving it. I didn't need to read it again. I had already committed every word to memory. It hadn't been published yet, but I knew it was only a matter of time. The draft sitting open on my computer monitor was from *The City Times*. It was the story Charlie gave to that relentless reporter.

I wanted to be angry. I wanted to lash out, to hurt someone. But I couldn't get past the shock of what I had read.

Why didn't Justine tell me?

I picked up my cell phone and dialed her number. It went straight to voicemail. Again.

I glanced up at my computer screen and scrolled to the top of the article. I pushed the computer mouse away, not wanting to see the words any longer. Instead, I stood up and went to the window. I stared out at the city, the East River coming in to view. The sun was low in the sky and glittered off the water's surface, but I wasn't really seeing it. My head was too full of childhood memories. They flashed fresh in my mind as if they only happened yesterday.

"Justine! What happened?"

"I don't know," she says through her sobs.

"Why do you have dad's gun?"

"Mommy's going to be so mad. I ruined my shirt!"

I shake her.

"How did this happen?" I ask her again.

Her face goes blank and she looks strangely at me through vacant eyes.

"Alex, do you know where my blue dress is? The pretty one with the flowers. Mommy likes when I wear it."

She didn't answer my question then, just as she wasn't answering my calls now. My sister knew. She knew the whole time. Her betrayal sliced through my heart and tore at every fiber of my being. I racked my brain trying to come up with a reason for her deceit, but I came up empty handed. I thought about the years I spent searching for an answer, searching for *her*, never knowing the answer lied with the one person I thought would never betray me.

However, when I thought back, I should've suspected. I should have seen the signs. Her paranoia over a media circus was always over the top. I recalled the last time she came to me, fearful Charlie would leak our secret past – the one I had successfully buried to protect her.

"It's bad, Alex. He's been making threats."

"What do you mean? What threats? I'll kill the fucking bastard if he touched you again!"

"No, he didn't hurt me – at least not in the physical sense. He's been calling... a lot. I thought about just having his number blocked, but I was afraid to because of what he's been threatening. It affects both me and you."

I had been so angry with Justine that day for interrupting my interview with Krystina. The fear in her eyes was the only thing giving me reason to pause. She had been crying and shaking so badly, so I had been forced to set aside my anger. She needed my support, not my fury.

"It's alright. It doesn't matter what his threats are. He can't do anything to me. And I already told you – I won't let him hurt you anymore."

"No, no! You have to listen to me, Alex! Damn it! This is why I've been blowing up your phone. He's threatening to expose us – our past!"

"And how would he know about our past, Justine?"

"Because...because I told him! I had to tell him. It was part of my therapy a long time ago. And now, all these years later, I've barely made peace with everything. The last thing I want is a media circus. I couldn't handle it, Alex. I just couldn't."

I shook my head. If only I had looked deeper into her fears. I believed she was terrified of the press because she didn't want to relive it. Never did I think it was because she had something to hide. Yes, I had my own personal motivation to keep the past hidden, but it was never as strong as my will to shield her. I did all I could to erase what had happened. I gave us a fresh start, devoid of anything and everything that could link us to that terrible time in our lives. Everything I did was for her. It was always for her.

A quiet beep tore me away from my thoughts. It came from the alarm panel on the wall. Someone was coming up the elevator. I glanced at the cell phone lying on the desk. There was a text notification. I picked it up and swiped the screen.

4:46 PM, Hale: *Miss Cole is in the penthouse elevator and on her way to you.*
4:47 PM, Me: *Any issues today.*
4:49 PM, Hale: *None, sir. All is clear.*

By issues, I meant with the media, but I didn't need to explain that to Hale. He knew without my saying. He read the article and knew to be on high alert. I set the phone down and reclaimed my seat behind the desk. My muscles were tense, and my nerves were shot. I ran my hands over my face and took a deep breath.

I needed to show the article to Krystina before we left for Matteo's party. I didn't have a choice. In the off chance it was leaked, I didn't want her to be blindsided by any of the reporters attending the event. My eyes darted to the clock at the top of my computer screen. I didn't have much time to explain things to her. The doors opened at seven, and we couldn't be late.

"Alex, I'm home!" I heard Krystina call from the foyer.

She knew both the alarm system and Hale always alerted me to anyone's arrival, yet she always made her presence known upon returning home. Sometimes I wondered if it was her subtle way of ignoring the security around her. Whatever it was, I loved that my name was the first thing I heard from her lips when she came through the door.

"I'm in the office, angel," I called back.

When she came in, her arms were laden with packages.

"Wait until I show you the dress I got for tonight!" she exclaimed with excitement.

"Shit!" I swore and hurried out from behind the desk to help her. "Why didn't Hale or Samuel bring this up for you?"

I freed her arms of the shopping bags and set them on the leather sofa in the office. She waved me off dismissively.

"Oh, stop it. I'm perfectly capable," she chided. "Here, let me show you."

Her cheeks were flushed with delight as she began to tear through the packages. Clearly, she enjoyed her day of shopping.

And I'm about to ruin it.

I wanted her to continue enjoying this moment, even if it was over something as simple as a dress. She deserved it. I wanted her to have the opportunity to slip in to something new and model it for me. I envisioned her curves twirling in front of the full-length mirror as she inspected her reflection. To me, it didn't matter what she wore. That killer body of hers could make anything look sexy.

I briefly toyed with the idea of not showing her the article until after the party. The way she was acting was so very normal, and it came at a time when everything in my world seemed to be at odds. I hated to be the one to break her mood, but I knew I had to.

What I had to tell her could not be sorted out in just one conversation or through a few hours of heart-to-heart communication. This would take time, patience, and finesse, as I didn't know how she would react.

Reaching for her arm, I stopped her from rummaging through the packages and turned her to face me. I paused, suddenly hit with enough anxiety to film my skin with a sheen of sweat.

"No, angel. That has to wait," I told her. I led her over to the chair in front of my desk. "Sit down. We need to talk."

10

Krystina

"Alex?" I questioned. "What's wrong?"
The seriousness of his tone set me on high alert. I carefully took him in as he sat down across from me and ran his hands through his hair. Stress lines marred his perfect face and his jaw had that telltale nervous tick. He was obviously angry, but there was more. His coloring was off, ashen almost. Never before had I seen him wound so tight yet appear defeated at the same time. The strong man in front of me looked completely and utterly broken.

"Do you remember everything I told you about my past?"

"Of course, I do. Alex, tell me what's happened. You look like you've just seen a ghost. Is everything alright?"

"A reporter from *The City Times* got in to see Charlie last night. Charlie told him everything about Justine and me. About our past."

I breathed a small sigh of relief. From the way he looked, I thought something catastrophic had happened. I often thought Alexander worried too much about his past being made public.

His paranoia was something I could never quite wrap my head around.

"It will be okay. Like I said before, you worry about this too much. It was a long time ago. You were just a boy, Alex."

He stared blankly at the wall behind me, appearing lost in a memory, before turning his gaze back to meet mine.

"When I threw that gun in the Harlem River, I thought I destroyed the only evidence that would lead to the truth," he murmured. His words were quiet, but not quite a whisper. I was so confused. Alexander hadn't talked about the day of his father's death since that night on *The Lucy*.

What happened to suddenly bring this on? Why is he thinking about it?

"More than likely, this will be gossip for a short time, then people will move on." I paused as I realized what he had just said. "Wait a minute. You said you *thought* you destroyed it. Has it been recovered?"

"No, it hasn't been found. It doesn't need to be," he said sadly and turned the computer monitor to me. "You need to read this, angel."

I looked at the computer screen. It was an email forwarded from Hale. The original sender was from someone named Mac Owens. My eyes scrolled down the contents of the page. There was a title in bold font with the date and credentials listed below it.

Rags to Riches: Was It Worth the Price?
By Mac Owens
February 24, 2017

In 2012, I set out to do a piece on the self-made billionaire, Alexander Stone. As with most media interactions, Mr. Stone was aloof, offering little to no insight to his background. I dug further, only to hit one dead end after another. It appeared as though Alexander Stone never existed before 2003. After years of digging and research, I was finally able to find the one man who could shine light on the truth: Charlie Andrews.

Below is a recount of Mac Owens' exclusive interview with Charlie Andrews, one that will give insight to the mysterious billionaire, Alexander Stone. This interview, although not the most thorough or complete set of questions and answers, is the most extensive information available on Alexander Stone and his rise to power.

Note: The following interview contains graphic language and may not be suitable for younger audiences.

The interview went into details about Charlie's history with Alexander. It gave a recap of my kidnapping and the subsequent car accident that shattered Charlie's plans to get rich quick. Charlie was careful with his wording to the reporter, never once admitting guilt. Rather, he blamed Trevor for all of it.

However, we knew his angle and his plan to say he was just in the wrong place at the wrong time. The lawyers were prepared for it. My testimony alone was more than enough to convict him. Charlie mentioned a few times that Alexander grew up poor, but other than that, I had no idea why this interview had Alexander so rattled. None of what I was reading was new information.

"Alex, I'm not seeing –,"

"Keep reading," he interjected. "You know most of this so far. You can skip ahead to this part of the interview if you want to."

He pointed to a spot on the computer screen. I blinked, startled by the determination written on his face. It was alarming and I almost didn't want to keep reading. I wanted him to tell me what it said, but there was something about the severity of his posture that compelled me to do as he instructed instead.

Turning back to the screen, I found the place where Alexander had marked and continued on.

Mac Owens: The details of your trial have been kept remarkably quiet, Mr. Andrews. I understand you may want the chance to plead your case to the public. Is there anything you can tell me I don't already know?

Charlie Andrews: I need to give you everything. Background is important. I thought you came to see me because you wanted a story. The whole story.

Mac Owens: I do, Mr. Andrews, but everything you've said up to this point is hardly earth-shattering.

Charlie Andrews: Okay, Mr. Fucking-know-it-all. I guess you know all about my ex-wife murdering her father then, don't you?

My head whipped away from the computer screen to face Alexander.

"What!" I exclaimed. "What does he mean about murd –."

He held up his hand to silence me once more.

"No. I told you to keep reading. You can ask questions later."

I looked back to the monitor, but questions were racing through my brain at a breakneck speed. I pushed them aside and focused once more on the text.

Mac Owens: You have my attention now, Mr. Andrews. Go ahead.

Charlie Andrews: I knew that would do the trick [laughs]. Haven't you ever wondered about my dear old ex-brother in law's parents? My ex-wife's parents?

Mac Owens: I was never able to find anything on them. Not a name, not an address. What can you tell me about that?

Charlie Andrews: You haven't found anything because you're looking in the wrong places. You should start with the old projects that were torn down some years back. You know, the ones that were replaced with low-income housing. That asshole was behind that too.

Mac Owens: Behind what? Who's an asshole?

Charlie Andrews: I just told you. Aren't you listening to me? The projects. They were torn down by my ex-wife's brother, Alex. Said it was for charity or some shit like that. It was a crap excuse. I knew why they were torn down. He didn't want there to be evidence of what Justine did.

Mac Owens: The murder?

Charlie Andrews: Ah, now you're finally learning. Yeah, the murder. She killed her father. She was just a kid, but she did it. She told me herself a few years ago. Apparently, the old man came home in a rage. He was a big drinker. Justine hated talking about it. But she told me. She told me everything.

Mac Owens: How did she kill him?

Charlie Andrews: Shot him. Just like that [snaps his fingers]. Right in the stomach. The sucker never stood a chance. The way Justine described the blood, he probably bled out in a matter of minutes. Maybe it was deserved. Hell, I don't know. If he really did kill his wife, maybe that was his punishment.

Mac Owens: Wait, you lost me there. What about his wife?

Charlie Andrews: I don't know the details about that. Her body was never found. At least, I don't think it was. I only know what Justine told me. The father came home, stumbling around, saying he killed her — the wife I mean. Justine and Alex's mother. He told Justine nobody could protect her anymore. Said Alex couldn't save her either. Called him a weak little pussy. Still is if you ask me.

Mac Owens: So, he came home drunk and said he killed his wife, Alex and Justine's mother. What year did this happen?

Charlie Andrews: I don't know. Justine was about seven or eight. Practically a baby. I like em' young, but not that young.

Mac Owens: What do you mean?

Charlie Andrews: He came at her. Started touching her in all the wrong places, if you know what I mean. That's when she shot him.

Mac Owens: Then what happened?

Charlie Andrews: That's when things get kind of fucked up. All secretive-like. You know that guy who's always with Alex? Hale something or another? His bodyguard, I think. I don't know what his title is, but he looks like he could snap a man in half.

Mac Owens: I know the man you're referring to. What can you tell me about him?

Charlie Andrews: He was really close with that family. He's a military guy. He was home on leave when it all happened. I think he did something to cover it up. Justine's mother remained a missing persons case. The murder of the father went unsolved. Hell, there's not even a murder scene left to investigate since Alex had the place torn down. It's all one big cover up.

Mac Owens: Mr. Andrews, this is quite the tale. I'm not saying I don't believe you, but I've dug into Mr. Stone's past. I've never come across this. Do you have proof? As you can imagine, the story of an unsolved murder case connected to someone as influential as Alexander Stone would be easy to find.

Charlie Andrews: Like I told you before. You're looking in the wrong places. His name isn't Stone. It's Russo.

My vision became hazy. There was more, but I couldn't focus on the remainder of the interview as I tried to comprehend what I was reading. A million thoughts swamped my brain in waves, before the sound of a roaring tidal wave filled my head.

Justine knew what happened this whole time?

Had Alexander known? Did he not tell me the whole truth?

What about the building he tore down? Did he really do it to cover up more evidence?

Then my eyes zeroed in on the last thing I read. I felt my stomach pitch.

Russo.

I looked up at the man before me. He was the man I loved with every fiber of my being, but there were so many layers. Just when I thought I had reached the core, there was another layer to get through. I wondered if I would ever truly come to know the central reality that made up the man I wanted to marry. It was an unsettling sort of feeling and I couldn't stop the troubling question from leaving my lips.

"Who are you?"

Alexander

I HATED to see so much hurt and confusion in Krystina's eyes. A shocked silence filled the room and made the air feel stifling. I repeated her question again in my head.

"Who are you?"

A part of me didn't know the answer to that anymore. The man I thought I was, the man I created, was free falling into an abyss. Past and present melded and blurred the lines I had drawn long ago. The only thing I was certain of anymore was Krystina. She was my constant. She knew me like nobody else did. It was up to me to make sure she never doubted that.

"My birth name was Alexander Russo. I have not spoken the name in years. That person no longer exists."

"What do you mean he doesn't exist? He's you!" she exclaimed, her voice rising to a near deafening level.

"Krystina, stop yelling. There are things you don't understand."

"I'm all ears, Stone. Or Russo. Or whatever the hell your name is," she spat out accusingly. She was on the verge of hysteria. Her eyes flashed angrily. I couldn't blame her. As far as she knew, I told her everything about my past. Except for my identity.

"I legally changed my name after I turned eighteen years old. I am Alexander *Stone*. Not Russo."

"What about Justine?"

"Hers was legally changed as well. It was Stone until she married Charlie Andrews."

"No, I didn't mean her name. It's all this other stuff. You told me you didn't know," she said, her voice cracking over the last sentence. She no longer sounded hysterical, but more like she was fighting off tears. I also sensed a hint of betrayal, a feeling I understood all too well.

"I didn't know," I responded flatly. "Justine never told me. It's hard to believe she would hide something like this from me. I haven't been able to reach her to confirm it either. For all I know, Charlie made it all up."

She sat back, folded her arms, and seemed to be considering the possibility.

"Do you think he did?" she eventually asked.

"I don't know, angel. I just don't know."

I raked a hand through my hair in frustration and stood up to pace the room. My sister's deception mixed with my own self-doubt weighed heavily in my chest. I didn't want to jump to conclusions, but my instincts were telling me what Charlie said was true. Every word of it. I pinched the bridge of my nose, trying to will away the headache starting to form.

If only Justine would answer my damn calls!

"I'm trying not to be upset with you about this. Just listening to you, seeing how shaken you are." She paused momentarily and shook her head. When she spoke again, her voice was hushed, almost as if she were afraid to voice the words. "I think you know Charlie didn't make this up."

I turned to look at her. One glance at her expression and I could tell she was exercising restraint. With our gazes locked, I could almost see the pleading in her beautiful brown eyes. Like she was begging me to make her understand.

"My gut says Charlie's story is the truth. When I think back on things, certain behaviors and actions..." I trailed off, struggling to find the words to explain something I should have seen a long time ago. "Justine has always been the jittery, nervous type. It wasn't until about five years ago when she began her obsession with the media, the police, and that rundown shitty apartment building. I blamed the shrink she was seeing. I thought he was making her nuts. She became obsessed over a past we successfully buried. That I buried."

"Is that where your aversion for our sessions with Dr. Tumblin comes from?"

"That's part of it," I admitted. "She pushed me to rip down the old abandoned projects. I didn't argue with her rationale. It was another memory I could erase. Besides, the projects were condemned, full of rats. They became a home for the homeless and a paradise for the heroine junkies. When I proposed the Stoneworks Foundation clean it up, the city was more than happy to oblige. Neighboring streets had been advocating for the demolition for years. Fundraisers were held and federal grants came easily. Justine headed up the entire project. The rotten buildings were torn down and new ones went up in less than two years. Once that happened, she stopped seeing the shrink and was calm again."

"It could just be a coincidence. Maybe she was just trying to erase the memory like you said," Krystina suggested.

"Perhaps." I thought about the other thing Charlie said about my father and Justine.

If he touched her, like that...

I couldn't even finish the thought. Bile rose in the back of my throat. I couldn't think about it, about him and his stale breath and grimy hands. She was just a child. If he truly did the unthinkable, I could never live with myself.

I should have known. I should have protected her.

I stopped pacing and slammed my fist hard onto the desk.

"Alex!" Krystina jumped in surprise. I looked into her eyes. They were as wide as saucers and full of confusion. But worse, there was fear in them too.

Was she afraid of me?

I closed my eyes and counted to ten. Taking a few calming breaths, I opened them to look at her again.

"I'm sorry, angel. I didn't mean to scare you. This is just a lot to process. I suspect Charlie is going to try to use this as a bargaining tool to strike a plea deal and I only have so much leverage with the DA. At this point, I don't give a shit if it goes public. All I know is he can't get away with what he did to you. I have to get a hold of Justine to confirm or deny. There are just too many things I need answers to."

My mother.

Did he really kill her?

Had she not abandoned us after all?

I didn't voice my questions but hoped Krystina would connect those dots on her own. I looked at her, begging with my eyes for her to understand. When her gaze fixed on mine, we stared at each other without saying a word. A silent message seemed to pass between us. She nodded slightly, telling me she understood.

Tearing her eyes away from mine, she looked out the windows and shrugged indifferently.

"You could always deny it, Alex. Say the story isn't true. Claim fake news. It works for some people."

I laughed bitterly.

"I doubt anyone would believe that. Like Charlie said, there's a missing person and a dead body. Too many things don't add up."

She looked thoughtful, as if she too were trying to put together the pieces of the puzzle. It was no use. I had tried for years, yet here I stood with more unknowns than ever before.

"What about Hale? Charlie mentioned he might know something."

"Hale read the article. He hasn't confirmed or denied anything, but I also never asked him," I said and shook my head. A part of me was afraid to ask, as if subconsciously I knew he would confirm everything said. "I'll talk to him later tonight after the party."

"The party? Surely, you don't still want to go?" she asked in surprise.

"Want to and have to are two different things. We can't miss it. There's been too much build up over this grand opening. I want you to relax and enjoy the night. This is my problem to worry about, not yours."

"But you said there would be press coverage there. Are you ready to face this head on, especially during Matteo's big night?"

"Nobody knows any of this yet," I told her, motioning to the computer monitor still facing her. "The article hasn't been published. I don't know how he did it, but Hale bought me a few days. At the very least, I'll have time to come up with a statement. In the off chance it's leaked, and we have a paparazzi circus tonight, we won't be taking any of my personal vehicles. All are too conspicuous in the event we need to blend in. Hale has secured a limousine for our transportation instead."

She reached across the desk and placed her hand over mine. Her eyes searched mine.

"Alex, I know you have so many questions that need answering, but I have to ask. Did you only tell me your birth name because your hand was forced? Were you ever going to tell me?"

My jaw clenched. I knew my answer would hurt her, but she deserved the truth. No more lies. No more secrets.

"I thought about telling you, but then decided against it. So, the answer is no. I wasn't going to tell you, angel. Like I said, Alexander Russo no longer exists."

11

Krystina

The drive to Matteo's restaurant was spent in silence. It wasn't an uncomfortable silence, but one of mutual understanding. We were not going to talk about the article for the next few hours. Before we left the penthouse, Alexander promised to explain more to me after the party. However, I didn't want to wait. I desperately needed answers. I had to understand why Alexander hid his true identity from me, even if it was the legal truth.

"Shh, angel. Don't agonize over this," he had whispered to me in the elevator when we were making our way down to the awaiting limousine. He leaned into me and pressed his soft lips to my forehead. "The reason why doesn't matter. You know now and I promise to answer all your questions later. You look stunning and I want you to enjoy the evening."

He didn't have to say more. He didn't need to. I understood his push to enjoy the party. I knew it might be the last bit of fun we had in public for a while. His whole world was about to be blown wide open. His privacy, everything he held close to his heart, was crashing down around him. He didn't need me to question him. By the way his eyes silently pleaded with mine, I knew he needed my patience. And more importantly, my strength.

As the limousine turned down the street to where Matteo's restaurant was located, butterflies sprang to life in my stomach. I could see the line of people slowly trickling in. Lights were strung between lampposts, a beacon for those wanting to attend. As we pulled to a stop, the sign for the restaurant came into view. Even though I knew Matteo planned to name the restaurant after me, after the woman who had stolen the heart of his childhood friend, I still wasn't prepared to see the ornate sign over the doorway to the restaurant.

"Krystina's Place," I whispered.

"This is it, angel. Are you ready to go in?"

Alexander laced his fingers through mine as Hale came around to open the limousine door for us.

"I'm ready."

When we stepped out of the limo, I breathed a sigh of relief. There were no flashing lights from cameras, no reporters shoving microphones down our throats. I knew Alexander's story hadn't been made public yet, but I couldn't squash the worry over the what-ifs. Upon entering the restaurant, seeing the crowd of people mingling in a very normal way was a tremendous relief.

I glanced up at Alexander. His face went from tense to relaxed as he surveyed the room. It was apparent he was feeling the same relief I was. I squeezed his hand.

"I love you," I told him. He smiled, dropped my hand and wrapped his arm around my waist. He leaned in, as if he was about to say something, but the sound of a familiar voice calling from across the room interrupted whatever words he was about to speak.

"There she is! My guest of honor!"

Alexander and I both turned to see Matteo making his way over to us. Alexander slapped a hand on his shoulder when he reached us.

"Everything came together great, Matt. The place looks fantastic!"

"So, others have told me as well. I hope they are just as impressed with the food," he joked, but I could sense his nervousness. Turning to me, he took hold of my hand and placed a feathery kiss on the backside. "Krystina, my dear. You look as lovely as ever."

I blushed at his compliment.

"Thank you, Matteo. It's so good to see you again. And don't worry about the guests enjoying your food. I can personally attest to its excellence."

"You are too kind! Come now, I have a table reserved for you." He turned away from us momentarily to call over his shoulder. "Luca!"

A younger gentleman dressed in a black tuxedo appeared before us.

"Yes, Mr. Donati."

"This is Alexander Stone and his fiancée, Krystina Cole. Please see to it that they have whatever they need tonight." He paused and turned back to us. "Alex, Krystina, Luca will take you to your table. I need to check a few things in the kitchen. I'll be back out to join you in a bit."

"No worries, Matt," Alexander assured. "Do what you need to do. I'll handle the crowd out here."

"Thank you, my friend. *Mi scusi.*"

And in typical Matteo fashion, he rushed off.

"What did you mean about handling the crowd out here?" I asked, my voice just barely audible over the buzz of the crowd in the restaurant as we followed Luca to our table.

"There are going to be a lot of influential people in attendance tonight. I'll need to make the rounds, talk up

Matteo, his background, and etcetera. Before the end of the night, half the city will be making plans to dine here."

I thought back to the first time I came to this restaurant. It was my first unofficial date with Alexander. I smiled as I recalled the memories from that night. The restaurant hadn't been open for business yet, as it was still in the remodeling phase. I glanced around. It was a far cry from what it once looked like. The main dining room was now festive, elegant and classy.

"Mr. Stone, Miss Cole," Luca formally addressed us. "Here is your table for the evening. There is a cocktail hour taking place in the banquet room. If you'd like, you can mingle with other guests or simply enjoy a few hors d'oeuvres."

"Thank you, Luca." Alexander nodded. "Krystina?"

"Whatever you want to do. I'm yours to command tonight, Mr. Stone," I teased before immediately realizing my Freudian slip. His eyes narrowed, a dark primal need showing through the slits. "I mean, not – not like..."

I sputtered, unable to finish. Luca raised his eyebrows but recovered quickly before excusing himself awkwardly.

My cheeks flushed crimson as Alexander leaned in to whisper into my ear.

"And command you, I will. I'll have you begging to get out of that sexy dress of yours. But the necklace and heels, you'll be leaving those on."

My hand reached up to finger the intricate swirls of the triskelion emblem as I looked down at my dress. Smooth lines of royal blue chiffon poured down my body, held expertly in place with sapphire straps running over my shoulders and lined my back. It was the perfect dress for the woman who would be on Alexander's arm for the night. I knew he would be proud.

I leaned away from him, away from the lips hovering just close enough to my ear to send shivers down my spine.

"Don't you have a crowd to work over?"

"Don't remind me," he groaned. "I'd rather be working over something else right now. With you in that dress, I might be too distracted to be of any use to Matteo."

"I doubt that," I laughed. There was still the proverbial elephant that loomed around us, but our casual flirting allowed us to push it aside. "Let's go to the banquet room before all the hors d'oeuvres are gone."

We made our way into the banquet room and found an open cocktail table.

"Stay here, angel. I'm just going to get us some champagne."

I watched him walk away, enjoying the view as he went. There were very few things in life that made me catch my breath in awe. Alexander in a tuxedo was one of those things. The room buzzed with conversation, as wealthy businessmen, politicians, and restaurant reviewers mingled about and sampled the array of delicacies Matteo had set out. All were dressed formally, but only Alexander truly stood out in the crowd.

I watched him cross the room with a champagne flute in each hand as he came back toward me. His hair was smoothed back, his waves almost as black as the tuxedo hugging his broad shoulders. His stride was fiercely elegant and unmistakably sexy.

And he's all mine.

The love I felt for him surged through me. It didn't matter if he was Alexander Stone or Alexander Russo. I knew the man he was inside. I knew his heart, and it had captured mine.

When he reached me, he passed me a champagne flute before resting his hand on my hip in a blatant display of ownership.

"There's no doubt about it. You are the most beautiful woman in here," he whispered into my ear.

I laughed, the bubbly champagne matching the bubbly

mood I suddenly found myself in. Curious eyes glanced in our direction, but I didn't care. Being with Alexander in such a public setting was a rare occurrence. He made me feel like a princess among peasants. It was a heady sort of feeling.

"I'd like to say flattery will get you nowhere, but then I'd be lying. Just wait until tonight," I said promisingly.

"That's twice you've teased me this evening, Miss Cole. Are you trying to give me a hard on in public?"

"I would never dream!" I admonished and laughed again.

"Krys! Over here!"

I turned and saw Allyson waving in our direction. She was off in a corner and appeared to be talking to a man whom I didn't recognize.

I looked up at Alexander.

"You go do your thing. I'll go hang with Ally for a bit. Besides, I want to drill her about Matteo," I told him. His eyebrows rose questioningly.

"Matteo?"

"Never mind. It's girl stuff."

"Don't get too chatty," he warned. "I might have to punish you if you're gone too long."

His voice was a low rumble as a bad boy smile tugged the corners of his lips. It made my stomach flutter in anticipation of what that punishment might be. I rose up on my toes to brush a soft kiss over his lips. Despite my jeweled four-inch stilettos, he still towered over me.

"I can assure you, Mr. Stone. I'm counting on it."

Alexander

I DIDN'T WANT Krystina to leave my side, but I had networking to do. This was a momentous night for Matteo and I had a lot invested in my friend's success. I was sure she would be bored stiff with the dry conversations about to ensue.

Although I was curious over her comment about Matteo, I figured it was best if I didn't know the details. Men always flocked to Allyson and her charms. Matteo was not immune. I noticed the way he looked at her, but she always appeared to keep him out of arms reach. I hoped he had the sense to stay focused tonight, rather than get caught up with her, as I had seen him do so many times in the past.

After thirty minutes of working the room, I had a good feeling about the restaurant's future success. I stood around a tall table conversing and shaking every hand offered to me. The food was getting rave reviews, and the excitement was at its peak. The high was contagious. Even the press coverage was solely focused on the restaurant, their prying eyes staying away from me for once.

I scanned the room for Krystina. She had been gone a while, despite my warning. I was surprised to see she was no longer with Allyson, but instead talking to the mayor and his wife. Her smile was bright, and her audience laughed at whatever she just said. Apparently, I wasn't the only one working the room this evening.

Interesting...

Her eyes caught mine and I felt that familiar tug. I knew she felt it too. Reaching out to shake the mayor's hand, she excused herself and headed in my direction. I watched her hips sway ever so subtly under the blue chiffon gown and I couldn't help but to admire her choice in attire. Even her makeup was spot on. Krystina never wore much makeup, but tonight she had painted her lips a deep red and added smoky shadow on her eyes. She looked absolutely stunning and I was acutely aware of the men who stared. She had the attention of every able-bodied man in the room and she didn't even know it.

"Alexander," said a male voice to my left. Breaking my gaze

away from Krystina, I turned to see who was addressing me. I quickly masked my displeasure when I saw who it was.

"Vic," I greeted with a fake, plastic smile. The last thing I wanted to do was engage with Victor Carr, the Wall Street shark who had been after me about making Stone Enterprise available for public trade. His presence was a reminder of why I preferred private dinners over public ones.

"It's good to see you again. I know you're technically here for restaurant matters, but I'd like to talk to you about –," he began, but I silenced him by holding up my hand.

"It's not happening, Vic."

He let out an easy laugh.

"Not to worry. I wasn't going into market talks with you tonight. This is something different and merely just friendly conversation."

I doubted that, but still gave him my attention.

"Go on."

"There's a property in Pennsylvania you might be interested in. It has historical significance," Victor informed me.

"Historical significance means a whole lot of red tape. I tend to avoid that for obvious reasons," I said dryly.

"This one isn't up for sale. It's a hotel that needs investors to bring it back to its former glory. Considering your recent venture with Wally's Grocery Stores, I may have mentioned your name as an interested party."

"Again Vic, not my thing. Wally's was an economic decision. It was all about preventing job loss in the city."

"What if I told you this property was owned by Roger Hennessey?"

I paused then, considering what he was saying. Roger Hennessey was the driving force behind bringing European football to the United States. He planned to be at the ribbon cutting ceremony for Stone Arena. If it weren't for him, the stadium would still be a pipedream.

"That's interesting to know. I might look into it," I told him, careful to keep a poker face in play and not say any more. Victor Carr was smart. I knew he considered his referral a favor, one he might try to use as leverage to further push me about going public. I was about to comment on it when Krystina slid up beside me.

"Sorry, I got caught up," she told me.

"Is this the lady of the hour?" Victor drawled.

I gritted my teeth. I didn't like his tone. It was then when I remembered the other connection I had to Victor. He wasn't only a shark on Wall Street. He was also a member of Club O. I'd only seen him there a couple of times in passing, but it was enough that he'd remember my affiliation with the exclusive club. He knew the privacy rules, but there was something sinister about the way he fixed his gaze on Krystina. Seeing as though she was with me, it made it easy for one to assume she was also a member. There was no doubt he'd try to test the limits. My fists clenched as I tried to fight the rage boiling up. I knew I'd have to play this cool or risk exposure.

"Krystina, this is Victor Carr."

"It's a pleasure to meet you, Krystina."

Victor extended his hand to Krystina. I expected a handshake, but he lifted her hand to his lips to kiss the backside instead. I saw red.

Before I could react, Krystina pulled her hand away, not allowing his lips to linger. She reached up to touch my arm reassuringly and moved closer to my side. I wrapped a protective arm around her waist.

"It's nice to meet you too, Mr. Carr. How do you and Alex know each other?" she asked politely. I stiffened. It was an innocent question, but she had no idea how loaded it was.

"Vic works on Wall Street," I answered in a neutral tone.

"We also belong to the same country *club*," Victor added,

emphasizing the last word. I wanted to knock his fucking teeth out.

"Oh, I see," Krystina said easily, but I heard the realization in her tone. "I don't frequent the country *club,* Mr. Carr."

"You should," Vic taunted.

The hand resting on Krystina's hip flexed. She never flinched but covered my hand with hers instead. When she spoke again, her voice was sugary sweet, practically dripping.

"That place is a bit over the top for me and not really my style, if you know what I mean. Besides, Alex and I have been so busy since our engagement, there isn't time for frivolities such as the club. Isn't that right, dear?"

She looked up at me and smiled lovingly.

I blinked and was momentarily confused by her uncharacteristic swooning. It was then when I realized Krystina was making a point. She was telling Victor, in not so many words, she was not a club member. She was also saying she was committed to me and me alone. She saw through his game and was able to change the dangerous topic of conversation before I could even blink. I had forgotten how much she relied on her naturally quick wit. It was her secret weapon, one I was always trying to stamp out of her.

I didn't know how it happened, but at some point during the exchange, I found myself looking at Krystina with new eyes. For months, I had been fighting to dominate her both in and out of the bedroom. She was both my heaven and my hell, all wrapped up in one succulent package. However, I now had the realization I didn't need to fight that feisty nature anymore. I knew behind closed doors, when she was naked in our bed, I would always demand her submission and was certain she would irrevocably give it. I owned her body and she would forever be mine to command.

But it needed to end there.

My attempt to dominate her outside the bedroom was

wrong. It would kill her spirit and I wanted her to be true to herself. I loved this fiery woman beside me – quick tongue and all. To see her use that defensive weapon on someone else gave me an unexpected feeling of satisfaction.

My firecracker. My angel. And soon to be my wife.

At that moment, although I didn't think it was possible, I loved her even more.

"Yes, our engagement has kept us *very* busy," I agreed. I winked and smiled down at her. In a possessive move, I pulled her closer to me, silently sending my own private message to Victor.

"Engaged? I – I hadn't realized," he stammered. "I guess congratulations are in order."

A waiter walked by carrying a tray of champagne flutes. The timing couldn't have been more perfect. I grabbed two. I handed one to Krystina and kept one for myself, deliberately leaving Victor empty handed.

"A toast," I began and looked to Krystina. "To us."

"To us," she repeated.

12

Krystina

"I'm assuming that guy wasn't talking about a country club," I whispered to Alexander as we made our way to the dinner table.

"No, angel. He wasn't."

I looked around and wondered how many other restaurant guests were club members. The world I had once considered exclusive to a small portion of the population was obviously more common than I thought. I shivered as I recalled the way Victor eyed me up and down.

"Ugh, he just gave me the creeps."

"Yes, he has that effect on people," Alexander agreed with a hint of venom in his voice. "I often wondered how he became so successful. His personality leaves much to be desired."

When we reached the table, Luca was waiting for us with a bottle of wine in hand and a linen table napkin draped over one arm. Alexander removed his arm from around my waist so I could slide into the booth that had been prepared for us. His hand lingered for a moment, tracing over the line of my hip, before he moved to sit beside me. Once we were settled, Luca held out a bottle of red for Alexander to inspect.

"Tonight's main course will be Barley Risotto with Mushrooms and Gremolata. Mr. Donati has chosen to pair it with a 2006 *Villa Gemma Montepulciano d'Abruzzo Riserva.*"

The words rolled off his tongue with ease, although I didn't comprehend much more than barley, risotto, and mushrooms. I was reminded of how out of my element I could feel in Alexander's world sometimes. While I was getting used to it, I would never lose my appreciation for Thai takeout and cheap white wine. Conversely, Alexander seemed to know exactly what Luca said and nodded his approval. After removing the cork, Luca poured a small amount of red wine into a stemmed glass for Alexander to sample.

"Exceptional vintage," Alexander said with appreciation. He swirled the glass and took another sip before handing the empty glass to Luca.

After Luca poured the deep maroon liquid into two glasses, another server seemed to materialize out of thin air to place a basket of fresh bread and olive oil at our table. Steam wafted from the basket and provoked a rumble from my stomach. During cocktail hour, the only thing I managed to consume was a pancetta wrapped fig. While it was delicious, it was hardly enough to curb my appetite.

Once Luca and the other server were gone, I went to reach for the bread but Alexander beat me to it. Tearing off a piece of the loaf, he dipped it into a small bit of oil and brought it to my mouth. Accepting his offer, I opened my lips for him.

"You're beautiful. So enticing and radiant," he murmured.

I blushed at his compliment, never one to accept them graciously, as I moved my mouth around the warm and flakey crust. Swallowing the bread, I reached for my wine. However, Alexander caught my wrist and stopped me. As he had with the bread, he brought the glass to my lips. Feeling awkward over such a public display of intimacy, I gently pulled my wrist free and took the glass from his hand. I took a sip and met his gaze. His eyes were intense as always, but there was something more in them that I couldn't quite place.

"Matteo has really outdone himself. The wait staff he hired –," I began. I stopped short when I saw the way Alexander's eyes flashed hot. Smoldering almost. Baffled, I asked, "What is it?"

"I've asked once, but now I'm going to ask you again. Are you trying to give me a hard on in public?"

"What in the world are you talking about? I haven't done anything," I laughed.

"Angel, you're not wearing any panties."

My eyes widened in surprise.

How could he possibly know that?

But then I remembered the way his hand lingered on my hip right before we sat down at the table. I was fairly confident that was the moment he discovered the absence of my usual lace undergarment.

"Look, I didn't do it to be kinky," I tried to explain. "It's just that the dress is somewhat fitted through the hips and you could see my underwear and stocking lines through it. That's all."

"No stockings either?"

"Well, er –," I faltered. "I have on thigh highs."

His eyes burned even darker. I was familiar with that expression of burning hunger. I knew it all too well. Alexander was undeniably aroused. That knowledge caused a sudden tightening in my core and I squirmed a bit in my chair. To my astonishment, I felt his hand move up the side of my calf, over my knee and to my thigh. He squeezed, biting into the skin of my leg.

"No panties and not following my instructions. I did warn you there would be punishment if you were gone for too long," he reminded me. His voice reverberated through the hum of conversation and the gravely Louis Armstrong lyrics piping through the overhead speakers.

"I wasn't gone that long," I practically squeaked.

I tried to move away, but he gripped tighter and rendered me immobile. My pulse quickened as his hand traveled up further. My breath caught in my throat.

"Angel, any amount of time you're away from me is too long," he said in a guttural tone.

I looked around the room. People were everywhere, conversing and eating, completely unaware of what was happening at the booth in the corner. To the casual observer, we were just two people enjoying dinner together. At least I hoped. I silently prayed the tablecloth was long enough to hide Alexander's roaming hand.

Inch by inch, his fingers crawled. For some ludicrous reason, the Itsy-Bitsy Spider song began to play in my head. As Alexander got closer to the mark, I began to feel slightly panicked. I glanced around the room again. Nothing seemed out of the ordinary. All I saw were normal people enjoying a normal dinner. Except for our table. Nothing about this was *normal*.

"Alex," I hissed. "People might see!"

"So, what?" he replied to my horror. His voice was deep and husky, challenging me to deny him. When his fingers finally made contact with my sex, I sharply sucked in a gulp of air. My nipples tightened as he slid expertly over my folds until he found a slick bundle of nerves. The fear of being caught was appalling, yet so incredibly erotic at the same time.

He swiped up. Once. Twice. I stifled a moan as I tried to, once again, recall the length of the tablecloth.

It's long enough to hide. Isn't it?

It had to be. I was coming apart at the seams. It was all I could do to keep it together. The only thing stopping me from giving in was the fact Luca was approaching our table. I clamped my legs closed tightly, but my plan to make Alexander stop backfired. I only succeeded in locking his fingers in place.

"Alex," I breathed. "You have to stop. Luca is headed this way."

A knowing smile curled up the edge of his lips and his sapphire blues flashed hot.

"Oh, no. This is your punishment, Miss Cole."

My eyes widened from utter disbelief as I stared at him.

He couldn't possibly...

My little devil friend twirled with glee as the angel erupted into flames. Luca was getting closer and closer, his arms laden with a tray or something or another. Probably food. I didn't really care what it was. Alexander had to stop this madness. At the sound of Luca's voice, my head snapped to attention. I was sure my cheeks were flushed, but I put on the most innocent smile I could muster.

"May I present the first course of the evening. Artichoke Parmesan Crostini and marinated olives. I see you are enjoying the bread and *bagna cauda*. Can I get you anything else?"

Bagna what?

I couldn't process Luca's words. Alexander's woodsy cologne combined with his wandering fingers clouded my thinking. I grabbed my wine and took a sip in order to avoid speaking. The wine warmed my throat as it went down. I had barely swallowed when Alexander pushed a finger inside, twirling and teasing around my clenched entrance. I wanted to grind shamelessly into his hand, but I couldn't. We were in a restaurant. Luca was only a mere few feet away. However, none of that mattered to Alexander. He was intentionally driving me to the point of madness.

"I'm all set for now. Everything looks delicious," Alexander told Luca. "Krystina? How about you? Do you need anything?"

I was thankful I already swallowed my wine. If I hadn't, I

might have spit it out all over the table right then and there. I looked to Luca who was patiently awaiting my response. I tried not to think about the fingers still probing my sensitive tissues.

"I'm good," I told him, my voice sounding strained to my own ears. The warm trail that began with the wine was now ablaze with flames brought on by Alexander's merciless exploration.

"Very good then. I'll be back to check on you momentarily," Luca responded with a slight bow before leaving our table once more. He seemed completely unaware of my suffering, yet how I managed to get through that was beyond me. Air expelled from my lungs in a whoosh and I started to tremble.

"My, my. That was an Academy Award winning performance, Miss Cole. I'm impressed."

"I can't believe you did that," I hissed, struggling to maintain control.

Heat pulsed through the blood in my veins as he continued to stroke. Regardless of our setting, Alexander always knew how to get me off. My orgasm was building. I could feel it. I wanted nothing more than to spread my legs wider and grant him full access. I was so close, desperate to feel the incredible height only Alexander could bring me to.

However, I was intensely aware of the people around us. I would need to deliver more than an Academy Award performance if I wanted to conceal the pleasure that was seconds away from tearing through my body. My gaze met his. His stare was intense as he continued to massage my clit with rapid circles. I couldn't look at him. Instead, I closed my eyes and tried to be still, as if nothing out of the ordinary was going on.

My core had just begun to deliciously tighten, when all at once the incredible release I craved was viciously snatched away. I opened my eyes in shock and looked at Alexander. His hand was no longer under the table but reaching to sample the crostini. I stared in awe as he casually took a bite, chewed, then slowly licked his fingers clean.

"My favorite," he said and eyed me seductively. I knew he wasn't referring to the food.

He's toying with me.

Just fifteen minutes earlier, I was aghast at the idea of doing anything sexual in the middle of a crowded restaurant. However, in the blink of an eye, Alexander had me throwing caution to the wind, helpless under his magic. Now here I sat, about to combust from overwhelming sexual frustration.

A wicked smile wrapped around the finger he sucked, making me suspicious of the casual way he slid each finger between his lips. I knew then, this was not a game.

"You aren't going to let me finish, are you?" I whispered incredulously.

"Only I say when, angel."

My scowl turned into a full-blown pout. This was, without a doubt, the worst punishment he had ever doled out. It was nothing short of torture. I picked up my wine and threw back a huge gulp. Flustered by my desire and newfound irritation, I channeled my emotion into the food by adding a few olives to my plate. This was going to be the longest dinner of my life.

13

Alexander

K rystina and I exited the restaurant and made our way across the sidewalk to the awaiting limousine. The hired driver held open the door for us as we approached. I guided Krystina inside, before glancing over my shoulder to see Hale just a few feet behind us. Before he had the chance to climb into the front passenger seat of the limo, I motioned him over to me.

"Any word from Justine?" I asked quietly.

"No, sir. I can go to her condo if you'd like," Hale offered. There was sadness in the eyes of my security detail. It was an emotion that was uncharacteristic and somewhat alarming. Given the situation, I should have asked him what he knew about Charlie's story. But, for some reason, I couldn't bring myself to form the words. Just as I was stalling a more fervent attempt to find Justine. Something didn't feel right in my gut, compelling me to proceed with caution.

"Just wait. I'll give her another couple of days, then go there myself."

"Yes, sir."

I turned back to the limo and climbed inside beside Krystina. Once the driver closed the door, she slid over next to me and rested her head against my arm.

"Everything okay?" she asked.

I moved to wrap my arm around her, brought her head to my chest, and traced small circles on her shoulder with the tip of my finger.

"Everything is fine. I think the night was a huge success. The food critics loved the place. Matteo has a lot to look forward to."

"I didn't mean about the restaurant," she said, her words barely above a whisper.

I knew that, but I was hoping she didn't want to revisit the conversation we had before the party, despite my promise to answer her questions. The problem loomed over us all night. And while it never reared its ugly head, it was always lurking in the shadows.

"Justine hasn't answered any of my calls. She hasn't gotten back to Hale either. I'm concerned."

Krystina became quiet, but I knew my angel. I was sure she had a thousand thoughts running through her mind. More than likely, she was deciding on which one to voice first. She reached out, ran her hand up my thigh, over my chest, before coming to rest on my cheek. She pulled back slightly and looked up at me. Her dark brown eyes were full of patience, but I could see the questions swirling in their depth too.

"Why Stone?" she asked.

"Stone?"

"Yes. Why did you choose that?"

I looked up ahead. The limo had begun to move, merging into the late evening traffic. Hale gave me a sideways glance, alerting me to the fact we could be heard. Leaning forward, I pressed the button that would raise the privacy glass. I didn't mind if Hale heard our conversation, as he was one of the very few who knew the history of my name. However, the limousine driver was out of the question. I knew the story would most likely come out soon, but I needed to hang on to my identity for just a little while longer.

Once the privacy glass was all the way up, I tilted my head to look down at Krystina.

"My grandfather's name was Edward Stonewall. He was a European football player, or soccer player, as people in the United States call it. He played for Sheffield in the late nineteen forties, after the Second World War. He was a good defender, very good if the recounts I've read are correct, until he got injured. Leaving the sport was difficult for him. Fortunately, he had a young Italian wife to pick up the pieces," I paused and took a moment to reminisce. I looked out the window at the passing buildings. The nightlights briefly illuminated them and created a mesmerizing strobe-like effect. "Lucille Silvestri, my grandmother, was a force to be reckoned with. She took the money he earned and moved them both to the United States. She said they needed a fresh start."

"You said Stonewall. Did he shorten the name?"

"Yes and no. Everyone called him Stone, but it wasn't his legal name and it was not one he used. He didn't start using it until," I stopped momentarily and shook my head, not wanting to remember. "He didn't start using the name until Justine and I started having a hard time in school. Everyone knew about the Russo kids, their dead father, and missing mother. We couldn't escape it."

"The day of the car accident, the reason I went to the library," she began. Hurt showed in her eyes, tearing at my heart. I knew what she was going to say next, but I still asked.

"What about the library?"

"I told you why I was going there that day, Alex. I wanted to look into your family. I couldn't find anything online and I just wanted to help you. You could have told me all of this then, but you never said anything. Why?"

"Outside of the fact I wanted to keep the name dead and buried, there was also too much going on at the time. You were in the hospital and had barely begun to recover from your injuries when it came up. What was I supposed to say?"

"How about the truth?" she asked quietly, but I could still hear the accusation in her tone.

"No. The truth didn't matter. My grandmother, like she did for her and my grandfather years earlier, gave us a fresh start."

"How did she manage that? I mean, a story such as yours..." she trailed off. She didn't need to go into detail. I lived it.

"We moved to another part of the city. She enrolled us in a new school under the names Alexander and Justine Stone. It was around this time my grandparents legally changed their name to Stone. In doing so, it protected us and gave them anonymity from their previous life in England so as not to be easily discovered. Following my grandfather's wishes, Justine and I legally changed ours once we turned eighteen." I shrugged. "It was an easy adjustment because we had been going by Stone for years."

"Who else knows this story besides Charlie, and well, now *The City Times*?"

I considered her question. It was a fair inquiry, especially after the way I deliberately kept the information from her.

"Hale and his mother know. I just recently learned Justine told Charlie. I suspect Matteo knows too, but I'm not certain."

"You suspect?"

"Matteo's grandmother, my grandmother, and Hale's mother were all friends," I clarified. "Matteo is five years younger than me, so it's possible he doesn't remember the chaos of what went on back then. But he's dropped hints here and there which makes me think he knows. Either way, I can trust him to not say anything. Other than those mentioned,

Justine and I are the only ones who know about the name change. And, of course, now you know as well."

"What about Stephen or Bryan?"

"They don't know. Although, I have contemplated telling Stephen. He is my lawyer after all. Given the current situation, I suppose I'll have to tell him sooner rather than later."

She looked thoughtful for a minute before her eyes suddenly widened. She bolted up right.

"No! Alex, I think Suzanne knows too!"

"Suzanne Jacobs? Justine's friend? What makes you think that?"

"It was something she said on the night of the charity ball. I just passed it off as drunk ramblings, but now I don't know."

"Krystina, what did she say?" I demanded a little too harshly.

"It was nonsense, really. I haven't even thought about it until now. She kept carrying on about how I didn't know the real you. She was talking to me like I was just a silly child, but it was the way she said your name." She hesitated and shook her head. Her vision seemed to cloud as if she were trying to piece something together.

"What do you mean? What about the way she said it, Krystina?" I fought the urge to shake the answer out of her.

"She said I was naïve and emphasized your name, like your name was a joke. Then she said I didn't know as much as I thought I did. I don't know, Alex. It could be nothing."

I ran a hand through my hair in frustration. Justine was close to Suzanne. There was a good chance she did know.

"Fuck!"

"Alex, don't jump to conclusions. I could be wrong," she said and put a placating hand on my arm.

"She's a woman scorned. She'll talk. To hell with whatever stops Hale pulled out. If Suzanne does know, and *The City Times* finds this out, that's all the corroboration they need to publish." I sat back and pulled her close. "I'm sorry, angel. When I told you my story, I should have told you everything. I just didn't think my old name held any relevance. But now, with Charlie's interview, I know how everything looks."

She settled into my arms easily, her warmth comforting the mounting fear I was feeling.

"It's just a name, Alex."

"I wish it were only that, angel," I said and began to stroke the top of her hair. She had it styled up, bobby pins restricting her otherwise unruly curls. One by one, I began to pull them out, needing the feel of her soft locks between my fingers. She didn't protest, but rather assisted my dismantling of her elaborate up-do.

"It is just a name," she reiterated as she dumped a handful of bobby pins into her clutch. "You are Alexander Stone. While I might be hurt I didn't know all of this sooner, I understand why you did what you did. Others will too."

"No, Krystina. You're not seeing the big picture here."

I took her face between my hands. Her now free curls cascaded down over her shoulders. The passing streetlights reflected behind her, casting a halo effect around her head. She was a vision, an angel who would save me from eternal damnation.

"Tell me, Alex. What am I missing then?"

"The gun I threw in the river, while I might have been just a child, Charlie's interview is much more damaging than the actions of a distraught boy. The name change, my demolition of the old projects...those were decisions I made as an adult. I look guilty."

"Are you guilty?"

"I don't know, angel. I ask myself that same question every day."

14

Krystina

When we arrived at the penthouse, Alexander immediately went to the living room, grabbed a bottle of whiskey from the wet bar, and poured some into a lowball glass. No ice. Two fingers, not one. He threw back the amber liquid and poured another. I frowned. Alexander always exercised control when he drank. This was way out of the norm.

He braced his arms on the edges of the wet bar and dropped his head to his chest. His back was to me, but I could tell he was taking a few deep breaths.

"Alex?" I questioned cautiously.

"What?" he snapped but didn't turn around.

"What's wrong? You never drink that fast."

He picked up the glass holding his second round, stared at it for a moment, before tipping back the contents.

"Every man has his poison of choice. Today, mine's whiskey," he stated bitterly.

Alarmed, I moved toward him slowly, like he was a wild

animal that could be spooked at any moment. Slipping my arms around his waist, I moved my hands up to feel the slow and steady rhythm of his heart. We stayed like that for a long moment before he eventually seemed to calm. Turning toward me, he wrapped his arms tightly around my back and cocooned me to his chest.

"I'm okay, angel. I just need a minute."

I nuzzled my head into his shoulder as he stroked the length of my hair. I felt as though my heart might burst.

"Let me take your pain away." I lifted my head up to meet his gaze. Torment swirled within his pools of sapphire, so I offered the only thing I could to erase it. "Be with me."

He took my chin between his fingers and brushed his lips softly over mine.

"I want that," he murmured and ran a hand down my arms in quiet tenderness. A familiar warmth spread through me and I tipped my head further back, my silent plea for him to deepen his kiss.

Pushing my tongue past his lips, I explored the depths of his mouth, tangling my tongue with his. He matched my intensity, pulling my body tighter to his.

"Take me to bed, Alex."

His grip on me slackened, creating an unwanted space between us. I ached for him to return.

"I'm wound too tight, angel. I don't think..." he trailed off, seeming unable to find the words to express his thoughts. He began to turn away, but I placed a hand on his arm to stop him. I didn't understand his hesitation, but I didn't need to.

"I want you. In this moment, nothing else matters."

His eyes met mine, burning with an intense hunger I had never quite seen before. I reached up and slid one of the beaded sapphire straps of my dress down my shoulder. Repeating it with the other, I let the expensive material fall into a pool at my feet. Pantiless and clad in nothing but my bra and heels, I stepped out of the dress and moved to rejoin him. Bringing my fingers to the buttons of his tuxedo shirt, I slowly worked to expose his flesh. I needed the feel of his skin and his hard abdomen beneath my fingers.

"No. Wait," he said. He grabbed my wrists, stopping my hands from continuing their exploration. The pain and sadness were back in his eyes and I felt my heart sink.

"Why? You need this, Alex. We need this. Let me take your pain away," I repeated.

I searched his face, trying to read the emotions flashing across his features. I saw more than just pain and sadness. I also saw worry, fear, and anger. When he released his hold on my wrists, I cast my gaze down and saw that his hands were balled into tight fists.

"It's not what you think, Krystina. Too many things happened today. I'm afraid that," he paused and looked to the ceiling. "God, I'll lose my fucking mind if I can't get inside you soon."

I arched a brow in confusion and shifted a little. I struggled to ignore the growing ache between my thighs, as his mention of being inside me nearly caused my legs to turn to jell-o.

"So, what's stopping you?"

He came to me and pressed his forehead down to mine. His palms splayed over my hips as his eyes found mine. I moved my hands up to trail my fingers over his chest, appreciating every ripple of honed muscle as I went.

"I don't want to hurt you, angel," he whispered.

"You could never hurt me. I trust you. Lose control on me, Alex."

He needed it, but I needed it too. Perhaps it was selfish on my part, but I wanted nothing more than for him to own me, to unleash his dominance and take what he desired. I wanted to be entwined in passion, lost in a world where nothing else mattered except for the power only Alexander could wield over me.

"Fuck, Krystina," he growled. His eyes blazed with unhinged desire. "You don't know what you're asking for."

Perhaps I didn't, but it didn't matter to me. I meant what I said. I trusted him with my whole heart, mind, body, and soul.

He lifted me effortlessly and I scissored my legs around his hips. As he walked us to the bedroom, I swiped my tongue up the side of his throat, relishing in his scent and the subtle saltiness of his skin. When we entered the bedroom, he flipped on the switch for the lights. After adjusting the dimmer so the lights were only a subtle glow, he spun to pin me roughly against the wall. I felt a hand fist in my hair, tightening as my head was yanked back.

He ravaged my mouth like he was starving and I tightened my legs around him. His teeth bit into my lower lip, the sharp sensation cutting through me and intensifying the ache in my core. I was more than ready for everything he could give me.

Lowering me to the floor, he reached around and unfastened the clasp of my bra. The straps loosened and fell down my shoulders, freeing my breasts one by one. He captured a nipple between his teeth, teasing the hardened point, before trailing hot kisses down my body until he reached my wet sex.

"Alex," I whimpered, practically begging for more.

I intertwined my fingers through his hair, encouraging him to take more as a fire began to build. It flowed through me, hot like lava. After the way he kept me on edge all through dinner, it didn't take more than a few strokes of his tongue to bring me to the point of eruption. Alexander knew I was close and he intensified the pressure of his tongue. Focusing on the sensitive bundle of nerves, he sucked my clit with fervor that took my breath away.

White-hot flames overtook me, blinding me in a surge of

heat as I went over the edge. I shuddered as the climax rocketed through my body and nearly collapsed from the intensity. Alexander caught me, my body yielding against his hard lines as he carried me to the bed. Setting me down, I lay back and melted into the satin sheets.

"I'll be right back," Alexander whispered into my ear.

I heard the jingling of keys and knew he was going into the closet of toys. Despite the fact I had been living in the penthouse for over two months, I had never seen the inside of Alexander's closet of fun. I hadn't wanted to. For me, I enjoyed not knowing what was in there. The mystery added to the sexual angst, just as it was at that moment. Despite my recent orgasm, my core clenched as I wondered what Alexander might return with.

Maybe the vibrator again?

I almost purred as I recalled the few times he used it on me. I silently prayed I would feel that familiar buzz tonight.

Or perhaps the nipple clamps?

The taut peaks of my breasts instantly tightened at the thought. I closed my eyes in anticipation, anxiously waiting for him to return.

After a time, I began to get sleepy. I wondered what was taking Alexander so long. My mind was drowsy as I moved to sit up. Propping up onto my elbows, my vision came into focus. I saw Alexander sitting in a chair in the corner of the room. He was completely in the buff, lazily swirling the key for the closet around his finger.

"I'm sorry," I said groggily. Although I'd never admit it, I was beginning to realize I should have listened to his warnings about overdoing it this past week. "I must have dozed off."

Alexander dropped the key to the floor, stood, and walked over to me. Even though the lighting was dim, I could see the dangerous glint in his eyes. My eyes traveled down past his tapered V and settled on his long, thick erection looking impossibly hard. Instantly, I became wide-awake.

"Get off the bed," he ordered.

I did as I was instructed without question, having grown more than accustomed to following Alexander's bedroom commands without a second thought. In fact, I had come to relish in them. However, this time I paused as something caught my eye. I turned my head to the right and saw two long metal bars fashioned in the shape of an X at the foot of the bed.

The St. Andrews Cross.

Goose bumps raced down my spine from the prospect of being bound to it for the first time. Alexander always hinted around it, but he had yet to actually do it. During my brief slumber, he must have secured the rails that formed the cross. I eyed up the loops attached to it. A rush of heat crashed between my legs, the sudden burst of arousal catching me by surprise.

I looked at Alexander. He pointed with his finger, directing me to the front of the cross.

"I don't know what –," I began. I was going to tell him I didn't know what to do next, but I was silenced when his hand covered my mouth.

"No talking, Krystina."

When I nodded my understanding, Alexander removed his hand from my mouth. Taking hold of my hips, he positioned me closer to the cross. The cool metal pressed against my skin, the point of intersection coming just below my breasts. I shivered as another blast of goose bumps peppered my spine.

Moving at a painstakingly slow pace, Alexander bent to secure a soft leather cuff around one ankle, before moving to do the same with the other. Coaxing my legs apart, he was careful to steady my high-heeled clad feet so I didn't teeter. Once I was balanced, he bound each ankle to opposite legs of the cross. My exposed sex throbbed as he moved up my body, stroking and caressing my backside as he went. Pausing in his ascent, he fondled my folds and pinched at my clit, before pressing his thumb against the tight entrance of my rear. My breathing hitched, the pressure sending another wave of pleasure through me.

However, he gave me no satisfaction. Instead, I was left wanting as he continued moving up. His hands slid up and over my shoulders and down to tease my straining nipples. Using one hand, he took hold of one of my wrists. I expected him to secure a cuff to it, but he brought it to the pulsing juncture of my thighs instead. Interlacing his fingers with mine, he cupped my dripping wet sex, massaging the throbbing pressure point of my body. I moaned as our joined hands slid back up my abdomen, leaving a trail of moisture along my torso, before coming to a stop near my mouth.

"You felt it, angel. You felt how wet you are for me. Now I want you to wrap your lips around your fingers and taste how much your body wants this."

I turned my head to the side so I could see him, my arousal reaching an all-time high. Feeling wanton, I locked my gaze on his and slowly parted my lips to taste my essence. I licked and sucked, relishing the feel of his hard erection straining against my backside. He hummed in pleasure over my actions.

Removing my fingers from my greedy mouth, he procured more cuffs and secured them around each wrist. After fastening them to the cross bars above my head, he took a step back.

"Admiring your handiwork," I teased. Although I couldn't see him, I could feel it in the air when he tensed and immediately realized my mistake. I wasn't supposed to talk. I lowered my head, knowing he wouldn't be pleased. He *tsked* at me and stepped closer to me once again. From behind, he took my head between his hands and lifted it up. I could smell the whiskey on his breath as he slid his tongue up the side of my neck and bit at my earlobe.

"Look straight ahead," he told me. My gaze focused on the sight in front of me. In the mirrored headboard of the bed, I saw my bound reflection. I was open and spread wide, helpless to his mercy. My eyes met his in the mirror. A slow, satisfied grin spread across his face. "Tell me your safe word, Krystina."

"Sapphire," I breathed. His smile widened.

"Good girl. Now you're going to watch as I flog you."

15

Alexander

I took great satisfaction in the way Krystina's eyes widened in surprise over what was to come. I also saw a twinge of fear in them as well. As twisted as it was, my cock grew harder because of it. I didn't try to rationalize the thought, or even worry about the possibility of her being afraid. I was too focused on her body, all strung up, and that glorious ass just waiting to be marked. I ran a hand over the smooth curves, appreciating its beauty.

Almost unwillingly, I stepped away to move to the dresser. With the press of a few buttons, music filled the quiet room. However, the melody wasn't what I wanted. It was too soft, too calming. After a quick scroll through the playlists, I settled on a Breaking Benjamin song from the "Control" playlist. It was a dark tune. Cold. Yet, it was intense and penetrating, suitable for my current state of mind.

Picking up the flogger, I turned back to her and ran my fingers through the deep chestnut curls cascading down her back. I walked around her, appreciating the view in front of me, as well as her reflection in the mirror.

"Christ, you're fucking beautiful tied up like this," I murmured. She was the picture-perfect image of absolute submission. I absently wondered why I had taken so long to tie her up this way. A twinge of guilt hit me as an unwelcomed memory tugged at my subconscious, reminding me why I stayed away from using the cross. It was because I didn't trust myself. Having her tied up, helpless to my every whim, was dangerous.

I shook my head.

No. Krystina will be different. She has to be.

I loved her too much to hurt her. Yet, as I ran the length of the flogger through my fingers, I hesitated. Krystina's shoulders rose and fell, her breaths deep and even. She knew what was coming and was preparing herself for the first blow.

I touched her again and ran my palm over her waist, across the curve of her hip and down her thigh. She was a flawless hourglass. My hand paused momentarily near the top of her thigh-high stockings, torn over whether I should remove them to expose her creamy flesh or leave them in place. When my eyes rested on those fuck-me shoes, blood began to pulse in my ears.

I ran the leather through my fingers again, examining the texture. I smacked the whip against my palm, testing it, and the devil inside me came to life. I wanted to rule her. To own her. My desire to see her flesh a beautiful shade of red was overwhelming. With the flogger in hand, I raised my arm and delivered the first lash.

SNAP!

The sound of leather on her skin was like music to my ears. Krystina didn't even flinch, all too familiar with the feeling the first jolt brought to the senses. Her head lolled back as she relished the sensation.

"Eyes on the mirror, angel," I reminded her. She promptly obeyed, her obedience an aphrodisiac that made me want to fuck her into oblivion. I brought the flogger to her skin again, not bothering with my usual care to make sure I struck in a different place. My need to mark her was too fierce, my dominance taking control. Slowly, lash after lash, I peppered her skin until it was glowing pink.

With every one of her moans, my dick hardened to the point of pain. She was mine, and she was at the mercy of everything I had to give. I eventually lost all track of time and the number of lashings I doled out. If I had been thinking clearly when we began, I would have told her to count them herself. It was no matter. The skin on her backside was already heavily marked, having received enough blows that they would still be visible come morning. I paused and rubbed a hand over her reddened ass. I imagined fucking that ass until I exploded and my seed poured down the lengths of her firm thighs.

I looked at her reflection in the mirror. Her eyes were glazed as she struggled to maintain focus, enthralled in the pleasure and pain I gave her. Endorphins would eventually kick in, but she wasn't quite there yet.

Just a little more, angel. I promise it will be worth it.

I channeled my promise to her with a soft caress to her swollen clit. It was hard with need and I itched to sink my cock into her, craving the restriction of her tight walls. I went to my knees and swiped my tongue over her vulva, the soft touch a dramatic contrast to the whipping she had been receiving. I groaned as I licked through her silk and breathed in her scent. Digging my fingers into her hips, I plunged my tongue in and out. I licked inside her, fucking her, feeling her spasm around my tongue.

"Ah!" she cried out, breaking her obedient silence as she tugged on her restraints.

I pulled my head away and stood up. Wrapping a hand

around her mass of curls, I formed a ponytail. I jerked her head close to my lips and looked at her reflection. Her mouth was open and slack. I yanked harder on the strands of her hair and whispered a warning into her ear.

"Be quiet."

Turning the flogger over in my palm, I squeezed it until my knuckles turned white. Sweat began to bead on my neck and back as I prodded the handle against her entrance. I watched her in the mirror as she fought her heavy-lidded eyes, absorbing the feeling. She was so worked up, her body responsive to even the slightest of touch. I quickly pulled the handle away, not wanting her to come just yet. Her orgasm would be mine, but not until I was buried balls deep in her heat.

With a flick of my wrist, I brought the leather straps around to strike one of her nipples. I aimed again, this time snapping it against the other one. I watched as they hardened and puckered, all while Krystina quietly whimpered her desire.

"Does this feel good?"

She nodded and I lavished more whips, one by one, inch by inch, down her body until I came to her sweet spot. I tormented her with gentle flicks at first, but I needed more. I wanted her to feel the same fire that surged through my veins.

Lose control on me, Alex.

My palms shook with adrenaline as I recalled her words. I ached to slap her, the need to take exactly what she offered burning hot. I wanted to take her. To claim her. To break her. I craved it with every fiber of my being. My breathing became more erratic and I felt my mind begin to slip away, a monster taking control of the restrained man underneath.

With one swift motion, I snapped the leather hard over her clitoris. She cried out, her words unintelligible. I didn't chastise her for speaking this time. I wanted her pain. I wanted her screams and desperate pleas. I needed them. My compassion and restraint slipped away as I hit her fiery nub again. Then again, denying her any sort of reprieve between lashings.

"Alex! I can't...I can't," she choked.

"You can and you will."

I spoke with more authority than I ever had with her before, the devil inside me now completely unleashed. She was nearing her limit, but I wasn't finished with her yet. I wielded back, striking her across both cheeks hard, her screams fueling me with unexplainable euphoria. I needed to see the pink blaze spreading over her skin turn to a deep red. Pausing, I ran the leather down the length of her spine. She stiffened under it, her body tensing in protest.

"No...please," she whispered.

I took in her reflection again. Her eyes were glossy and her body hung limply from the cross, almost haggard. Her gaze met mine in the mirror. It was like she was fighting off a sex-induced coma, but not necessarily in a good way. Pain was written plainly on her face. But worse – desperation stared back at me.

My clouded vision cleared, and I staggered a few steps back. I knew that look. I had seen it the last time I had a woman tied to a cross. It wasn't here, at my penthouse, as I had never used the custom features of my bed before meeting Krystina. I was at Club O.

If I focused hard enough, I'd still be able to hear the pulsing rhythm of the club music as I ascended the steps to the private suites. I squeezed my eyes closed tight, trying to block out the memories from that night. It hadn't ended well. I had completely lost control. I couldn't even recall the woman's name, but perhaps I had never asked. I only knew I ignored her pleas for me to stop, and I never heard the safe word she'd sworn she used. I had crossed a line, one I vowed to never cross again.

It was a long time ago, but not so long that I could forget the lesson I learned. Tonight, Krystina's expression was like a ghost from the past. Never before had I worked her over like I just did. The flogger fell from my hand and hit the floor with a thud as the realization hit me.

She had been ready to use her safe word.

"Forgive me," I whispered in a voice, so low, she couldn't hear.

I hurried to remove her cuffs, first her wrists, then her ankles. I spun her to face me, crushing her weakened body to my chest as I placed a palm on her cheek. I wanted to kiss every inch of her beautiful body and make the pain, the pain I caused her, go away. I tilted her head up to look at me.

"I'm so sorry, angel."

I stared into the depths of her expressive eyes, desperately trying to get a read on what she was thinking.

"Why are you sorry?" she asked. Her voice sounded sluggish, but she seemed genuinely confused. It caught me completely off guard. I had expected her to sound despondent, or perhaps even angry. Either emotion would be deserved.

"There's a line between pain and pleasure. I crossed it and pushed you too far. I showed no discipline. I never should have –," I stopped as she brought a single finger to my lips to silence me.

"Did I use my safe word?"

"No, but..." I shook my head. I didn't think she did, but I had been so lost in the moment it was possible I didn't hear it. Just like the last time. The high I got from inflicting pain was an inherited sickness from my father. I knew I was like him the moment I broke the rules with the unnamed woman at Club O. Tonight I confirmed it. Only this time, I had hurt the woman I loved.

"But nothing," she insisted.

"Angel, you told me no. That should have been enough to make me stop."

She shook her head.

"You're the one who taught me the importance of a safe word. You said the word no could be misunderstood."

"Don't make excuses for me, Krystina. I know what I did," I spat out bitterly, feeling ashamed.

"Listen to me. When I said no tonight, I meant no more flogging because I needed release, Alex. Nothing more. Call me twisted, but I was incredibly turned on. However, I will say you did test my limits," she admitted. Her mouth tilted up in a wry smile as she reached around to rub her backside. "We probably won't be able to do that again anytime soon. I might need a few days."

Then she let out a quiet laugh. Like it was funny.

She's joking? How can she possibly be so flippant right now?

"Krystina, no. I..." I trailed off, unable to find words to describe how much of a bastard I was.

"Alex, what's really the matter?"

"What's the matter?" I repeated incredulously. "You should be livid and lashing out at me. I know what I did. The marks on your back are proof. I'm a monster and you deserve better."

"Stop this right now!" she exclaimed forcefully, catching me by surprise. She wasn't quite shouting, but I winced nonetheless. "You can't keep insisting I know everything about you, but then try to convince me you're not good for me. I know you, dammit! I know what's in your heart, but it's like you're trying to convince you and me both that you are something you're not."

"No, it's just that I don't want you to forget where I came from. I know what's inside me, just waiting to come out. I can mask it, but it's always there, Krystina."

"You're not your father, Alex."

"His blood runs through my veins. I can't change that, nor can I forget it."

"No. You are different. I gave you permission to lose control, yet you didn't." She paused and tilted her head to the side contemplatively. "Or, perhaps in your mind, you did. You shouldn't be so hard on yourself, Alex. You have always read the reactions of my body and today was no different."

I searched her face as a million emotions flooded through me. Her eyes were so expressive. If I looked hard enough, I could see into the depths of her soul. She was a warrior, wild and strong, and so beautiful. It hurt to look at her. She didn't put up with any bullshit yet having such a strong woman willingly submit her body to me made me hard. She was perfect and, at times, I wondered if she were real or if she really was an angel sent to save me.

The gravity of my actions, of what I did to her, was a crushing weight to my chest. I didn't deserve her patience and understanding. Her strength and determination were something to be revered.

I'm such a fucking asshole.

I couldn't erase what I did, but I needed to do something – anything to ease my guilt.

"Lay on the bed. I'm going to rub some cooling gel on your back."

She shook her head back and forth again.

"I don't need you to do that. My back is fine. A little raw, but fine."

Her devotion to me was unnerving. She made me feel like I was worthy of it, even when I wasn't.

"Let me make this up to you, angel. What do you need?"

She looked up and slid her hands over my cheeks to cup my face between her palms. Her fingertips, so soft and smooth, moved over my skin until her thumb rested on my bottom lip. I leaned into her gentle touch.

"I need you to let go of your control, Alex. For real this time," she said softly. "Let me make love to you."

16

Krystina

Taking Alexander's hand, I led him around to the side of the bed. With a gentle nudge, I coaxed him to sit on the edge. Leaning down, I skimmed my lips lightly over his.

"It's your turn to trust me," I whispered.

Slowly, I returned to a standing position. Walking over to the dresser, I turned off the dark tunes Alexander had been playing. I wanted to create a different atmosphere and take him to another place, one free of the demons plaguing him throughout the day and during the black hours of the night. But most importantly, I needed him to see that he didn't hurt me. I was familiar with that haunted look in his eyes. He had been recalling some memory. Whatever it was didn't matter and his guilt was completely unfounded in my opinion.

After switching to the "Persuasion" playlist, I selected a song by Glades, and lit a few candles. I closed my eyes for a moment, allowing the dreamy and melodic vocals wash over me. I needed to erase the dark energy from the room and replace it with something beautiful. It wasn't for me, but for Alexander.

Not wanting to be worried about balancing in my stilettos, I slipped the shoes off my feet and tossed them in the corner. When I turned back to Alexander, he was still seated on the bed, watching me with interest. Shadows danced over his features from the flickering candlelight. My breath caught in my throat, my adoration for this enigma of a man suddenly overwhelming me.

Stepping towards him, I bent to give him a slow and lazy kiss. Lowering to my knees, I took his thick and virile cock into my hand. His breath hissed between his teeth as I closed my lips around the lush head, flicking my tongue around leisurely before taking him further into my mouth. He was hot and silky soft. His taste ignited my senses and I greedily sucked, worshiping his manhood.

Alexander fisted his hands through my hair, encouraging me to take more. I lowered my head further until I felt him hit the back of my throat. Tightening my lips, I pulled back to swirl my tongue around his broad head, before lowering down to suck him in long, drawing pulls.

"Yes. Take it deep," he groaned and arched upward.

My sex tightened from his pleasure as I moved over him, his thick veins throbbing against my tongue. I worked him over until his grip on my hair tightened. His thighs bunched as his shaft swelled deep in my throat. His breathing became ragged and I knew he was close.

I pulled back, not wanting him to come just yet. I wanted to feel him inside me when he did. I looked up at him. Our gazes locked, the raw hunger in his eyes mirroring my own. Slick with anticipation, I stood and moved to straddle his hips. I positioned the tip of him to my entrance and lowered onto the scorching heat of his erection with painstaking restraint. He pierced me, stretching me inch by divine inch, until he was entrenched in the recess of my core. I absorbed the pleasure and disregarded the pain that always came when he was rooted so deep.

"Oh, god," I moaned. I needed this. I needed him.

"You're perfect, Krystina." He slid a finger down my cheek and over my collarbone. "I don't deserve you."

"Shhh. Don't say things like that."

With my hands braced on his shoulders, I began to move in a slow and steady rhythm, showing him with my body how much I was irrevocably his. He caught my face in his hands, brought my head down, and kissed me hard. I moaned against his lips, the intensity of his kiss sending shockwaves through my system as I continued to ride him. He broke away, his breathing ragged as his hands flexed over my hips.

"You're beautiful," he said, his voice thick with emotion. "I want to give you everything you need. I never want you to feel afraid, but only safe and cherished."

The intensity of his words nearly leveled me and my heart ached from the love I felt for him. Emotion clogged in my throat and it suddenly felt like he wasn't close enough. I needed more of him.

"More," I breathed, wanting every sensation only Alexander could make me feel.

He pushed up, and I tightened around him. His motions were determined, matching me thrust after thrust. I gripped at his shoulders, feeling his rippled muscles bunch beneath my palms. We moved together and a fine mist of sweat began to cover our skin. I kissed him again, our breaths mingling as we rose to new heights. Our hands roamed in tender caresses of exploration. I thought I had the lines of Alexander's body memorized, but at that moment, it was as if we were new lovers discovering each other's bodies for the first time.

I pushed him back against the sheets and we rolled, Alexander's hard body covering mine. Caging me between his arms, he held me captive as he reared back. Before I could comprehend the shift in power, he shoved inside of me with a force that took my breath away. He withdrew, teasing me with his cock, before ruthlessly plunging back in. His eyes met mine. His gaze was transfixed with an almost reverent intensity. Never before had I felt so close to him. So connected.

"Play with your nipples," he commanded.

With every inch of his length buried inside me, I couldn't think. All I could do was focus on the beautiful man above me, his powerful commands ruling my body. I did as I was instructed without hesitation. My hardened nipples brushed against my fingertips. He watched me with a dark expression, captivated by the sight. He moaned and his jaw clenched as he rocked into me slowly. Encouraged by his reactions, I pinched the straining points and massaged the round shape of each breast. Before long, I was overflowing with arousal. I released my breasts, needing something more to hang on to. Something hard, solid, and strong before I went over the edge. I reached up and dug my nails into his shoulders to brace myself.

"Oh, god," I breathed. I was so close.

"Fuck, Krystina. You're so goddamn hot. I want your orgasm. I need to feel that sweet pussy tighten around me."

Circling my clit with his thumb, he picked up his pace, never breaking the connection until I began to shake. My muscles clenched beyond my will as he brought me closer to that glorious peak. He knew exactly how to please me, how to torment me with delicious pleasure, teasing me just long enough to ensure my climax would be cataclysmic.

"I'm almost there," I panted and tightened my legs around him. I trembled, losing more of myself with every passing moment. I became desperate, the promise of release all consuming.

"Now, angel. Give it to me now!"

With one hard thrust, he plunged deeper. My sensitive tissues rippled until I began to spasm uncontrollably, his words sending me into a heart-pounding orgasm. Colors flashed before my eyes as the rush surged through me.

"Alex!" I cried out and unraveled around him, my body overwhelmed with the sensation of blinding white heat. I was mindless, writhing against him shamelessly as I split apart at the seams. My fingernails clawed at his back, pulling him closer. His body shuddered before he stilled. Then all at once, his cock became impossibly harder, pulsing deliciously, as his own climax poured into me.

ALEXANDER LAY NEXT TO ME, mumbling in his sleep. His words were incoherent, but I knew he was dreaming again. Before long, he would begin thrashing and his skin would be covered in a cold sweat. I needed to calm him before the visions behind his eyes drove him to that point. I put my hand on the top of his head and ran my fingers through his hair. Pressing gentle kisses to his cheek, I murmured soothing words.

"Shh, Alex. You're okay. You're a powerful man. You're not a boy. It's only a dream. I'm right here with you."

I continued to whisper soothing words to him until his breathing became soft and even. Shifting over onto my side, I pressed my back against his hard torso. Even though he was spooned up against me, the steady rhythm of his chest rising and falling assured me he was sleeping peacefully.

Thirty minutes later, I felt like I had been lying awake for hours. After this past week, I should've been exhausted and sleeping too. But, for the life of me, I couldn't get my eyes to close. I glanced at the clock on the nightstand and watched as the neon red digital numbers changed to reflect five minutes after one in the morning. I suppressed a groan.

I wish I could just shut my brain off.

Unfortunately, that wasn't going to happen. I was too

consumed with worry over Alexander. Knowing the Sandman wasn't going to find me anytime soon, I slipped quietly from the bed, pulled on one of Alexander's t-shirts and a pair of comfy sweatpants.

I looked back down at the bed when I heard him stir. He didn't wake but rolled over onto his back. The arm cradling my head before I got up was still draped across my pillow. His chest was bare, the hard lines of his body highlighted by the moonbeams shooting through the room. At that moment, he looked so peaceful. It was a stark contrast to how he was just a little while ago. I fought the urge to reach out and touch him, but I didn't want to risk waking him up. Instead, I padded barefoot into the kitchen to make myself a cup of decaf tea.

As I waited for the kettle to boil, I searched my brain for some way to help the man I loved so much. This was the tenth night in a row I woke to the sound of him mumbling and thrashing in his sleep. He never spoke about the contents of his dreams, but his cold sweat told me all I needed to know.

Thankfully, tonight I was able to settle him down before he fully woke up. If he had, neither of us would be sleeping right now, as Alexander always felt too guilty about disturbing me. If he didn't hate the mere mention of therapy so much, I may have demanded he go on his own, without me. Forget couples' therapy. We could do without. For now. At the present moment, Alexander's healing was so much more important.

I knew he was hurting and it was no wonder why he was having nightmares. When I considered all that had happened, I couldn't even begin to imagine the magnitude of what he must be feeling. Betrayal, confusion, and anger probably only tapped the surface of his emotions. I was worried he was reaching his breaking point, something that became apparent when I was strung up on the cross.

For the past five months, Alexander showed me many things from his world of BDSM, and each time we were brought to new and exhilarating heights. I had come to love his kinks. I craved them like a drug and I meant what I said to him tonight. He didn't really hurt me with the flogger.

However, there was something unusual about the way he delivered his blows this time. He didn't display his normal caution and precision, but rather seemed fraught and desperate. Alexander always made me feel cherished, his touches often bordering on worshipful. What happened tonight was not his usual behavior. And while we managed to connect in a way we never had before, it was hard to ignore the way it all began.

The water in the kettle began to rumble and I quickly removed it from the burner before it began to whistle. After selecting a tea bag from the canister Vivian always kept perfectly stocked, I brought the steeping mug into Alexander's office.

Alexander and I kept separate offices in the penthouse, so I was rarely in here. One of the spare bedrooms had been converted for me so I could have my own space. However, my office didn't have what I needed. If I wanted to find a way to help him, I had to read Charlie's interview again. The only way to do that would be to access Alexander's hard drive.

I flipped on the stereo, making sure the volume was low enough so as not to be heard from the master bedroom. Not bothering to change the station, I left Lapsley's "Falling Short" playing and took a seat behind Alexander's spacious desk. Sipping my tea cautiously so I didn't burn my tongue, I took a minute to enjoy the soothing feeling on my throat. It was feeling a little sore and I half wondered if I was coming down with a head cold. I prayed I wasn't. If I did, Alexander's lectures about getting more rest would go from nagging to excruciatingly painful in the blink of an eye.

I groaned at the thought.

Maybe Vivian has the medicine cabinet stocked with some vitamin C pills.

Setting the mug of tea aside, I made a mental note to check as I woke the computer with a shake of the mouse. The screen came to life, but I frowned when it lit up. It was password protected.

Damn!

I should have known better. I opened the top drawer of the desk in search of a scrap piece of paper it might be written on. I didn't find anything, but I did find a pack of Big Red chewing gum. I chuckled to myself as I continued to search the other drawers. Two of them were locked and I had no idea where he kept the keys.

I blew out a breath in frustration, tapped my fingers on the desk, and tried to think of what the password might be. For all I knew, it was some long encryption I would never be able to guess. But then again, this was his home office. Perhaps the computer security wouldn't be so strict. I pulled the computer keyboard closer to me and typed the first thing that came to mind: Angel62293.

I smiled when the computer unlocked and the screen came into view. I found his choice of password to be endearing and my heart fluttered. My password was Sapphire32383. Like the word angel, my computer was also protected by a word shared between Alexander and me.

And here I thought combining it with his birthday was clever.

Apparently, I wasn't all that smart. But at the very least, his predictability showed me just how close we had grown over the past few months.

Luckily for me, his inbox was still open and I was able to easily locate the article. I clicked on the email and read through it once more. The last time I read it, I barely comprehended it because I was too busy formulating questions in my head. This time, I was more careful to retain the details.

I read through its entirety, then read it again. I was looking for something, any small detail that would give me an idea of how to possibly fix this for Alexander. I didn't want the interview to become public. With his sister's possible deception in the mix, he didn't need anything else on his plate. He had already suffered enough.

I stared at the article for so long, my eyes burned and my neck began to ache. I stretched my head from side to side. I couldn't figure out what Charlie had to gain by releasing this. I tried to remember what it was Alexander said about Charlie.

"I suspect Charlie is going to try to use this as a bargaining tool to strike a plea deal and I only have so much leverage with the DA."

I wasn't sure how this could be used as a bargaining chip. A crime was a crime, regardless of the pull Alexander had. My testimony was more than enough to convict Charlie, not to mention the phone records shared between Charlie and Trevor. But...

That's it!

A plan started to formulate in my head. I couldn't believe I didn't think of it before. However, I paused for a moment, contemplating my impulsive idea. The last time I tried to help Alexander, I ended up in a coma. Alexander would be furious if I attempted to do anything again.

Screw it. My husband-to-be needs me right now and I'm the one holding all the cards.

I quickly exited out of the email containing the article and opened Alexander's sent bin. I scrolled down and located the email he forwarded me the day before. It contained the details about the trial date. It had been moved up, and I didn't have much time to act. After reading the information I needed, I exited out of the email and set the computer back to the way Alexander had left it.

It was after two o'clock in the morning when I quietly slipped back into the bedroom. Before climbing into bed, I made a quick stop in the master bath and was pleased to see there was a bottle of vitamin C in the medicine cabinet. I popped a couple of tablets. There was a lot to do and a cold brought on by exhaustion was not on the itinerary. I needed to be healthy and rested if I wanted my wits about me to do what I had to do.

Moving back into the bedroom, I slipped under the sheets and settled in beside Alexander. He didn't wake, nor did he stir. I was happy to see he was still peaceful. Resting my hand on his chest, I nestled into the crook of his arm. His body was warm against me as I placed a feather-light kiss to his pectoral.

"Don't worry, baby. I've got this," I whispered.

17

Krystina

I spent all of Sunday cursing the myth that was Vitamin C. The full-blown head cold I was trying to prevent had shown its ghastly face.

Alexander doted on me for most of the day. He called Vivian and asked her to come to the penthouse with a batch of her to-die-for chicken noodle soup. Unfortunately, I could barely taste it, but I still appreciated the gesture. In an attempt to stop Alexander from shoving cough syrup down my throat, I rested under a blanket on the couch and convinced him to have a Star Wars marathon with me. As I listened to Chirrut chant "I am one with the Force, the Force is with me", I couldn't help but wish the power of the Force would be with *me* so I could get rid of my cold. There was too much to do, and I couldn't let a ridiculous head cold slow me down.

Alexander didn't know about my grand master plan to help him and I was positive he would not go along with my idea. I struggled with my conscience, but I knew I had to keep him in the dark for the time being.

However, he never strayed far from my side, his presence always just around the corner. While I appreciated the care Alexander and Vivian lavished on me, it ended up being a very frustrating day. Pulling out my laptop to collect the few pieces of information I needed was nearly impossible. My conscience played tug of war every time I snuck a peek at my cell phone under the blanket to gather what I needed. I told myself it wasn't lying, but for his protection – despite the fact my angel had planted herself on my shoulder for most of the day and chastised me.

By the end of the night, I somehow managed to get what I needed. Now here I was, Monday morning, with my guns locked and loaded. Even though I was miserable from feeling sick, I knew the untimely head cold just might work to my advantage.

I sneezed when the elevator doors opened to the floor that held Turning Stone Advertising, a reminder of how I was going to have to get through the day sniveling into a tissue. Over-the-counter cold suppressants had become a major food group over the past twenty-four hours and I could only hope the meds would kick in soon.

"Good morning, Regina," I greeted my assistant in a nasally voice. She looked up at me in surprise.

"Morning, Miss Cole. Are you sick?"

"Just a stupid head cold. Nothing major. Is the team ready to meet about the Beaumont project?"

"I just saw Clive head into the main design room. The rest of the team is here as well. The strategy session is scheduled for eight-thirty, so I expect the rest will be in to meet you and Clive shortly."

"Perfect. Please tell them I'll be in there momentarily. I just have a couple of calls to make, then I'll be in with my files on Beaumont."

Regina nodded, and I continued on toward my office. When

I entered, I quietly closed the door behind me and leaned my head back against it. Closing my eyes, I thought about the phone calls I had to make. Once I set things in motion, there would be no going back.

Can I really do this?

I shook my head, knowing that questioning whether or not I could do it was irrelevant. I had to for Alexander. When I opened my eyes, I was surprised to find a mixed bouquet of lilies and blue delphiniums on my desk. I frowned in confusion as I walked over to the desk and pulled the card from the holder.

I hate that you're not feeling well. Since you refused to stay home today, I thought these might brighten your day.
- Alex

At first, I smiled. Until a twinge of guilt hit me for not being forthcoming about my plan. The angel's voice sounded loudly in my head.

Liar!

The voice got louder and louder causing my heart to thud hard in my chest. The self-condemnation grew as I fired up my computer and pulled up Alexander's schedule for the day. I took note of when he'd be tied up in meetings, knowing he wouldn't be looking for me during those times. Removing my cell phone from my purse, I located the phone number I was able to obtain in an email correspondence from a few weeks back.

Guilt-ridden angst caused me to shake as I began to dial the private cell phone number for Thomas Green, the Manhattan District Attorney who was heading up Charlie's trial.

"DA Green here."

I swallowed the lump in my throat and summoned the most confident voice I could muster.

"Hello, Mr. Green. This is Krystina Cole."

"Hello, Miss Cole. What can I do for you today?"

"Actually, I was wondering if I could come in to see you today."

"Today? Is everything alright?" he asked, seeming confused.

Everything wasn't alright, but the most important thing at that moment was setting up a face to face meeting. I did not want to do this over the phone. Facial expressions and body language told too much of a story.

"I need to talk to you about my testimony."

"Okay," he paused, sounding even more perplexed. "I don't know what else there is for us to go over, but I'd be happy to meet with you and Mr. Stone –."

"No!" I nearly shouted, forgetting my composure. "Not Alex. Just me please. And I'd appreciate it if you didn't mention our meeting to him."

"Well, I ah..." he hesitated. I huffed out a breath of frustration over my own stupidity. I should've predicted he'd want Alexander to be present. I would have to say something more to convince him.

"Look, Mr. Green. Something has just come to my attention that could affect my testimony. I'm going to have to pull the client attorney privilege on this one."

"With all due respect, Miss Cole. You're a witness, not my client. I work for the city, so that rule doesn't really apply here."

Shit! Think, Cole. Think!

I scrambled to try to come up with a way to persuade him to my way of thinking. I didn't want to show my hand just yet, but I was desperate.

"I see," I began evenly. "While that may be true, you need me for this case. Am I correct?"

"Yes..." he trailed off cautiously.

"You don't have a solid case without me. If you want my

testimony, I must insist this meeting stay between just the two of us."

There was a long pause and I could only assume he was weighing his options.

"I understand. Let me just pull up my schedule." While his words were agreeable, his voice sounded terse, like he was annoyed with the situation. The last thing I needed was for him to be uncooperative. Trying to sound as sincere as possible, I acknowledged his efforts to meet with me.

"I understand this is sudden. Thank you for agreeing to meet, Mr. Green."

I heard the shuffling of papers for a moment before he spoke again.

"I'm due in court in thirty minutes, but I should be free by noon. I can see you at twelve-thirty today if that works for you. My office?"

"Yes, your office is fine. I'll be there then."

After I hung up, I took a deep and calming breath. Then I tried counting to ten, but it didn't seem to help. My nerves were still jumping as I looked up the second phone number I needed to dial. This call was even more nerve wracking than the last, as I was still apprehensive about whether or not I could follow through with my plan.

"*The City Times.* How can I direct your call?" asked the female phone operator.

"Yes, hello. I'm looking for a Mr. Mac Owens."

"Mr. Owens is off site today. Can I direct you to somebody else, or would you like me to put you through to his voicemail?"

"Oh, um...voicemail would be fine. Thank you."

After she patched me through, I waited on the line until a gruff male voice could be heard, telling me to leave a message.

"Mr. Owens, my..." I hesitated before continuing, then swiftly decided to not leave my name. I would leave a bit of detail on what my call was about instead. "I'm interested in talking with you about a story. It has to do with Charlie Andrews. If you could please give me a call back at your earliest convenience, I would appreciate it."

I rattled off my phone number and quickly hit the end button. My heart was racing and the ball of nerves in my gut felt heavier than a wrecking ball. It worsened as I pulled up my calendar, the same calendar Alexander referenced to obtain my schedule, and began typing in a fictitious doctor appointment for twelve-thirty.

It's better this way.

Nonetheless, guilt weighed heavily in my chest as I gathered the Beaumont files. Grabbing a box of tissues on the way out, I tried to force the pangs of my conscience aside and made my way to the design room to meet my team.

Clive, my lead marketing coordinator for Turning Stone, already had design drafts and mockups displayed on the flat screens when I entered. He was writing notes on the white board and looked up upon my arrival. He raised his eyebrows when he saw me.

"No offense, Miss Cole, but you look terrible."

"Thanks," I stated dryly.

"I know this planning session is important, but do you want to reschedule?"

I looked around the room at the other eight people assembled and ready to go. A part of me did want to reschedule, but it wasn't because I was sick. It was because I felt too anxious to concentrate on the job at hand.

"No, I'll be fine. I want to be well prepared for Friday's meeting with Sheldon Tremaine. Beaumont Jewelers is too big of a contract to risk. Let's do this."

Alexander

I STOOD in the doorway of my office and shook the hand of Sheldon Tremaine. He was just leaving after a very productive meeting. Ironically, while Krystina was discussing the advertising strategy for his business with her team, he had been meeting with me.

I had asked Sheldon to come to my office to discuss his business appointment with Krystina later in the week. I also wanted to discuss commissioning Beaumont Jewelers to create a piece of jewelry I would give to Krystina as a wedding gift. His work was impeccable, as was proven with the triskelion necklace he had made for her, but the commission also gave me leverage. I used it to solidify the promise that he'd commit to advertising with Turning Stone.

"I'll get a design drawn up for you and send it over, but I think I know exactly what you're looking for," Sheldon assured.

"I'll look forward to it. It's a pleasure doing business with you."

"Likewise, Mr. Stone."

After Sheldon left, I went back to my desk and pulled up my calendar – my real calendar.

Setting up the meeting with Sheldon had been tricky. I couldn't type his name in my calendar or I'd risk suspicion from Krystina if she happened to look at my schedule for the day. Instead, I blocked the time out as being in a meeting with George Canterwell, knowing full well Krystina wouldn't disturb me if she knew I was meeting with the old miser. Laura, on the other hand, was completely thrown off when Sheldon Tremaine showed up. She had merely tossed me a strange look but didn't ask questions. She knew better.

I glanced at the clock. Stephen and Bryan were due in my office in less than fifteen minutes. The architect would be here at three to meet with both Krystina and me about the house in Westchester. I absently wondered if she remembered to clear her schedule. Moving the mouse, I clicked over to her schedule. I stopped short as I went over her appointments for the day.

Doctor?

I hadn't realized she scheduled one. Instinctively, I picked up the phone to call her Primary, but then stopped myself.

Give her room to breathe.

Fighting my gut instinct was a challenge, but I replaced the receiver nonetheless. Krystina had a head cold. I told myself it was natural for her to schedule a visit to the doctor. I also knew she had Samuel with her. She would be fine.

I looked up when I heard a knock on my office door. Stephen poked his head in.

"Come on in," I told him. "Where's Bryan?"

"He's just down the hall, chatting it up with some new intern. He'll be here in a minute I'm sure."

"Christ! He knows the rules. Go tell him to put his dick back in his pants and get in here."

Stephen smirked.

"Sure. The rules. Go ahead and tell him that yourself. I'm pretty sure he'll remind you of how your relationship with Krystina started."

I scowled at him.

"That's not the point."

"Ah, come on. Cut the poor guy some slack. He's always so serious and buried in numbers all day. Let him get his kicks when he can."

"Last I checked, Bryan didn't have any issue finding his kicks," I stated dryly.

My statement wasn't meant to be funny, but Stephen found it hilarious for some reason. I pursed my lips in annoyance. He was still laughing when Bryan finally decided to saunter in.

"What's so funny?" Bryan asked.

"Your dick," Stephen announced.

"Huh?" Bryan asked and raised an eyebrow.

"Yes, your dick. It's not allowed in the interns," I reminded him. My statement caused Stephen to laugh even harder.

"Shit! Did you just make a joke, Alex?"

I rolled my eyes at him.

Always the jokester.

Bryan, as if sensing my irritation, sat down in the chair next to Stephen and held up his hands in surrender.

"Sorry, Alex. I'll keep it to myself."

"You'd better," I warned. "She's probably too young for you anyway."

"Well, Krystina is a lot younger than –."

Stephen howled with laughter again, his face turning ten shades of red.

"I tried to warn you, Alex," he said when he caught his breath. I shook my head but couldn't help but to crack a smile.

However, my smile was short lived, as I had important matters to discuss. I was about to lay a bombshell on my accountant and lawyer. Because they were also friends of mine, I knew they'd be more than a little shocked over what I had to tell them. My only defense was I had met them in college, and well after I changed my name to Stone. I would explain it to them like I had explained it to Krystina, and say Alexander Russo no longer existed. I could only hope they didn't feel betrayed like she had.

"Alright, recess is over you two. I have something important to tell you both. It isn't good. Stephen, depending on how things shake out, I'll more than likely need you and your legal team," I told them.

My overly serious tone caused Stephen to sober immediately. Both of them looked at me curiously. A ball of dread formed in my gut. In a few minutes, I would show them *The City Times* interview given by Charlie Andrews. Once I did that, even more people would know about my past. After all these years of keeping it hidden, it only took one conniving weasel to blow it all up.

"What's going on, Alex?" Bryan asked.

"Bryan, as my accountant, I'll need your input on protecting my assets. Again, depending on what happens, I don't know the financial ramifications."

"What the fuck, Alex! Spit it out. What's wrong?" Stephen demanded.

"Charlie Andrews."

18

Krystina

I looked at the clock. It was nearing noontime. Feeling confident about what my team and I had accomplished, I grabbed my purse and slung it over my shoulder. It was time to meet with the DA. I tried not to be nervous as I made my way to the elevator, but it was as if my trepidation grew with every step I took. I stopped short when I spotted Samuel standing near the doors.

Shit!

I had completely forgotten about my hired shadow. Between this and the conversation with the DA, I was quickly learning my grand master plan had way too many holes in it.

Note to self...I'm terrible at scheming.

"Headed out, ma'am?" he asked.

"I'm just going to a doctor appointment, Sam."

"I'll pull the car around," he told me and moved to press the down button for the elevator.

I had a sinking suspicion he wasn't referring to my Porsche sitting and collecting dust in the parking garage. If I knew

Alexander, he had assigned Samuel his own set of wheels. If that was the case, it could be very problematic. I couldn't afford to have Samuel follow me. If I wanted to ditch his watchful eye, I'd have to get creative.

"No, it's okay. There's no need for you to come along," I told him in my most innocent voice. The coughing fits plaguing me all morning were suddenly absent, so I faked one for added effect.

"I'm sorry, ma'am," he said hesitantly, as if he was unsure as to whether or not doctor appointments were in the rule book. "I'm going to have to clear that with Mr. Stone."

And the plot thickens...

"He's really busy today in meetings. I wouldn't bother him. Besides, he's the one who actually scheduled it for me," I lied, but felt somewhat shocked at how easily it rolled off my tongue.

"Yes, ma'am. But I'm supposed to accompany you whenever you leave the office."

"Sam," I said and placed a reassuring hand on his arm. "I can assure you, Mr. Stone understands the importance of privacy when it comes to my doctor appointments. The doctor's office is only a few blocks away, so I'm going to walk. Trust me, this is perfectly okay."

Yet another pang of guilt hit me, knowing I was taking advantage of the fact Sam didn't know the ropes yet. If he listened to me, I knew he would be in some serious hot water.

"If you insist," he said, but his voice was laced with doubt.

It wasn't until the elevator doors shut when I could breathe a sigh of relief. One thing was for certain – keeping up this charade was not going to be easy. I could only hope it would all be worth it in the end.

I hadn't lied when I told Samuel my doctor was located just a few blocks down from Cornerstone Tower. However, it had been the only truthful statement I made during our brief conversation. I thought of that as I neared the embossed glass door of a building that read LifeCare Health Center. My doctors name, along with the many others in the practice, were listed beneath it. To me, each name was a representation of the many lies I had told over the past few hours. They were like a beacon for my deceit. I was almost grateful when the doors opened and a woman and a small boy exited onto the street.

I watched them as they scurried to the curb to hail a cab. The woman, whom I assumed to be the boy's mother, turned to the boy and placed a woolen knit cap over his head. Dark ends, nearly black, stuck out beneath the winter head gear and I was reminded of Alexander's hair color. The boy looked up at me, watching me with pale blue eyes, as I passed by them. For some reason, my conversation with Allyson during our shopping trip came to mind.

Babies.

The cold wind whipped around me and I shivered. However, I wasn't sure if my shiver was from the frigid temperatures or from the trepidation I felt over having children. I shook my head. That was the last thing I needed to think about at that moment.

Get your head in the game, Cole.

Pulling my iPod from my purse, I popped a set of purple buds into my ears and listened to the sultry voice of Claire Guerreso as I continued on another four blocks. When I finally reached the building that held the District Attorney's office, I was freezing. I stepped inside and rubbed my hands up and down my arms. My cheeks warmed, thawing from the cold of the outdoors. The winter temperature did little to help my sniffling and I had to stifle a sneeze. Looking around, I spotted a restroom just down the corridor leading to the DA's office. I made a quick detour so I could blow my nose and freshen up before my meeting.

After popping a couple more cold medicine tablets into my

mouth, I looked at my reflection in the mirror of the ladies' room.

Geez, Clive was right. I do look terrible.

I ran a hand over my unruly curls in an attempt to smooth them out. I frowned when they refused to tame. Rather than fight it, I fastened a hair tie to create a lose ponytail at the nape of my neck. Digging into my purse, I pulled out my compact, added a bit of powder to my nose and freshened up my lipstick. I looked better, but not great.

A glance at the time on my cell phone screen said it was twenty-eight minutes after twelve. I had stalled long enough. It was show time.

My palms began to sweat from anxious nerves. I rubbed them against the material of my pantsuit as I made my way toward the DA's office. His secretary, or at least I assumed she was, looked away from her computer screen when I arrived. She must have been new, because I didn't recognize her from my previous visits.

"Hello," I said. "My name is Krystina Cole. I have a meeting with Mr. Green at twelve-thirty."

She smiled politely and motioned to the door behind her.

"Yes, Miss Cole. Mr. Green is expecting you. You can go right in."

Summoning all the courage I could muster, I thanked her and pushed through the door that would lead me to Thomas Green.

The room I entered wasn't anything fancy, but simple. There were comfortable cushioned chairs surrounding a long wooden table. Cherry bookcases filled the walls, overflowing with a countless number of legal volumes. The setting was familiar, as Alexander and I had attended several meetings with the DA over the past two months. During that time, not only had we talked about my testimony, but Thomas often recounted stories about his six-year-old fraternal twins, Olivia and Tommy. The small bit of knowledge I had about his personal life might serve me well during this meeting.

Thomas Green's desk was at the far end of the room, but that wasn't where he sat. Instead, he was at the polished wooden table pouring over manila folders full of documents upon my arrival. His wire rimmed glasses were pushed down near the tip of his nose. He looked up when he heard me come in and shoved the glasses to rest on top of his salt and pepper hair.

"Miss Cole," he greeted. "Always a pleasure."

"Likewise, Mr. Green. New secretary?"

"Oh, no. She's a temp. My secretary is out sick. It's that time of year," he stated sardonically. Despite the light attempt at sarcasm, his voice was tense and matched the tone he had when we spoke over the phone earlier that morning. When he pressed his lips together and frowned, I wondered if he was just as apprehensive as I was about this meeting.

He stood and extended his hand to shake mine, but I shook my head.

"Like you said, it's that time of year. I'm fighting a bit of a head cold myself, so you probably don't want to shake my hand. I'm sure your wife wouldn't want you bringing it home to your kiddos," I said lightly and smiled, hoping I could ease some of the tension with the mention of his wife and children.

He quickly pulled his hand back and returned my smile.

"You're right. They just got through a bout with the flu. Rebecca would have my head if I introduced a new germ to Olivia or Tommy," he laughed. He motioned to the chair in front of his desk. "Please have a seat."

"Thank you. Other than the recent flu, how is your family doing?"

As I sat down in the offered chair, Thomas walked around to his side of the desk. After he sat, we talked briefly about what his children were doing in school and about his wife's latest endeavor to become an independent consultant for a new fad makeup company. After a while, he leaned back and looked at me curiously.

"So, now that you're up to speed on my family happenings, I'd like to talk about why you're here. I've been a bit perplexed since your phone call this morning. So much so, I managed to get out of court early and spent the last hour reviewing the case files," he admitted and motioned to the table covered with manila folders. "What's so pressing that you had to see me today?"

Not wanting to beat around the bush, I gave it to him straight. Or, at least, as straight as I could without jeopardizing Alexander and Justine.

"It's Charlie's trial date."

"What about it?"

"I know it's been moved up. I need you to move it back."

His eyebrows raised in surprise.

"I can honestly say I didn't expect that to come from you, especially with the amount of pressure Mr. Stone has been exerting on everyone to proceed. The jury was selected a month ago and the presiding judge is anxious to move forward as well. I can't change the date unless you can give me a significant reason as to why you need it moved."

I hesitated, choosing my next words carefully.

"Mr. Green, as you know, one of the charges Charlie Andrews faces is extortion. You should know he's up to his old tricks. A reporter was able to meet with him."

"What do you mean? He's supposed to have a strict no visitor's policy," Thomas said disbelievingly.

"I'm aware. I think it had something to do with a rookie prison guard. I don't know the details. Either way, I have reason to believe Charlie is going to use the story to get Alex to back down on some of the charges. I need you to postpone the trial until I can kill the story."

"Miss Cole, that won't be necessary. No matter what this supposed story is, I have no intention to drop charges or strike any sort of deal with Charlie Andrews."

"I believe that. However, Charlie can't know that."

"I'm sorry?" he asked, seeming genuinely puzzled.

I shook my head in frustration. Trying to convince the DA to do what I needed without specifics was going to be more difficult than I anticipated.

"Look, Alex is a very influential man in this city. You have first-hand knowledge of this."

"I do, but it's not only the city, Miss Cole. His influence spreads across the country."

It does?

I tried to process what he meant, wondering what else I didn't know about my future husband. I knew Alexander had a slew of business dealings and properties in the city, many of which I didn't know about. However, I didn't know his reach went beyond New York. I had never even thought to ask. I pushed my unease over that bit of information aside, knowing my current conversation was much more important than Alexander's real-estate holdings.

"Mr. Green," I implored. "Charlie knows things about Alex – things Alex does not want to be made public. I can't tell you the details of it, but just the threat of exposure is devastating to him. That's why I need you to buy me time. I need you to make Charlie believe you *are* considering a plea deal. I'm hoping, if you do that, it will make Charlie thinks he has a shot at a plea and will retract what he said to the reporter."

"Miss Cole – Krystina, if I may," he said, and I nodded. "You're not giving me much to work off of here."

I sat back and bit my lip, fretting over what I should and shouldn't say. My hands were twisting nervously in my lap, when it suddenly came to me. I couldn't tell him the whole story, but I could remind him of something Alexander once said.

"Did you go to the Stone's Hope Gala? The fundraiser from a few months back?"

He narrowed his eyes suspiciously at me. I couldn't remember if Thomas was there that night, but Alexander told me the newspapers and local networks reported on the speech he gave at the gala for a full solid week afterward. Even if Thomas wasn't there, it was fair to assume he would have at least heard about it. However, if he was actually present and was witness to the emotional words pouring from Alexander, the better positioned I would be.

"I was there. Why do you ask?" Thomas questioned cautiously.

"If you were there, then you must have heard Alex's speech."

"Yes," he confirmed slowly, but I could see the dawning in his eyes. Alexander had told a story in that speech. *His* story, although the people in attendance didn't know that. Nonetheless, Thomas Green was anything but stupid. He was already connecting the dots. Instead of repeating the speech, I switched tactics.

"Can you imagine if your children, little Olivia and Tommy, came from a life like that?"

Thomas seemed to visibly shudder.

"No, I can't," he admitted honestly. "My kids are loved. Protected. If only you could see some of the cases that come across my desk. They can be brutal sometimes. As for the speech Mr. Stone gave, are you telling me it was..."

He didn't finish his question, but he didn't have to. My sad and pleading eyes told him what he needed to know.

"Please, Mr. Green," I whispered.

He leaned back in his chair, removed his glasses from the top of his head, and ran a hand through his thick hair.

"I want to help you. I really do. If Mr. Stone was speaking about his own childhood at that gala, I can't blame him for wanting to keep it hidden."

"But?"

"But I don't think you're giving me the whole story here."

I began to fidget and squirmed a little in my seat. I was going to have to be more open, but the thought of betraying Alexander even more than I already had, tore at my heart.

"Alex will kill me for saying this, but I see the front he puts on – all big, bad, and mysterious. But that's just it. It's a front. He views his privacy as the only protection he has from his memories. I don't want him to relive it, or worse, endure press speculation that could cause more damage. I have to protect him. That's why he doesn't know I'm here. That's why I tried to pull the confidentiality card with you."

He seemed to be contemplating his words before he leaned forward on his elbows and looked me square in the eyes. When he spoke, he adapted a softer tone.

"It's not often I have people in my office who remember the names of my wife and children and ask after their well-being. I think you have a good heart. And, as much as Mr. Stone tries to come off as a hard ass, I think he does too. I've gotten to know the two of you pretty well over the past couple of months. I want you to talk to me – off the record. Not as a DA, but maybe as a friend."

I shook my head, knowing what he suggested was out of the question. Perhaps we had gotten to know each other well, especially when we were discussing the connection I had with my abductors. He knew Trevor wasn't only a part of the kidnapping, but also my rapist. However, I only divulged that information because it was needed for my testimony. I certainly wouldn't consider Thomas Green to be someone I could openly confide in about Alexander and Justine. Their secrets were so much bigger than mine had ever been.

"I already told you. I can't, Mr. Green. As it is, I've said too much. I'm sorry, but it's not my story to tell. You're just going to have to trust me."

"And if I don't?"

I frowned, not wanting to give him an ultimatum. It wasn't my style, but I was desperate. I narrowed my gaze at him and kept my tone neutral, yet resolute at the same time.

"The trial is just over three weeks away and I don't know if that will allow me enough time to do what I need to do. I'm not asking you to drop the case, I'm just asking for time. Only you can make that happen. If you don't, I'll retract my statement and planned testimony. I'll do anything to protect the man I love. I'm doing this for him, Mr. Green."

He laughed then, but it wasn't in humor. It sounded more stoic than anything else.

"Mr. Stone once told me you're stubborn as hell. He couldn't have been more right."

I smiled sheepishly.

"Yeah, well...so I've been told from time to time."

"You were pretty emphatic about seeing Charlie go away for a long time. I don't believe you would actually throw it all away, especially without good reason. I'm not saying I'll try to push back the trial, but your conviction has me curious. What's your plan?"

I exhaled the breath I hadn't realized I'd been holding. I finally felt like we might be getting somewhere.

"I need to get to the reporter. I'm hoping to give him a new story so he won't publish the one Charlie gave."

"Who is the reporter?"

I hesitated before continuing, but ultimately decided honesty was the best policy at this point.

"Mac Owens. From *The City Times*."

"I've heard his name before, but don't know him personally. He must not cover many trials," he mused before continuing. "I don't know what Charlie Andrews told this Mac Owens guy, but it must be big. You've already said you can't tell me the details, so I won't ask for them again. However, whatever story you plan to replace it with has to be bigger. You know that, right?"

I closed my eyes, knowing this was another potential hole in my grand master plan. I didn't know if I could go through with what I needed to do, not to mention the fact I didn't know if Mac Owens would even go for my offer. However, I refused to just sit on my hands.

"That's up to Mac Owens to decide, I guess. But I have to try."

"I'll be perfectly honest. No judge will allow me to move the trial date based on what you've told me. However, what I can do is pay a visit to Charlie and feel him out. If he's going to push for a plea again, I'll need to plan accordingly. I don't meet again with the presiding judge for another week. You have at least until then to do what you have to do. Take advantage of the time. You probably won't get any more than that."

I resigned myself to take what I could get at this point.

"Thank you so much, Mr. Green," I told him, feeling relieved he didn't continue to pump me for information. I was about to stand up to leave, but then I remembered something. "You'll keep this meeting between us, won't you?"

The corners of his mouth shifted to form a frown, but he eventually nodded his head.

"I will for now. But if Mr. Stone finds out I've been to see Charlie Andrews, he's is bound to ask questions. I will only be able to avoid his calls for so long," he warned.

"I know," I acknowledged and began to fidget again nervously. "I'll be in touch after I talk to Mac Owens. Keep your fingers crossed for me, will you?"

"You're going to need more than superstition on your side, Krystina."

"Trust me. I know that too."

Thomas Green and I said our goodbyes and I told him I would keep him posted on my progress. Even though I didn't achieve what I set out to do originally, I still felt somewhat optimistic about the DA meeting with Charlie.

As I was walking down the corridor to exit the building, I felt my phone buzz in my purse. I pulled it out and saw it was a text from my mother. I had no idea what she wanted, as I didn't read the text. I was too distracted by a different notification also on the screen. I had a missed call. No voicemail was left, but I recognized the number. It belonged to Mac Owens.

My heart started to race. He must have returned my call when I was meeting with the DA. I slid my finger over the touch screen to unlock the phone. I wasn't due to meet Alexander and the architect until three. Hopefully I could arrange a meeting with the reporter sometime between now and then.

Too preoccupied with what I would say during the phone call, I was paying little attention to anything around me as I began to dial Mac Owens. Unexpectedly, I slammed into a person in front of me. I stumbled back and my phone went clattering to the floor.

"Shit!" I swore and bent over to retrieve it quickly.

That damn cold medicine is turning my brain into a hazy fog.

When I stood back up to apologize to the person I had so rudely bumped into, I froze.

It was Hale.

19

Krystina

Time moved with no sense of reason as I followed Hale out to the waiting Porsche Cayenne. His determined footsteps echoed down the steps and onto the pavement toward the car, drowning out the noises of the city. When he opened the car door for me, his glare was icy. He never looked at me that way before. It was almost frightening.

I'm so screwed.

I got into the car and Hale closed the door behind me. I waited as he walked around to get into the driver's seat. As soon as he was seated, I started rambling.

"Hale, I'm sorry. I don't know how you knew where I was, but you seem angry. Please don't tell Alex about this. He'll be –."

"Miss Cole!" he snapped. He turned around in his seat to face me and held up his hand. "First of all, I have access to the GPS tracking on your phone. You know this. Now imagine my surprise when Samuel comes to me about your supposed

doctor appointment. You and I both know you didn't have a
doctor appointment."

I shrunk under his words. Hale wasn't just angry. Yes, his
tone was near murderous, but there was worry in his eyes too.

"No, I didn't have a doctor appointment," I whispered,
feeling ashamed. "Are you going to tell Alex?"

He pursed his lips to form a tight line.

"Tell me why you lied and ditched your security detail," he
demanded, rather than answering my question.

"Like I said, I'm sorry. I just didn't know any other way."

"Any other way to do what?"

A sudden wave of emotion hit me, and tears began to sting
my eyes. Perhaps it was from lack of sleep. Or maybe it was
because I was just caught in the act. No matter what the excuse
was, deep down I knew the underlying issue. It was because I
was overwhelmed with worry for Alexander.

I blinked the tears back, feeling frustrated. I didn't know
how to explain this all to Hale. I didn't know how to explain the
many nights Alexander was tormented by nightmares. I didn't
know how to describe the shadows plaguing his eyes during
the mornings afterward. But most importantly, I was fraught
with worry over the possible legal ramifications Charlie's
interview might hold for Alexander. There were no words to
depict how bad my heart ached over the possibility of losing
the person I loved above all else, and all because of a gambling
addict's greed. The compulsion I felt to save Alexander from
the past, to make it disappear for him, was overpowering.

*Hale is Alexander's protector. If he couldn't do the very thing I
was seeking to do, what made me think I had that power? I'm a
nobody.*

Suddenly, I felt foolish. There would be no satisfactory
explanation for my actions. The lies, the sneaking around. I
had always been a straight shooter. However, I had irrationally
allowed desperation to take over who I was. In fact, desperation

didn't even begin to describe how I felt. I yearned, with every fiber of my being, to go back to the place Alexander and I had been when he proposed to me on a hilltop in Westchester. At that moment, it had been just us. Now, it was as if it were the two of us against the world.

How had so much changed so fast?

The tears I had been holding back came flooding down my cheeks. Words came bubbling out of me as the pent-up frustration boiled over.

"I just...I just needed to do something!" I sobbed. "The article, Charlie, Justine. Alex's constant quest for answers. The threat of losing him. Everything! I tried therapy with him and it was a disaster. I've tried to get him to talk it out with me, but he shuts down – especially after he's had a nightmare. I don't know what else to do! I can't just sit by and watch him suffer anymore, Hale. I just can't. It's not fair that he's being threatened the way he is. He was just a child and he doesn't deserve this!"

Hale watched me curiously and his expression softened, revealing a certain amount of compassion over my sudden outburst.

"Vivian was right," he eventually said.

"Vivian?" I asked, confused as to why he would bring up Alexander's housekeeper – our housekeeper.

"She was right about the nightmares. She had her suspicions and she voiced her concerns to me. Not to mention, I'm familiar with the haunted look Mr. Stone has at times. I saw it often when he was a boy. You just confirmed what I suspected."

I sat quietly for a moment, composing myself as I contemplated Hale's words. I thought about Vivian and how she was always there, yet she wasn't. I barely saw her, but I knew she was in the penthouse several times a day. Whether she was delivering fresh laundry, bringing groceries, or preparing a meal, our meetings were always polite and brief. For me, getting to know her was an odd concept, as I still wasn't entirely comfortable with the idea of having a housekeeper. I didn't know how to act. However, I was now beginning to regret not getting to know the woman who had been with Alexander for years.

How much does Vivian know about Alexander's past?

I made a mental note to try to engage in conversation with her in the very near future.

"What were you doing at the DA's office, Krystina."

Hale's words broke me away from my thoughts. As he sat there, waiting patiently for my answer, I knew hiding the truth from him would be futile. Knowing Hale, he'd find out anyway. I hastily brushed the tears from my face and composed myself.

"I'm trying to help Alex, but I need time. I was hoping Thomas Green would be willing to push the trial back."

I went on to explain everything that transpired since I read the article. Well, mostly everything. I left out the part about my experience on the St. Andrews Cross for obvious reasons. When I finally got to the part about my plan to talk to Mac Owens, Hale's eyes darkened again.

"Did you tell the DA about the contents of the unpublished article?"

"No, absolutely not," I quickly replied. "I would never jeopardize Alex or Justine like that."

Hale seemed to relax a bit, but his expression remained bleak.

"You will not talk to that reporter, Miss Cole."

His tone mirrored one Alexander would take with me sometimes. It was maddening.

"But I have to try something!"

"You're a smart woman, but you're being incredibly naïve at the moment. Mac Owens has been trying to dig up dirt on Mr. Stone for years. What kind of story could you give him that would convince him to drop the one he's always wanted?"

I slumped back in my seat, not sure if I wanted to tell him about what I wanted to do. Hell, I wasn't even sure if I *could* do it. Just the thought of it caused my heart to pound with trepidation.

No. I have to do it. It's my only shot.

"I kept thinking of all the press reports and speculation Alex constantly warns me about. He keeps me hidden away and shielded from reporters at all costs. However, I know how reporters were chomping at the bit over Trevor's death." I paused for a moment, my mouth tasting like ash at the mention of his name. "He came from a prominent family. His father was the CEO of some dot com company and used to be a member of the New York City Council. The details of Trevor's involvement in my abduction were kept very hush, hush. I can only assume his father paid people off."

"What are you trying to say, Miss Cole?"

"The presiding judge decided to keep Charlie's trial closed to the public. Closure was decided because of decency concerns – because of the testimony I have to give about my history with Trevor. At first, I was grateful, but now I realize I can use it to my advantage. Considering the press was denied details about Trevor's involvement in the accident, they are bound to be miffed about being shut out of the trial. I was thinking of offering an exclusive interview of sorts, a personal recount of my experience with the son of an influential family."

Hale rapidly shook his head back and forth.

"Are you trying to tell me you were going to give the story of your rape to Mac Owens?" he asked in disbelief.

The idea turned my stomach, but I didn't waver.

"Yes. If that's what it takes to get the heat off Alexander, so be it."

"Mac Owens is slime. He's not a gossip columnist, but an

investigative journalist looking to make his mark any way he can. He'll sensationalize your story like you can't imagine and publish the one about Mr. Stone. He'd never agree to a trade. You'd basically be offering him a two-for-one deal. There isn't a decent bone in the man's body. You can't talk to him. It will destroy you. Not to mention, Mr. Stone would be murderous if you became a victim of the press."

I blew out a breath in frustration. Hale was most likely right, but I was hard-pressed to come up with anything better. It was beyond irritating. It wasn't like I wanted to make my sordid tale public. In fact, the idea scared the hell out of me. But I had to do something.

I tilted my chin up stubbornly.

"Well, help me then. Let's work together to shut this down, Hale."

I tried to come across strong, needing to be a goddamned super hero looking to join forces and conquer evil, but Hale wasn't buying it. He afforded me a small smile and shook his head.

"I know you have the best intentions, but I think you've gotten in over your head here. Tell me, Miss Cole. Have you ever Googled your name?"

"Uh, no. Why?"

"Because you're engaged to Alexander Stone, that's why. You should keep yourself informed and know what you're getting into before you make rash decisions. You need to forget this plan of yours and just trust me. I'm working on the situation. Let me handle it. It's what I do. Right now, the best thing you can do for Mr. Stone is be there for him. That's all."

"I'm trying, but sometimes I don't feel like it's enough," I said quietly.

Hale didn't respond but seemed to be mulling over his thoughts before he turned to face forward and put the car in drive. After signaling and merging into traffic, he spoke again.

"Miss Cole, before you started coming around, Mr. Stone was a hard man. Even unforgiving at times. You changed him. I suspect that could be the reason why he's having nightmares." He paused and looked at me in the rearview mirror. His eyes were pensive.

"What do you mean? How could I possibly be the reason?"

"You made him feel again, Miss Cole. You don't need to embark on some grand crusade to protect him. You already have all the power you need."

We didn't talk anymore on the drive back to Cornerstone Tower. Having just experienced the longest conversation I've ever had with Hale, there didn't seem to be anything else to say. I didn't ask again about whether or not he would tell Alexander about my visit to the DA. There was no need to. I knew he wouldn't, even if the words were left unspoken.

When Hale and I pulled up to the towering fifty-story structure, I looked up to the sleek spire topping the building. Low lying gray clouds hid it from view. It was as if it disappeared into nothingness, embodying the answers I searched for but couldn't see. I still didn't know what I was going to do. I was so conflicted, not knowing if I were coming or going. But, at the very least, I felt like Hale and I had come to an understanding.

Once I was back in my office, I sat at my desk and pondered over the conversation I had with him. He told me I had all the power I needed. It was just up to me to figure out how to use it. However, the comment he made about whether or not I had ever Googled my name was nagging at me more than anything else.

I was due to meet Alexander and the architect in about an hour. I had plenty of work to do to pass the time, but I couldn't concentrate on it. On a whim, I turned toward my computer and opened the online search engine. I typed in KRYSTINA COLE NYC. I felt a sense of déjà vu, as I had once completed a similar search when I was trying to discover who Alexander was. I remembered the numerous articles I found on him, but nothing prepared me for what a search of my name revealed.

The number of results that populated were astounding. What was even more shocking were the publications my name was listed in.

This can't be right. It's got to be someone else with the same name as me.

My name was listed in everything from local online blogs to *Rolling Stone*. I scrolled down the list, one by one, in utter disbelief. I didn't know how I was unaware of this until now. But then again, I wasn't in the habit of Googling myself and Alexander forbade me to use social media. I was starting to see why.

As I read through the many news links, I found most of them were about Alexander with my name tossed in here or there. However, there were some speculating about our relationship and I began to get angry. If I read one more article about how I was a supposed gold-digger, I might scream. Not now, nor was I ever, after Alexander's money.

There were several pictures of me, many of which were taken at a few events Alexander and I attended. It was sort of surreal, as I hadn't even realized our picture was being taken at the time. However, there were other photos of just me. These were the pictures that really grated on my nerves. They varied in location. Some were taken as I waited in line for coffee at La Biga. Others were taken in random parts of the city as I went about my day. Each image was captioned with arbitrary things, such as the name of the designer for the clothes I wore or the notation of a recent haircut. They even knew the name of my hair salon.

What the fuck?

The intrusion was infuriating. But it was also scary. A chill raced down my spine and I couldn't help but to think of Princess Diana's fatal car crash and the paparazzi. While I wasn't nearly as popular as the beloved Royal, the invasion of privacy she must have felt had to mirror my own to some extent. Suddenly, Alexander's insistence on a bodyguard didn't seem all that unreasonable anymore.

As I continued to click through the links, I came across an article about Alexander written by Mac Owens. It was dated five years back and published by a newspaper I had never heard of. I skimmed through the text, not finding much of it interesting. In fact, the content was pretty dry, despite its lengthiness. It mostly spoke of Alexander's wealth and speculated income. There were references to property holdings extending from New York all the way to the Florida Keys. It reminded me of my conversation with Thomas Green about how far Alexander's influence extends. While I was sure Alexander didn't keep this information from me deliberately, I decided it should be something we discussed before we were wed.

Considering Mac Owens' current project with Charlie, finding an earlier piece he had written about Alexander was ironic. I exited out of the article and switched up my search. I wanted to see if he had published anything else related to Alexander or Stone Enterprise.

I didn't find anything else, but I did discover Mac got his start in journalism at a well-known tabloid. There were pages and pages of links, many of which gave the reader stories about local and world-renowned celebrities. The more I read, the more my stomach began to turn.

Hale was right. Mac Owens was not a stereotypical gossip columnist, but an investigative journalist – one who thrived on digging up dirt about celebrities, politicians, and other public figures. What Hale failed to mention was this man destroyed families, reputations, and in some cases, marriages of unsuspecting people. Seeing what he did made me sick.

And I planned on talking to this sleaze bag...

Perhaps that was why Hale suggested I Google my name. He must have known the direction my search would take. No matter what his reasons where, I learned more than I wanted to learn. Mac Owens could be potentially dangerous in more ways than one. I no longer had any intention to meet with him in the future. Instead, I planned to heed Alexander's demands regarding my protection. I may not always like following his orders, but I needed to remember there was *always* a reason for giving them.

20

Alexander

"Hi, this is Justine. Please leave a message."
I hung up my cell phone and tossed it on the desk. For the third time today, I was sent to my sister's voicemail. She wasn't even answering emails. I was confident she'd respond to the email about the Carnegie Medal of Philanthropy, but even that didn't entice her to resurface.

Where the fuck is she?

I pinched the bridge of my nose, feeling the beginning of a headache coming on. I ignored the documents I still needed to sign and the flood of emails that needed to be sorted. I had been working non-stop since eight that morning, but Justine had been on my mind through it all.

The location service setting on her phone was turned off, so Hale was unable to locate her that way. I had Bryan pull up the expense reports and credit card statements, but I still came up empty. The only thing I found were a few ATM withdrawals made in various parts of the city. Each one was for three hundred dollars. Wherever Justine was, she was using cash.

At the very least, that bit of activity led me to believe there wasn't any foul play. Nevertheless, I planned to go to her condo later on just to make sure. Cautious instincts or not, I could not put it off any longer.

I roughly pushed away from the desk and stood, slamming the chair into the expansive window behind me. I needed a mental break. Between Justine, Charlie's case, that goddamned article, and the tension between Krystina and me, my nerves were shot. While Krystina and I seemed to be in a better place than we were a few days prior, there was still a faint strain looming between us and I didn't know why. The only positive thing in my life seemed to be business. Everything was running smoothly, all the puzzle pieces fitting nicely together. It was my one constant.

I paced back and forth in my office, a sort of restless energy settling over me. My normal life, one I strived to keep measured and controlled, had been in a tailspin for months. No matter what I did, there always seemed to be another shoe that dropped. I raked my hands through my hair in frustration before pounding my fists against the window glass.

The sound of my fists against the glass made me pause. I quickly dropped them to my sides and took a few calming breaths. I needed to get a handle on my temper. Fate was giving me the ultimate test. All the strain and turmoil over the past six months could have broken me. It hadn't, although I came scarily close to losing it a few times. Nonetheless, the challenge wasn't over. I still had to find the resiliency to withstand the future. If not for myself, then for Krystina.

A good sparring match with my personal trainer always worked to diffuse my rage. I might have considered calling him that afternoon, but a glance at my watch told me Krystina would be here any minute. We were supposed to meet with Kent Bloomfield, the architect I hired to draw up the plans for the house in Westchester. However, little did she know, I canceled the appointment. Instead, I requested the blueprints be sent to my office. I would review them personally with her, but I knew she wouldn't be happy with me for canceling with the prominent architect.

As if on cue, the door to my office opened and Krystina entered. Her face looked flushed, almost feverish.

"Hey, handsome," she greeted with a smile, despite the fact she sounded like hell. I immediately crossed the room to go to her. I drew her into my arms and placed a palm to her forehead.

"How are you feeling, angel?"

"Better as the day goes on. I sound worse than I actually feel."

"Are you taking your medication?"

"Yes, Dr. Stone," she teased and pulled away. "Every four hours on the nose."

"Speaking of which, how was your appointment?"

She blinked, as if confused, before her eyes cleared again. More than likely, she'd forgotten I had access to her calendar.

"Oh, um...good. Just a cold like I thought."

Her eyes darted around the room nervously and her hands began to fidget. Something was obviously bothering her. Since we hadn't spoken at all during the day, I wondered if she was upset that I peeked at her schedule. However, I sensed it was something else entirely.

"What is it, angel?"

She moved over to the seating area in my office and sat down on the plush loveseat. Resting her elbows on her knees, she squeezed the bridge of her nose.

"I Googled my name."

Fuck.

Although I knew she might do something like that eventually, I had hoped to shield her from the press speculation for as long as possible.

"What made you do that?"

"Curiosity, I guess," she shrugged.

"I suggest you don't make a habit of doing that. I'm sure you read a lot of untruths."

"I did. So many were calling me a gold-digger. You don't think that, do you?"

I laughed at the absurdity as I sat down next to her.

"No, angel. I don't think that. I tried to give you a portion of my company, yet you refused. Remember? That's why I don't think you should Google too often. Tabloid rumors have the ability to hit an individual's natural insecurities. It can ruin them if they choose to let it. Don't let the rumors get to you."

"I won't. But I have to say, I was surprised to see how popular I've suddenly become. I guess you're a bigger deal than I realized."

Her tone was light, but I saw the wheels spinning.

"Don't go there, Krystina. Don't feed the beast. You know who I am. I just don't brag about my wealth, that's all. How much money I have or what properties I own is not their business. Unfortunately, public records make it hard to hide certain things, but all they have is speculation about the rest."

She took a deep breath and sighed.

"I know you're right. It was just so strange to see my picture everywhere. Now I understand why you want Hale or Samuel with me all the time."

My fists clenched. I knew the pictures she was referring to. The intrusion of her privacy was maddening. The fact that her face was all over the internet drove me absolutely insane. And I hated that I had no control over it. The only thing I could do was ensure she was always protected.

"Does that mean you'll stop arguing with me about it?"

She smiled sheepishly.

"I suppose I should," she murmured. She glanced down at the table in front of us and noticed the roll of blueprints for the first time since she arrived. "Oh! Are those the plans? But wait – where's Kent Bloomfield?"

"I cancelled him. I thought we would go through the blueprints ourselves first."

She narrowed her eyes suspiciously at me.

"You knew I was looking forward to being a part of this process, Alex. Why would you cancel him?"

Her tone was accusing, almost lecturing, and it set me on edge.

"I don't feel like dealing with people anymore today," I answered testily. My tone was gruff and I felt her body stiffen beside me. When I spoke again, I adapted a gentler approach. "Look, prying eyes just seem to be everywhere lately. I want a break from it. I know this is important to you, but I need you to meet me in the middle on this. I want to discuss the house plans amongst ourselves. Just me and you, angel. At least for today."

Her eyes searched mine, so expressive, yet I couldn't tell what she was thinking. Seeming to come to a decision, she placed her hand on my knee and gave it a light squeeze.

"Okay. Let's have a look at what you've come up with so far."

"Thank you," I told her, appreciating her agreeability. Leaning in, I pressed a chaste kiss to her temple before pulling the blueprints out of the clear tubular case. I unrolled the plans and spread them out on the low table in front of us. Krystina leaned forward and inspected the drawing. I had already reviewed it, so I allowed her time to absorb the layout and waited for her to speak first. After a moment or two, she gasped.

"Alex, this house is huge! I won't be able to keep up with anything this big!"

I laughed.

"I can assure you, ten-thousand square feet in that neck of the woods is small by comparison."

"But why in the world would we need seven bedrooms?"

"Maybe I want six kids," I said, waiting to see how she would react. I didn't really want that many children. In fact, I didn't know if I wanted the responsibility of even one. However, I would be open to hearing Krystina's thoughts on the subject. My statement was only meant to feel her out. A look of panic flashed across her face before she quickly recovered.

Interesting...

Unfortunately, that fleeting expression was all I got from her. She didn't take the bait. Instead, she pointed to another area of the plans.

"There's a massive carriage house on the back corner of the lot. Who is that for? And what's this? An eight-car garage?"

She fired off one question after another, her eyes widening more with each one. I needed to put her mind at ease.

"Relax, angel. The extra bedrooms are for overnight guests, such as your mom and Frank. Westchester is a bit of a hike, so I suspect Allyson or Justine might stay on occasion as well," I explained. My heart tightened at the mention of my sister, but I continued on. "Hale will be in charge of security on the property. Vivian will be responsible for keeping up the house and the grounds. Each of them will have their own private suite in the carriage house."

"They are just going to pack up and move with us? Where do they live now?"

"One floor down from the penthouse," I told her, somewhat surprised she didn't already know that. "They are aware of the move and have agreed to it. Don't worry about that. In fact, they are pleased with the arrangements. The extra rooms in the carriage house are for whomever Vivian decides to hire to assist her with her duties. She likes it because the staff she brings on will be right on site."

"The staff?" she asked, her voice sounding slightly high pitched. She was recognizably overwhelmed.

"Krystina, look at me," I ordered. When she turned her

head, her chocolate brown eyes seemed to grow impossibly larger in her beautiful face. I took her chin between my thumb and forefinger. "I never wanted the domestic life before you. A house in the suburbs just wasn't for me. But now that I want it, I will only have the best for you. For us. The sooner you come to terms with that, the easier time we'll have with planning our new home."

"I'm no stranger to nice houses, Alex. My mom and Frank have a nice four-bedroom. But before Frank, my mom and I lived in a small apartment," she said, shaking her head in disbelief. "This house you planned...it just seems a little over the top."

I grinned.

"Have you ever known me to do things any other way?"

She relaxed then and returned my smile.

"No, I haven't."

Then she laughed. Instantly, the mood in the room shifted and my shoulders relaxed. All the tension I felt twenty minutes earlier just slipped away. The sound of her laughter, no matter how bleak of a mood I was in, would always brighten my world. It amazed me. She amazed me.

I reached up to touch her face again. I ran my hand over the soft line of her jaw, before cupping her cheek and turning her head to face me.

"You're beautiful," I told her.

Her cheek warmed under my palm from the unexpected compliment.

"Cut that out," she said as the delicate blush deepened. She playfully swatted my arm.

"Cut what out?"

"That look in your eyes. It's like you want to throw me down and devour me."

"Maybe I do."

I removed my hand from her cheek and slid it between her

thighs. Pressing my thumb against the material of her slacks, I exerted pressure in all the right places. She closed her eyes and leaned into me. Then, rather abruptly, she pulled away and sneezed. Not once, but twice.

"Damn it!" she swore and she reached into her purse for a tissue. "Sorry. I'm not very sexy right now."

I chuckled, amused by her irritation.

"I need you to feel better, Miss Cole. I left you alone last night so you could get your rest." I paused and flashed her a wicked smile. "But my cock won't be patient for much longer."

"Your sexual appetite is absolutely insatiable. Do you know that?" She shook her head at me, then stood to throw away her tissue. When she returned, she looked back at the blueprints. "So, tell me about this eight-car garage. Are you planning to buy enough cars to fill it?"

Her tone was somewhat mocking and I grinned at the sarcasm I'd come to love.

"I already have enough to fill it," I stated with a deliberate hint of arrogance. "Well, technically I have seven, one of which is yours, and a bike."

"How did I not know that you had eight vehicles?" she asked incredulously.

"You never asked. Two of them only get pulled out in the summer months. We haven't been through a summer together yet, so I never thought to mention it. However, I did tell you collecting expensive cars was a hobby of mine."

"You did, but..."

I could tell she was over thinking again. No surprise there.

"What's going on in that inquisitive brain of yours?"

"I just feel like lately...I don't know. There's so much I don't know about you. Well, not you personally, but about your world. Your business and your possessions." She paused and shook her head. "I know it shouldn't matter, but it kind of does. Am I making sense?"

"You're making perfect sense, but it doesn't matter right at this moment. You'll know about all of my holdings soon enough."

"What do you mean?"

My newfound good mood instantly vanished. One minute we were planning our home, then the next I was feeling the sharp slap from reality. It was a reminder that we may never be free from it. I sighed, a heavy tiredness settling in my bones. I didn't want to have this conversation today, but there was no use putting it off. She would know everything in a few days anyway.

"Depending on what happens with this fucking news reporter, I might need to protect my assets. There are too many unknowns at the moment. As we speak, Stephen is drawing up papers to transfer everything over to you in the event something happens to me."

Krystina's brow furrowed. If she was shocked at what I told her, she didn't show it. Instead, she looked sad and confused. Her eyes searched mine as she placed a hand over mine.

"Everything will be okay, Alex."

"We don't know that."

"Let's not talk about what-ifs. Okay?"

"We need to," I asserted. I pulled my hand from under hers and pushed the blueprints aside. "In fact, we should discuss some of it now while we have the time. There are things you need to know about my assets."

She shook her head.

"Alex, I will look forward to the day when I can learn all about it. I'm actually kind of excited by the idea. But I want to do something else right now."

My eyebrows rose when she unexpectedly stood, grabbed her coat, and slung her purse over her shoulder.

"And what might that something else be?" I asked curiously.

"Well, you know I was surrounded by car talk for years because of Frank. I'm sure my stepfather will want to hear all about your collection. Take me to the storage facility. I want to check them out."

I wasn't sure where this sudden need to see my vehicles came from. I was sure she had an angle, as Krystina rarely did anything without purpose. But whatever it was, I was grateful. The distraction might be good for me.

Perhaps it would clear my head before I made the trip to Justine's place.

Almost immediately, a knot of dread formed in my gut at the thought of going to my sisters. I tried to suppress it as I stood to help Krystina into her coat. Once she had it buttoned, I pulled her into a fierce hug. I held her tight and breathed in the scent of her hair. It was always a soft smell, like magnolia blossoms on a warm summer day. After a moment, I pulled back and fixed an intense gaze on her.

"Thank you," I murmured.

"For what?"

"For always knowing exactly what I need."

21

Krystina

Alexander and I took the Tesla over to the storage garage. It was further away than I would have imagined, well outside the city, and took us over forty minutes to get there. Occasionally, I would sneak a few glances at him out of the corner of my eye. He seemed tired. The stress lines marring his face made him seem so much older than he really was. But worse, I didn't like his tone when he mentioned Stephen drawing up transfer of asset papers. I wasn't sure what that entailed, but Alexander sounded resolute, almost like he was giving up.

When we pulled up to the front of the building, he got out of the car and came around to open my door. Taking Alexander's hand, I allowed him to guide me into a standing position. I smiled up at him and recalled Hale's words about the power I possessed. Perhaps the way for me to save Alexander was to remind him why he needed to keep fighting. It was part of the reason I suggested the impromptu drive over. The trip to the storage facility was meant as a distraction from the unfortunate situation around him, but I also hoped it would make him see some of the things he would be giving up.

Alexander pulled a key from his pocket and unlocked the door that would lead us into the garage. However, instead of a garage, we entered into a hallway of sorts and were presented with another door. Alexander pressed his palm to a glass screen mounted on the wall to the right of the door. The screen seemed to scan his palm, then flashed green. When he moved his hand away, a pin pad appeared on the glass and he typed in a series of numbers.

"High tech," I mused aloud, wondering why in the world there would be so much security at a parking garage.

"It's necessary. There's a lot of money in here. Now give me your hand."

Without waiting, he took hold of my wrist and pressed my palm to the screen.

"What are you doing?" I asked in confusion.

"Protecting my assets. It's a good thing you suggested coming here today, or else I may have forgotten."

He held my hand in place until the screen flashed green again. Alexander then entered more numbers into the pin pad and I heard a click. I could only assume it was from the door unlocking.

"Forgotten about what?"

"To give you access. In the event I'm...inaccessible, you may need it."

Instantly, my heart constricted from a wave of sadness. I knew he was referring to the potential repercussions from Charlie's interview, and I found all this talk about transferring his wealth to me to be unsettling. I didn't want Alexander's money. I only wanted him.

Will people believe Alex tried to cover it up? What is the statute of limitations for Justine? Could either of them really face jail time?

I didn't want to think about the possibility. Alexander was

surrounded by a slew of wealthy and powerful people. From lawyers to judges, someone was bound to know what to do about this. After all, they were only children at the time. I had to believe everything would work out and I forced my trepidation aside.

Once we entered, I scanned the massive space. The first two spots were empty. However, the third space held the 1931 Bugatti, the same car we had taken to the Stone's Hope Gala. When my gaze traveled past the Bugatti, I gasped. The need for so much security was suddenly very clear. The vintage car wasn't the only thing with an expensive price tag.

"Alex! Are you freaking kidding me?"

I hurried across the expansive storage garage to come face to face with a car that took my breath away.

"You like?" he asked, coming up beside me.

"This is insane. You actually own a Ferrari?"

"A Ferrari Sergio to be exact. There are only six of this design in the world."

I was practically drooling over the sleek red and black convertible. I reached out, but then pulled my hand back, afraid to mar the hood with my fingerprints.

"Frank is going to lose his mind when he hears you have this."

He laughed and pointed to the far end of the garage.

"Come here, angel. Let me show you this."

Taking hold of my elbow, he led me past an Aston Martin and a Jaguar, two luxury vehicles that seemed to pale in comparison to the Ferrari. We stopped in front of a Ducati motorcycle. The model or year I couldn't be sure of, as motorcycles had never been my thing. However, regardless of my tastes, I couldn't help but to admire the sleek lines. I imagined being strapped in behind Alexander, with the speed and power between my legs. I ran my hand over its leather seat and looked up at Alexander.

"This is a very sexy piece of machinery."

He came up behind me and circled his arms around my waist.

"I never took you for a biker chic."

"I'm not really, but then again, I didn't think you were into the whole MC thing either."

"Eh," he said with a shrug. "It's a toy really. Matteo used to own a bike. I only bought this so I could go riding with him on occasion. But he sold his when he was trying to start up the restaurant, so I don't ride often anymore. Now, I'll venture out of the city only once or twice in a summer and let her rip. I thought about selling it or giving it to Matt, but I like it too much. It's good when I want to clear my head."

"I can imagine the exhilaration. The need for speed. The power."

"You have no idea, angel," he murmured into my ear.

I tried to picture Alexander on the bike wearing one of his designer suits. The idea was almost comical. But then I pictured him in jeans and a black leather jacket.

Now that's something I could get used to.

My core tightened, thinking about how much I loved his ass in denim. I could visualize myself sitting behind him on the bike, my legs straddling his hips as I clung to his hard body. Just the simple idea of our bodies pressed together was enough to be a total turn on. The tightening in my belly intensified and began to travel south. I could almost feel the wind whipping my hair as the scenery flew by, my crotch pushing against him.

Perhaps I am a biker chick at heart...

Lost in my fantasy, I didn't notice the way his breathing had increased. Before I knew what was happening, Alexander's arm shot out and he grabbed me. Spinning me around, he pinned me against the Jaguar parked next to the bike. He pushed me backward, pressed my spine against the hood, and covered my body with his.

He buried his face into my neck and breathed in deeply. Peppering kisses along my hairline, he moved over my ear and bit my lobe. I threw back my head, welcoming him to take more, as his lips traveled down my neck. I was suddenly desperate, feeling as if it had been way too long since he'd been inside me. Considering how regularly we normally had sex, my recent head cold put a major damper on things. I no longer just *felt* like it had been too long – it *was* too long.

Untucking my blouse, he shoved it up roughly over my breasts. He bit down, capturing a nipple through the lace of my bra. My back arched as the taut peaks immediately hardened in response.

When he moved back up to my neck, I reached down and slid my hand between us, searching for the buckle of his pants. He shifted slightly to give me easier access. Freeing him from the restriction of slacks, he moaned when I grasped his hard erection and began to pump. The sound of his moan because of my actions was a heady feeling, and it just might have been the sexiest sound I'd ever heard.

"Jesus Christ, Krystina," he grunted. "You, on the hood of my car, is the most erotic thing on the planet. I want to fuck you. Right here. Right now."

If his words weren't enough to unravel me, his fingers were. His hand slid down my belly, under my waistband, until he reached my wet slit. His forefinger circled my nub furiously, as if he was in a hurry to get me off. As if he were just as desperate as I was. I wanted that, but I wanted him inside me even more. I continued stroking him, my grasp tightening around his cock, as he plunged two fingers inside to stroke my walls.

"Oh, god. Yes. Just like that!" I cried out, my screams echoing off the concrete walls of the garage. His talents never ceased to amaze me. At times, I felt like I could orgasm with just a simple look from him. Ours eyes met, and I saw his were a blazing inferno of desire, as he continued to push me higher and higher.

The unexpected sound of a cell phone ringing interrupted us, so loud and intrusive, I almost thought it wasn't real.

"Shit!" Alexander hissed and removed his hand from my body. "It's Hale."

My frustration came out with an exaggerated exhale.

What the hell!

Knowing Hale only called if it was important, I released my grip on his cock and collapsed against the hood so he could take the call.

Fumbling in the pockets of the pants that were below his hips, it took him a minute to dig out his cell. I smirked, the vision almost comical. Once he located it, he pursed his lips in annoyance.

"What is it?" Alexander barked into the phone. After a moment, his irritated expression turned to worry. I sat up in alarm.

"What's wrong?"

He held up a finger to silence me.

"I'll be right there," Alexander told Hale. He hung up the phone and looked down at me. "It's Hale's mother. She fell and is being transferred to New York-Presbyterian Hospital. I'm going to meet him there. I'll drop you off home along the way."

I recalled Alexander telling me about Hale's mother a few months back. She was diagnosed with early-onset Alzheimer's and was living in a long-term care facility. Hale struggled with the situation, especially since his mother's moments of clarity had recently become less and less frequent.

"I can come with you," I offered.

Alexander seemed to contemplate something before he shook his head. The haunted look was back in his eyes.

"No, angel. It's not that I don't want you there, but I have to stop at Justine's place afterward. I probably should have mentioned it to you before now. I don't expect her to be there. However, if she is, I need to have a conversation with her. Alone."

I nodded my understanding and reached for his hand.

"As long as you know to call or text if you need anything. I can have Samuel drive me to meet you if needed."

After tucking his manhood back into his pants, he kissed the top of my head and pulled me close.

"The only thing I need is for you to be home waiting for me. I believe we started something that needs to be finished."

He tried to come across as playful, but I wasn't buying it. The shadows I managed to chase away from him were now back. The only thing I could do was to do as he asked.

"I'll be waiting," I promised.

22

Krystina

After Alexander dropped me off, I found Samuel waiting for me in the lobby. Alexander had called him on the drive back, so I knew he would be there to greet me and escort me up to the penthouse. However, as much as I was dying to shed my high heels for the day, I had a pit stop to make first.

"Samuel, do you know which apartment Vivian's is?"

"Yes, ma'am."

I cringed, still hating the way he addressed me, but I didn't bother to correct him this time. Some things were just ingrained.

"I want to stop by there for a bit. Would you mind taking me there?" He hesitated. I couldn't blame him after the way I ditched him earlier in the day. He needed assurance, so I added, "You can be with me the whole time."

Nodding, we walked over to the bank of elevators. Instead of entering the one exclusive for the penthouse, we stepped inside the lift that led to the apartment suites. When we reached Vivian's floor, Samuel pointed down a long corridor.

"This way, ma'am."

As we passed the doors for the residences, I absently wondered which apartment was Hale's. Samuel stopped about halfway down the hallway, in front of a door with gold numbers which read 4812. Surrounding the numbers was a decorative wreath made of faux twigs and spritzes of flowers.

"Is this her apartment?"

"It is," he told me.

"Thank you, Samuel," I said and smiled my appreciation. I stepped in front of the door and rapped on it three times.

"Just a minute," Vivian called from the other side of the door. I heard the sound of a security chain and the unlocking of a deadbolt before the door opened. "Why, Miss Cole! What a pleasant surprise."

She greeted me with a bright smile, making the lines around her eyes crinkle. I suspected she was in her early sixties, but I couldn't be sure. She didn't have a ton of wrinkles, but a smooth face only marred by lines from years of smiling. Her dark hair was swept up into a bun, the streaks of gray prominent within the knot. She was wearing an apron, as usual, and appeared to be dressed comfortably underneath. It was later in the evening, and I worried I would disturb her. However, her attire didn't suggest she was going to bed anytime soon.

"Hello, Vivian. May I come in?"

"Of course, my dear!"

She stepped aside and motioned for me to follow her. She led me over to a long cherry wood dining set and pulled out a chair for me to sit at.

"Thank you," I told her as I sat down.

"You still look a little flushed. How are you feeling? Can I make you a cup of tea or coffee? What about dinner? Have you eaten?"

I laughed.

"I'm fine, but thanks. I actually just wanted to come by and say thank you for the soup. It was very kind of you. In fact, I'm feeling considerably better than I did yesterday."

Despite what I said, Vivian walked into the kitchen and set up an ornate looking percolator used for brewing coffee.

"That's wonderful to hear," she called over her shoulder. "Samuel, would you like a cup?"

I turned to look behind me. Samuel stood just inside the door. He was like a statue.

"No, ma'am," he replied, his expression remaining stoic.

Vivian just shook her head and continued on with her task. While she prepared coffee, I looked around her apartment. Just as I imagined it would be, her space was tidy and neat, but not nearly as modern as Alexander's penthouse. Vivian's home was decorated with more traditional trends. The apartment had an open floor plan, larger than I would have expected, with a large kitchen, living room and dining area all within my view. Despite the open concept, it didn't feel cold like the penthouse did at times. Vivian's was warm and inviting.

When she returned, she carried a tray with two steaming cups of coffee and an assortment of cookies. I could use the coffee, but I avoided the cookies. I had lost a few pounds during the weeks I was in the hospital and I was determined to keep them off. I wasn't sure, but there was something about Alexander seeing me naked every day that kept me motivated, and sweet treats didn't get along very well with my hips or my behind.

"I appreciate the coffee, but really. You didn't have to go through the trouble, Vivian."

"Nonsense. I don't mind," she assured. She added a few dollops of cream to her cup, then looked quizzically at me. "So, tell me. I'm sure my chicken soup isn't the reason you're here. What can I do for you?"

I blushed over the fact she was able to sense an ulterior

motive for my visit. I smiled and tried to keep my response light.

"I'll be honest, I'm not used to having a housekeeper. I wanted to get to know you a little better. After all, you are the woman who washes my underwear," I joked.

She gave me a soft smile, a gentle one matching the look in her eyes.

"I wondered how long it would be before you came to see me. I'll admit, you held out longer than I thought you would."

I blinked, unsure of what she meant.

"I'm sorry?"

"Never mind. I'm just getting ahead of myself," she dismissed. "So, you want to know about me. Well, I've lived in this building for twenty-seven years. I came to work for Mr. Stone a little over ten years ago. It was right after he bought the penthouse. He was so young, obviously new to his wealth, but smart. So very smart. I mostly did basic cleaning for him a few times a week just for some extra cash. It wasn't until...well, until later when I began working full time."

I noticed the way her expression grew sad. To my surprise, her eyes misted over. Curious, I couldn't help but to ask her what was wrong.

"What is it, Vivian?"

Instead of answering right away, she pulled a tissue from her apron pocket and dabbed the corners of her eyes. Folding it back up, she waved her hand back and forth as if suddenly embarrassed.

"Oh, don't mind me. You'd think after all this time, I'd be able to talk about my deceased husband without getting all weepy."

"Oh! I'm so sorry. I didn't mean to –."

"No, no. It's not you, dear. I'm just a silly old woman. Now, where was I?" She paused and seemed to be trying to collect her thoughts. "A year after I started working for Mr. Stone, my husband passed away. I loved my dear Wilson something fierce, but with his death came a mountain of debt I couldn't pay. When I told Mr. Stone I would need to move, he wouldn't hear of it. He paid off the debt and offered to pay me a regular salary if I stayed. That's when I started working for him full-time. His only stipulation was I be available at all times. Considering all he did for me, I couldn't refuse him."

I gave her a wistful smile and felt my heart melt. I thought about what he did for Wally's, my former employer, and how he saved the grocer from going under. I thought of Hale's mother and about how Alexander paid for her stay at one of the best long-term care facilities in the city. And now, I had another story about Alexander's generosity.

Vivian and I talked for another thirty minutes. I learned she didn't have any children or grandchildren she was tied down to, so making the move to Westchester with us would be simple. After a while, I became incredibly comfortable with her and I regretted not getting to know her sooner. There was something familiar about her, like she was the grandmother I'd never known. My grandmother passed away right after I was born, so I have no memory of her. However, if she were alive, I imagined her to be much like Vivian.

Perhaps it was that connection which compelled me to bring up the topic I had been thinking about since I walked into her apartment.

"Vivian, I'm worried about Alexander."

Vivian's eyes darkened, yet they were sad at the same time.

"That's honestly the reason I thought you came to see me today. I know he's struggling, but don't let that scare you off. You're good for him. He needs your spunk."

"I love him very much, Vivian. I'm not going anywhere," I assured her. "You've been with him for a while now. What do you know about his past?"

I deliberately left the question open ended in an attempt to feel her out. I didn't know how much Vivian knew and I didn't want to betray Alexander's confidence.

Vivian sat back in her chair and folded her hands in her lap. She nodded slightly and seemed to contemplate her words before speaking. I almost wondered if she were the one feeling *me* out. When she spoke again, her voice was cautious.

"I know enough to know he can't be at peace until he has answers. He's a good man. Hard at times, but good. He lets his past define him. Sometimes that's good. Sometimes it's bad."

"How is it good?"

"Just look at all the work he does with his foundation. Take the woman's shelter for example. I suspect there's an underlying reason for that project."

I nodded my agreement.

"I've often suspected the same. I just wish I could help him more, you know?" I shook my head sadly, feeling frustrated over the situation.

"Oh, but my dear! You do help him! You are his Dorothy!" she exclaimed. I was genuinely confused.

"His what?"

"Do you remember Dorothy, from The Wizard of Oz, and her ruby slippers?"

"How could I not? It's a classic," I laughed.

"It is a classic, but there's a metaphor there too. With her ruby slippers, Dorothy had the power all along. You have a similar power, Krystina. And for Mr. Stone, you are the only place he calls home."

23

Alexander

I walked down the steps of New York Presbyterian Hospital and headed toward the parking garage. Hale's mother was a little banged up, but it was nothing serious. After ensuring she would have aides around the clock, I left Hale alone to visit with his mother. Her mind was absent today, her clouded vision a telltale sign she was somewhere else. Nonetheless, Hale felt obliged to stay with her, so I told him to take as much time as he needed. Samuel had already been briefed on the situation and I assigned him to some of Hale's duties accordingly.

By the time I climbed into the Tesla, it was nearing eight o'clock. Justine's three-story brownstone condominium was on the Upper West Side, located about four miles from the hospital. Traffic would be light at this time of day, so I knew it wouldn't take me more than fifteen minutes to get to her place. However, time had a funny way of playing tricks on the mind, especially when you're trying to put something off. The drive seemed to only take seconds. Before I knew it, I was parked outside her home.

As I stood in front of the brick structure, the knot of dread that had formed on the drive over seemed to sink lower in my gut. I wanted her to be home, but I was also afraid of what she would say. I almost didn't want her to confirm Charlie's story, as once she voiced her betrayal out loud to me, there would be no going back.

I walked up the steps and knocked on the door. No answer. Rather than knock again, I pulled out the key I had for her condo and unlocked the door. The lights were off, making it clear she wasn't home. I flipped on the light switch in the entryway so I could survey the interior.

Everything inside was chic and modern, decorated in various shades of white, silver, or gray. There was the occasional splash of color here or there, but other than that, the interior of her home reminded me of the décor at Stone Enterprise.

I smiled to myself, reminded of the memory of the first project I gave to Justine. It was right after I purchased the building that housed Stone Enterprise. When I acquired the fifty-story building, my knowledge about the Federated-May merger helped to negotiate a lower than fair selling price. The building was a steal, but it needed a lot of updating if I wanted to lease out some of the floors at a premium rate. Justine had been the one to find Kimberly Melbourne.

Together, floor by floor, they worked tirelessly to make Cornerstone Tower one of the poshest office buildings in the city. After seeing Justine's organization and exceptional results with the project, I decided to appoint her as head of the Stoneworks Foundation. It gave her something to do, as well as offset the stipend I gave her every month for her living expenses. I played it off as a win-win situation for the both of us. Although, the truth of the matter was, I had ulterior motives for keeping her close. By working with her on a regular basis, it allowed me to keep an eye on her when she was married to Charlie.

I walked further inside the apartment, looking for some sort of clue for where she might have gone. Nothing appeared out of place. However, framed pictures on the mantel of the fireplace caught my attention. They didn't used to be there. Curious, I went over to look at them and picked up the first snapshot.

It was a faded Polaroid of Justine with my mother. From the looks of it, it was taken at the home of my grandparents. Justine couldn't have been more than three years old in the picture. My mother appeared to be laughing, her eyes alight with humor.

That would have been before her first trip to the hospital. Before the asshole beat her to a bloody pulp.

My mother's blue eyes, eyes that matched my own, never shone bright after that day. I swallowed the lump in my throat and moved on to the next picture. Both Justine and I were in this picture, with my mother in between us looking down at me. Even in the picture, I could see the love in her eyes. Fall leaves were scattered around us and I recalled the day it was taken. My mother, grandmother, and Hale's mother had taken Justine and me to Central Park. We had a picnic of peanut butter and apples, Justine's favorite food. Even now, I could almost taste it. I could nearly smell the crisp autumn air.

I wondered where Justine had gotten the pictures from. I wanted to feel bitter about seeing them, but I couldn't. The expression on my mother's face in both pictures showed how much she adored us. The thickness in my throat tightened and I had to blink back the moisture in my eyes. I couldn't afford a moment of weakness.

Where are you, Justine?

I set the picture down and shook my head in an attempt to

rid myself of the memories. I had to get a grip. Looking at the old pictures was like ripping a scab off a wound, but there wasn't time to reminisce. And there certainly wasn't time to become emotional. There was too much at stake.

I walked upstairs and into her bedroom. I opened the closet doors and found her clothes neatly lined up on hangers. The bed was made, the comforter pristine and crisp. Nothing seeming out of place. I went into her bathroom, but there wasn't even so much as a toothpaste smudge in the sink. Unable to find any sort of clue for her whereabouts, I headed back downstairs to the kitchen.

Once again, I found everything to be neat and tidy. There wasn't a glass in the sink or a food crumb on the counters. It was almost surreal, as if nobody lived here at all. If I hadn't already seen the clothes in her closet, I may have actually believed that.

I looked to the ceiling and reached up to rub my temples. A part of me expected she wouldn't be here. But another part of me hoped to find her curled up in her bed, fraught with worry over the interview Charlie gave. I didn't know if she knew about it, but she had to have. It was the only explanation for her disappearance. I truly believed Justine was running scared.

I turned to make my way out the of kitchen, disappointed I wasn't able to find any answers. I paused when I saw a small scrap of paper under the kitchen table. Bending to retrieve it, I saw it was a receipt for a parking garage in Brooklyn. Yesterday's date and time stamp was printed on the top.

Brooklyn? Why the fuck would she be in Brooklyn?

I pocketed the receipt, unsure of what to think. I only knew, as soon as Hale was back, I would ask him to look into it. Perhaps there were traffic cams in the area that would reveal something. Between Hale and Gavin, my ingenious computer tech, they were bound to come up with some answers.

Just as I turned the key to lock up, my cell rang. I glanced at the screen. It was Matteo.

"What's up, Matt?"

"Hello, my friend! Have you seen the papers?"

My stomach dropped. Hale had assured me he stalled the publication of Charlie's interview.

"The papers? What about them?"

"The reviews!" he exclaimed, sounding completely exasperated.

I breathed a sigh of relief, suddenly realizing what he was talking about. He was calling about the restaurant.

"The reviews," I repeated. "No, I haven't seen them yet. Sorry. It's been a hectic day."

"You're killing me! Look them up, man. They are good. Really good actually."

"That's great to hear, Matt."

My voice was detached, even to my own ears. I didn't mean to sound like I didn't care. I had a lot invested in his success, but I just couldn't feel his excitement at that particular moment.

"What's wrong?" Matteo asked, obviously picking up my tone.

"Nothing. Just tired," I told him and forced myself to match his enthusiasm. "I think we need to celebrate. What do you say?"

"I think that's a great idea. Let's plan for Friday if you're free. The restaurant closes at nine. We can hit a club or something. One of the ones Allyson goes to maybe. Check with Krystina and maybe the four of us can go out together."

I raised my eyebrows as I climbed into the Tesla. I was sure we would not be going to any club Allyson frequented. If I was going to go out, we would do it my way. Still, his mention of Allyson made me pause. Switching over to Bluetooth, I continued the conversation and pulled out of the parking space.

"Allyson," I said, letting her name hang in the air as a statement rather than a question.

"What about her?"

I smirked at his evasion. He knew exactly what I was talking about.

"What's your interest in her?"

"She's a cool girl. We have fun together. That's all."

"Why do I think there's more to it?"

I heard Matteo sigh through the line.

"Don't over think it. Really, there's nothing between us. She's not the one for me."

"If you say so," I said disbelievingly. If there was something going on between the two of them, they were both being very tight lipped about it. "I'll talk to Krystina, but I'm sure Friday will be fine. I'll give you a buzz later in the week and we can work out the details."

"Sounds good. *Ciao!*"

After I ended the call, I texted Krystina to let her know I was headed home.

Today
8:49 PM, Me: On my way.
8:50 PM, Krystina: Are you hungry?
8:51 PM, Me: Only for you, angel.

She didn't respond, but I could imagine the smirk on her face after reading my reply. She would probably say sex was always on my brain. It was, but I couldn't help it with her. It was just so goddamned good. However, sex was far from my mind at that moment. Mental exhaustion was hitting me hard. The chill I felt at Justine's had slowly crawled back into my bones after I ended the call with Matteo. Now, I just wanted to get home to Krystina. I needed her warm body wrapped around mine more than ever before.

Once I reached my building, the elevator's ascent to the penthouse seemed to take impossibly long. When the doors finally opened, I hurried inside, eager to wrap my arms around the woman I loved. To feel her. I called out to her but she didn't answer. I kicked off my shoes and loosened my tie as I made my way to the kitchen. That's where I found her.

She was in front of the long marble counter, her back facing me, as she prepared a light dinner for us. I could see the outline of her iPod in the back pocket of her snug jeans. Earbuds were in her ears and her hips slowly swayed to music I couldn't hear. Sandwich and salad fixings were spread over the counter, but I wasn't even hungry for it.

Damn, I could watch her for hours.

She had such a tiny waist, but it was followed by curves that made me hard enough to drive nails. The gentle side to side movement of her hips made me want to fuck her and the independent questioning mind of hers that challenged every dominant instinct I possessed.

My earlier thoughts about not wanting sex quickly dissipated as I came up behind her and encircled her into my arms.

"Oh!" she gasped. She plucked the buds from her ears and draped the cord around her neck. "You scared me. I didn't even hear you come in."

She turned in my arms to look up at me. I leaned in, buried my face in her neck, and breathed deep.

"I could have watched your sexy hips move for hours. What were you listening to?" I asked.

"Rise Against," she told me.

I pulled away, took one of the earbuds, and placed it in my ear. "Roadside" was playing, a male and female duet about separating lies from truths. How much the song seemed to mirror my own life was ironic.

I silently watched Krystina as I listened to the song for

another few moments. I thought about how she always related everything to music. In a way, she had passed her love for music on to me, as I found myself choosing music to fit my mood more than I ever had before.

"Interesting song choice," I quietly observed. I returned the earpiece to her and she shrugged.

"It's a good tune," she dismissed. "I made sandwiches."

She was changing the subject, but I didn't mind. Instead, I leaned into her once more.

"I don't want sandwiches. I want you," I groaned into her ear.

"So why don't you have me?" she suggested. My cock instantly went rigid.

She reached up and laced her fingers through my hair, sliding through and tugging slightly. Her fingers on my scalp never felt so good. I pulled her closer, until my erection was pressed against her firm stomach.

I expected her to ask about Justine, but she didn't. Instead, she just melted into me and held me tight. I closed my eyes at her touch, moved and aroused by her display of understanding and affection. It made me want her all the more. And now. The food could wait. I needed her long legs wrapped around my waist. My dick was now throbbing, aching. I wanted to take her to bed and press her roughly to the mattress. So that's what I did.

I lifted her and carried her to the bedroom. We shed our clothing without saying a word. We didn't have to. She knew what I needed. I crawled over her body and widened her legs, dominating her and taking what I wanted. She gave willingly as I shoved into her hard. I fucked all the pain, betrayal, and anger out of my body. I used her to feel good, and she let me.

The pain I felt while at Justine's apartment was replaced by pleasure. The betrayal was replaced by affection. My anger dissipated into passion as I rocked into her. Like the song, I was separating the lies from the truth. And Krystina was my truth. My only truth.

I pushed my mind into a freefall of orgasmic oblivion so I could no longer think. When Krystina's nails bit into my biceps, I felt the only thing I could feel when I was with her. I felt alive.

24

Krystina

The hot stream from the shower felt good against my neck and back. I hated the idea of getting out, but I had an important day ahead of me. The week had been incredibly busy, one day seeming to blend in with the next. However, it had been an extremely productive four days as a whole. Before I knew it, Friday was here.

As I stood in front of the bathroom mirror and towel dried my hair, I felt optimistic about the day ahead. My head cold was completely gone and I had a full schedule planned. Not only did I have a pitch appointment with Sheldon Tremaine, but there was a night on the town planned. I may have been looking forward to that more than anything else. Alexander and I needed a night out. It would be good to have some good old-fashion unadulterated fun for once. No networking, no business, and no stress. Just drinks with friends.

Alexander came into the bathroom just as I was putting the finishing touches on my makeup.

"Beautiful as always, angel," he told me and leaned in to

nuzzle my neck. I breathed in his scent, freshly showered with a hint of woodsy aftershave. It wreaked havoc on my system. You'd never know I had awakened that morning to the feel of Alexander's manhood slipping inside of me. Our love-making had been warm and tender, a sweet morning wakeup call. I couldn't think of a better way to start the day. However, if he didn't stop trailing kisses over my neck, I'd soon be looking for something much rougher.

"God, you smell good," I murmured.

His lips moved over the line of my jaw until he met my lips. Not caring he would ruin the lipstick I'd just applied, I gave into the moment and returned his kiss. He had been different over the past couple of days. I couldn't pinpoint what it was exactly, but he seemed more relaxed. I could still sense tension in him, but it wasn't consuming him the way it had been.

The article was still a threat, but it had yet to be released. I wasn't sure why Mac Owens hadn't published and I didn't particularly care. He called me three times this past week, but I dodged every one of his calls. I wondered if Charlie decided to recant his story after a visit from the DA. I hadn't spoken to Thomas Green since our meeting, but I knew I would have to call him soon to let him know I dropped my plan. It was a risky idea anyway and I had failed to come up with anything better. Yet, as Alexander deepened our kiss, I was reminded of Hale and Vivian's words.

You are the place he calls home. Just be there for him.

Perhaps it wasn't the grand plot I was originally going for, but it was exactly what I was doing. I wasn't sure if I'd go so far as to say I had a special magical power, but simply being there for Alexander did hold some merit. Maybe that was why he seemed different. Whatever it was, I only knew I didn't want to see him in misery anymore. If my show of support was all he needed, so be it.

Eventually, he pulled away. I was left feeling empty, already missing the feel of his lips. I was about to pull him back to me but stopped short when I spotted his face. His lips and the area around his mouth was heavily smudged with pink lipstick.

"Ah, pink is not your color, Alex. Let me help you with that," I laughed.

He chuckled when he realized what I was referring to.

"You don't think so?" he joked.

"No, I don't. And I think your employees would agree." Grabbing a makeup wipe from my cosmetic bag, I wiped away the evidence of our kiss. He studied me while I cleaned the lipstick from his face. His gaze was so intense, I found myself blushing. "What are you looking at?"

"You. I love looking at you."

My cheeks heated and flushed a deep shade of red. Unable to withstand the fire in his gaze, I turned to throw away the wipe and began to fidget with the little jars of makeup on the counter.

"Well, you're not so bad yourself," I murmured.

"Krystina, look at me," he demanded. He grabbed hold of my arm and spun me back to face him. Cupping my face between his hands, his gaze met mine. His eyes were stormy with emotion. "I love you. I hope you know just how much."

I wasn't sure what brought on this sudden display of affection. I wasn't going to complain, but I was curious.

"Of course, I know. I love you too, baby. What brought this on?"

He dropped his hands and took a deep breath.

"I had a dream. Another nightmare last night."

I froze. Although I awoke to his thrashing regularly, I didn't last night. Even if I had, Alexander wouldn't have told me about the dream. I never asked for details and he never volunteered them. I figured, when he was ready, he'd tell me.

"Oh?"

"Yeah. I was looking for you. Well, at first it was my mother, then you. When I finally found you, there was something wrong." He paused, seeming far away in thought. "The details aren't clear anymore, but I do remember you were bleeding from somewhere. Normally, that's when I wake up. But I didn't this time for some reason. The dream kept going. When I tried to help you, to hold you...you walked away from me. You left."

I placed my hand gently over his heart.

"Alex, I'm right here. It was only a dream."

"I know that, angel," he agreed and offered a faint smile that didn't quite reach his eyes. "But you've been different this past week. You haven't argued or fought with me. Hell, you haven't even questioned my demands."

"That sounds like a complaint. Isn't that what you've wanted since we first met?" I teased, trying to keep the mood light. When he reached up to tuck a loose curl behind my ear, I leaned into his palm.

"I wanted your submission, yes. You've given it where it matters most, but it's more than that. You can be so goddamn unpredictable that you drive me crazy, yet you haven't been pushing me like you normally do. You simply seemed to know what I needed and you gave it to me. Because of that, I was able to think."

"Think about what?"

"I feel like I've been out of my fucking mind lately. Except, then I see you. Then I touch you. When that happens, I can somehow forget everything. I've come to realize nothing else in the world matters as long as I have you, angel. I might lose it all – my business, my cars, my penthouse. But I don't care. I am nothing unless you're with me."

My heart began to pound. I didn't like his tone. Not one bit. There was a certain amount of finality to his words and it was scaring the living hell out of me. My eyes began to burn and I had to blink back the threatening tears.

"Alex..." I trailed off, unable to complete the sentence that would bring my fears to life.

"I'm going to talk to Thomas Green."

I knew what he was planning without him even saying it. He wasn't going to talk to the DA about Charlie's trial, but about the interview. And the past.

I immediately shook my head back and forth in denial.

"No. You can't!"

"I need to get this out in the open. I can't keep living like this. And now, with Justine missing, staying silent won't help matters if there is a case."

"Wait, just don't. Not yet. There has to be another solution."

"Not one that would satisfy me. I need to get this story out on my terms. The only reason Mac Owens hasn't gone public is because Hale reminded him he needs another source to corroborate Charlie's story. As of right now, he doesn't have one. It's only a matter of time before he does."

I thought about the many times the reporter called me over the past few days. It was my fault, but I wondered if he would have called regardless. I began to wonder if there were others he tried to contact, when I remembered Suzanne Jacobs.

"Justine's friend, Suzanne. Do you think she'll talk to him?"

"I don't know if he's made that connection yet. In any case, Hale has put a tail on Suzanne just in case."

"So, there's still hope. Maybe if you or Justine, wherever she is, can talk to Suzanne first then –."

"My mind is made up," Alexander cut me off firmly. "I'm going to call him on Monday and set up a time when Stephen and I can meet with him. Stephen doesn't seem to think there's a case, but I'm tired of being on edge, not knowing when Owens will publish. He eventually will, and I'm prepared for a PR nightmare. I'm just hoping that, if it happens, it occurs after the ribbon cutting ceremony for Stone Arena. However, no matter when it's released, if cops are sniffing around it will look worse for me. It's better if I come forward first."

"Are you sure about this?"

"I've been hiding my past for too long. I've told you countless number of times to stop living in the past. Well, now it's time for me to take my own advice. You know me – *all* of me. You know what I am inside. No one's ever seen me the way you do, Krystina. So please, no matter what happens, I need your assurance that you'll stick by me."

"Of course, I would! I don't know how you could think otherwise, but –."

"Shhh," he said and held his finger up to my lips. "I don't know what Monday is going to bring, so I just want to enjoy the weekend with you. No more talking about any of this. Don't worry, angel. For all we know, nothing will even happen. But, if it does, I'd like to have a few days of normalcy. Can you do that for me?"

My throat tightened painfully as I stared into the depths of his sapphire eyes. So many emotions swirled within them. Love. Fear. Pain. He had been through so much.

How could I not give him this?

I didn't speak, but simply nodded my agreement and slipped my arms around his waist. Before Alexander went to the DA, I would have to tell him about my meeting with Thomas Green. However, as I clung tightly to Alexander, that was the least of my concerns. I was too busy worrying about how I was going to get through the next couple of days of pretending like everything was alright.

THE WORK DAY was drawing to a close. My office door was open and I could hear my staff buzzing about meeting for happy hour after they punched out for the day. They deserved it.

Together, we managed to nail the pitch to Sheldon Tremaine and land a three-year contract with Beaumont Jewelers. It was the largest commission Turning Stone Advertising has had to date. It was almost hard to believe.

Even now, as I stared at the half million-dollar wire transfer on my computer screen, I couldn't wrap my head around what this meant for me or for Turning Stone. The commission put us on the map, making us a major player in the New York marketing scene. It was a dream come true and I almost wanted someone to pinch me just to make sure it was real. Nonetheless, as exciting as this moment should be, I was having a hard time feeling it. Alexander's words from the morning loomed over me, making it hard to be excited about much of anything.

I pushed back from my desk, stood, and walked over to the large floor to ceiling windows in my office. Normally I loved taking in the view Alexander had gone through great measures to give to me. However, today the picturesque view of the city's skyline was blurred with low lying clouds. The sky was gray and bleak, a reminder of my current mood. I would be heading up to Alexander's office soon and knew I had to shake it off. He didn't want me to worry and, while I promised him I wouldn't, it was going to be difficult to keep up the façade. My only hope was the evenings plans of music and dancing would distract me enough to keep up the act.

I tore my gaze from the sky when I felt my cell phone buzz through the pocket of my navy striped blazer. I fished it out and looked at the screen. It was my mother. We had been playing phone tag all week. A part of me wanted to just ignore the call, as I wasn't feeling up to the wedding conversation I wanted to have with her. Yet, at the same time, it had the potential to be exactly what I needed to perk up my spirits. Talking about wedding plans with my mother could go one of two ways. Either she would piss me off by trying to talk me out of it – *again*. Or she could be excited to start planning. I hoped for the latter as I swiped the screen to answer the call.

"Tag, you're it," I said upon answering. She laughed.

"Hi, love. I saw you called yesterday, but I was tied up with Frank all day. He's shooting a new television commercial for the dealership and he wanted me to be in this one. I don't know why. He knows I despise being on camera. They lie when they say the camera adds ten pounds you know. It's more like thirty."

Her tone was light and I took it as a sign that she was in a good mood.

"You're skinny as a rail and beautiful. Cut it out," I told her.

She rambled on and on about the troubles with the camera crew and the shoot. I let her talk, grateful she was choosing mindless chatter over her normal doom and gloom. After about fifteen minutes, her story concluded and she switched topics.

"How are things with you? How is Allyson?" she asked.

"Ally is the same old. She's been really busy with work, but I managed to nail her down for a bit last weekend."

"Oh? What did you do?"

Here it goes.

I superstitiously crossed my fingers.

"Actually, we went wedding dress shopping. I asked her to be my maid of honor too."

"I see," was her only response. I inwardly sighed.

"Yes, Mom. I'm still getting married, and I'd really love for you to be on board with it. I mean, come on. You're my mother. I want you there to help me plan things. You know, to do the whole mother daughter thing."

She was silent on the other end of the line for a moment. When she finally spoke, her tone was softer, yet still somewhat hesitant.

"Have you set a date?"

"Not yet, but I did find a dress designer yesterday," I told her, hoping to appeal to her love of fashion to persuade her.

"After shopping with Ally, I decided to skip a store-bought dress and have one made. I have a consultation scheduled in a few weeks. I don't know what your schedule looks like, but I was wondering if you'd like to come down and go with me. I planned it for a Friday, thinking you might want to spend the weekend in the city."

I paused and held my breath as I waited for her response. I rarely encouraged my mother to spend weekends with me. I loved seeing her and Frank, but a weekend with them usually left me completely exhausted. Like oil and water, I never blended well with my mother for very long. I hoped my invitation showed her how important my marriage to Alexander was to me.

"What's the day of the appointment? And what kind of dress did you have in mind?"

A slow grin spread across my face as an unexpected wave of happiness washed over me. I didn't realize it before, but now, with my mother on board, it made everything so much more real. I was really doing this.

And soon, I would be Mrs. Alexander Stone.

25

Krystina

I poked my head inside the door to Alexander's office at five-thirty.

"Hey, are you ready to –."

I stopped short when I saw he was on the phone. He waved me in and motioned for me to have a seat in the chair in front of his desk.

"That's fine. I'll be there at nine tomorrow. Will you be back by Wednesday?" He paused, and I assumed it was to allow whomever was on the other end of the line to speak. "Good. I don't think Samuel would be able to handle it at such short notice. Krystina and I are going out tonight and he'll be driving us. I'll brief him before we leave."

He must be on the line with Hale.

As I waited for Alexander to finish his call, I sat back and gave myself a moment to drink in his powerful frame. He stood behind his desk chair, his fingertips drumming against the back of it. His suit coat was off, which allowed me to appreciate the naturally wide span of his shoulders. He looked powerful, and nothing like the vulnerable man I had seen this morning.

He fixed his blue gaze on me, as if noticing I was watching him. He winked, before pivoting gracefully to pace the large glass window. A part of me wondered if he was deliberately giving me the opportunity to check him out completely. After all, it was no secret that I loved to look at him. I would never get used to the impact of his face, so strong and masculine, with his sculpted cheekbones and lips that were both sensual and wicked. The devil peeked his head out from behind my shoulder and I shivered. It was far too easy to imagine Alexander's lips pressed against my body.

Easy, girl.

I averted my eyes quickly before I pounced on him. I had left the office door open and I was fairly certain Laura wouldn't appreciate seeing an X-rated office party.

When Alexander ended the call, he sat down in his desk chair and beckoned me with one finger to join him. He had that familiar gleam in his eyes, dark and primal. I raised my eyebrows in surprise, swearing he must have the ability to read my mind. I glanced behind me at the door.

"Hold that thought," I told him. Standing, I hurried over to close and lock the door, then went back to Alexander. Feeling thankful I opted for a pantsuit over a skirt today, I easily straddled his hips. Alexander pulled me into his arms and pressed a warm kiss to my lips. It started off sweet but evolved slowly and seductively into something so much more. I felt him harden between our layers of clothing and I nearly moaned. I pushed down, seeking the friction to satisfy the building ache. However, instead of pressing against me like I wanted him to, he pulled back to look at me.

"How's my angel?"

"I got to stare at you for the past five minutes, so I'd say I'm doing pretty good."

"Is that so?" he murmured and brought his mouth to my neck. "You liked what you saw."

He didn't phrase it as a question, but more like a statement. It was completely arrogant but, for some reason, I found it to be inexplicably hot.

"I did," I breathed and tilted my head to the side, wanting him to ravage me. Sometimes I wondered if I would ever get enough of him. I was already desperate for him, yet we were just intimate less than twelve hours ago. Perhaps it was because of my fear of what may or may not be coming on Monday. Or maybe it was suppressed excitement over landing the Beaumont deal. I also thought it could simply be the fact I was undeniably addicted. I suspected it was a little bit of all three.

"That was Hale on the phone," he murmured in between bites to my neck and nips on my collarbone. I arched against him, encouraging him to take more.

"I assumed."

His hands continued to roam, but he never stopped the conversation as he untucked my blouse. His hands slid up my back and deftly unhooked my bra. He cupped my breasts in his palms and began to knead.

"His mother is leaving the hospital to go back to the long-term care facility in the morning."

"Hmmm...that's good to hear," I murmured. It was great news, but I didn't particularly care to talk about it. I wanted to focus on his fingers that were pinching my aching nipples.

I reached down in between us and began to unfasten his belt.

"I'm going with him in the morning to bring her back. Also, don't forget to clear your schedule for the Stone Arena ribbon cutting ceremony. It should be an all-day –." He stopped and hissed when my hand wrapped around his length. "Fuck, Krystina!"

"I don't want to talk," I told him as I captured his lower lip between my teeth. He chuckled, his lips vibrating against mine.

"Why, Miss Cole. I never thought I'd hear you say those words."

Without warning, Alexander reached out and swiped his arm across his desk. Everything, minus his computer, went crashing to the floor. I heard the shattering sound of glass.

"Alex! You broke somethi–."

"Shh. You said you didn't want to talk, so shut up," he growled. Lifting me effortlessly, he stood and lay me back against the cool surface of the desk. "Take off your pants."

Feeling weakened by the command and edge in his voice, I used one foot at a time to kick off my heels. His eyes were scorching, dark with unexplainable need, as he watched me shimmy my pants down my hips and over my thighs. I began to sit up so I could take them off the rest of the way, but he pushed me back down and did it for me instead.

After removing the knee-high stockings from my feet, he began to slowly work up my body. He placed hot, open-mouthed kisses over every inch of exposed leg flesh as he went. When he reached the apex of my thighs, he breathed deep.

"I love your scent," he groaned and pressed his face against the lace of my panties. "I've been hard all day from thinking about you like this. On my desk, spread wide for me."

I arched under him, needing him to remove the fabric barrier between my sex and his mouth.

"Alex, I need you. Your tongue. Please," I shamelessly begged. Not needing any more convincing, he looped his index fingers under the side of my panties and tugged them down. Grabbing my ankles, he spread my legs apart, exposing my sex already wet with arousal. Standing between my thighs, he leaned forward and slowly unfastened the buttons of my blouse.

The lights in the office were on, and the sky was just dark

enough where anyone in a nearby building would be able to see exactly what was happening in Cornerstone Tower. Instead of being worried about it, I felt an incredible surge of excitement. It was strange and twisted. Indecently wanton. It wasn't that I wanted others to see us, but the idea gave me an unexpected thrill.

I heard the weight of his pants and belt hit the floor before he shoved my legs apart further. He lowered himself and moved in, taunting me with slow and velvety tongue strokes over my throbbing bundle of nerves. Heat crept over my skin as that familiar moment of bliss built. I knew it wouldn't take me long, as I was already drenched with desire before his tongue made contact. However, right before I could go over the edge, Alexander pulled back and stood to his full height. Grabbing my hips, he yanked me toward him and notched at my opening.

"Come around my dick," he ordered.

In one swift thrust, he tore into me so deep, I was nearly brought to tears.

"Ah!" I cried out but found myself suddenly muffled when his hand clamped down over my mouth.

"As much as I love your screams, you have to be quiet. This room isn't soundproof. Do you understand?"

I nodded. He released his hand but didn't move inside me. Instead, he stayed still. I could feel him fully rooted deep, my walls rippling as I slowly adjusted to his wide girth. I was panting, anxiously wondering how long I could keep quiet. Desperation overwhelmed me.

"Alex," I whispered.

"Yes, angel."

"I need you to fuck me. Hard and fast. I won't be able to stay quiet for long."

A grin spread over his lips, primitive and wicked, as he took hold of my hands. He brought them to the edge of the desk on either side of my hips and curled my fingers around the edge.

"Hang on tight," he told me. Bracing myself for the pounding I desperately craved, I gripped the mahogany wood so hard my knuckles turned white. He reared back, and with one swift thrust, he slammed into me hard. Then again and again, until he took my breath away. He always knew what I needed, like he knew my body better than I did. I hooked my ankles around his hips, urging him deeper into me. With each powerful drive, he edged me closer and closer. Fire spread through my veins, heating me limb to limb as he rocked into me.

I gasped, relief and ecstasy flooding my senses as the tension mounted. Knowing I was close, he lifted my hips from the desk and drove in hard, hitting the spot that made everything turn white behind my eyes. My body seized around his and he groaned. I clenched my teeth to stifle my screams as he rolled into the last few strokes to take us both over the edge.

Krystina

THE AFTERMATH of our unexpected sexual frenzy left a whopping mess all over the floor. Papers, pens, and a shattered mug littered the carpet around Alexander's desk. Yet, as I picked up the pieces of the broken ceramic and deposited them into the trash, I found myself smiling. We wrecked the place in our dying need to get naked, but I didn't particularly care. Grabbing a quickie in the office was definitely something we needed to do again. I felt fantastic and more energized than I had all day.

As I began to button my blouse, I noticed Alexander watching me from the other side of the room. His wardrobe was already intact and he appeared completely put together, like we didn't just engage in wild animal sex on his desk. I, on the other hand, was still a fantastically crumpled mess.

He was standing next to a tall file cabinet, his fingers drumming on the top like he was deep in thought.

"What?" I asked, as I slid a leg into my trouser pants.

"Once you're finished sorting yourself out, have a seat," he said.

Alexander removed a legal-sized manila folder out of one of the filing cabinet drawers. It was thick with documents and made a loud thud when he dropped it on his desk.

"What's that?" I asked.

"Provisional authorization to control my assets. I need you to sign it."

The fiery energy I had been feeling was instantly snuffed out by his words. I stopped buttoning my slacks and shook my head.

"Alex, you said we weren't going to talk about this stuff this weekend."

"We don't have to talk. You only have to read and sign on the dotted lines," he told me matter-of-factly.

"Can't it wait? We don't even know what the DA will say."

"Just sit down, Krystina. Don't make this more difficult than it needs to be."

I sat in the chair, but I had no intention of signing anything. I wished he would stop being so pessimistic.

Alexander began to flip through the pages and explain his list of assets. I found my eyes growing wider and wider with every word he spoke. Many of his property holdings were high rise buildings. Some offered lease agreements, others had condominiums for individual sale. I expected as much. However, I didn't anticipate hearing they were not only U.S. based, but international. From the Florida Keys to Brussels, Alexander held real-estate all over the globe. One location even had a golf course. I knew Alexander was wealthy, but I had completely underestimated his worth.

He was a self-made empire.

When he began to explain how each property was maintained by various property managers, I began to feel overwhelmed. When he told me he set up bank accounts in my name, ready and waiting to be filled with an astronomical transfer of funds, pure panic set in.

Feeling stunned, I shook my head again. I didn't want any of this to belong to me. The only thing I wanted was for Alexander to be with me. Material possessions meant nothing unless he was a part of the package. Not to mention, I wouldn't even know what to do with everything he owned. The idea that I could make decisions for his company was ludicrous.

"Alex, I'm not signing this."

"Stop being obstinate. This is only a provisional agreement. It will only take effect if something were to happen. If there's an investigation, I can't afford a possible freeze of my assets, particularly the liquid ones. Stone Enterprise wouldn't be able to operate. Too many of my properties are intertwined, and they rely on a steady cash flow."

"Alex, I can't have this responsibility! I don't know the first thing about what you do!"

"You don't have a choice. This is bigger than your wants and desires, Krystina. Hell, it's not even just about my real-estate holdings either. You're forgetting about the foundation. I mean, imagine what would happen if the funding to the women's shelter was cut off. You need to sign. But rest assured, there are provisions in here that require Stephen and Bryan to advise you as needed until I can take back control of the company."

I thought about what he was saying.

Until he can take back control. This isn't permanent.

"This is only a temporary thing?"

"Yes," he confirmed.

I pursed my lips. By signing everything over, even if it was temporary, he showed an extraordinary amount trust in me. However, I knew I couldn't sign the documents while there was a secret between us.

"Before I sign, I need to tell you something about Thomas Green."

Alexander's head snapped up from the documents to look at me.

"What about him?"

My heart began to pound loudly in my chest. I didn't know how he would react to my deceit.

"I went to see him," I blurted before I could chicken out.

His eyes narrowed and he leaned back in his chair. Folding his arms, he stared pointedly at me.

"Why did you go see the DA, Krystina?"

I told him about what I did and how I decided against my original plan. I thought about leaving Hale and Samuel out of the story. I didn't want to get them in trouble. However, if I were really coming clean, I knew it would be best to lay it all out there. The truth never stays hidden for long anyway.

I made sure to reiterate that I didn't divulge the contents of the article or his past to the DA. I wanted to reassure Alexander no harm was done, but I couldn't get a read on him. The entire time I spoke, he never said a word. His jaw ticked, so I knew he was angry. Other than that, I had no idea what he was thinking or feeling about my confession.

When he stood up and stalked to the door to grab his overcoat, I panicked.

Is he not going to speak to me now? Does he not trust me anymore?

I had to know what was going on in his head.

"Alex, talk to me. What are you thinking?"

"I'm thinking you need to sign those fucking documents now so we can go home," he snapped as he roughly pushed his arms through the sleeves of the coat. "I'm starving and I want to grab something to eat before we get ready to go out."

He still wants my signature. He still wants to go out.

I took it as a good sign, but I knew he was fighting to control his anger. I couldn't afford to piss him off anymore. Grabbing a pen, I pressed it to the paper and quickly scrawled my signature over the required pages.

"There. I signed," I said. I dropped the pen and stood up to walk over to him. "Now please, Alex. Tell me what else you're thinking."

He turned to face me as I approached and took a step toward me. His blue eyes penetrated me, flashing fiercely. Feeling intimidated and unsure of what that flash meant, I moved back a few paces. He continued toward me until my back was against the wall. Placing his palms against the wall on either side of me, he boxed me in.

"You. Drive. Me. Crazy."

I winced from the way he punctuated each word.

"The situation we're facing is driving *me* crazy, Alex," I whispered. "I had to do something."

"You shouldn't have gone to the DA. As for Mac Owens, that idea was just fucking insane. How could you possibly think of putting yourself out there like that? All of your pain. Your suffering. Reliving it. Everything you went through would have been on the front page of every newspaper!"

"I know that, but at the time I felt it was worth the risk. Please don't be angry with me," I pleaded, even though I knew he had every right to be mad at me for lying and putting myself in jeopardy.

"But I am fucking angry with you!" he swore again ferociously. He slapped his hand against the wall, causing me to jump.

"I'm sorry, Alex. I was only trying to protect you."

He lowered his head, inhaled slow and deep, before

connecting to my gaze once more. When he spoke again, he wasn't nearly as gruff. Only resigned.

"I'm not worth that sort of risk, angel."

"Yes, you are. I would risk everything for you. Even if it meant leaving myself vulnerable."

"Look, this isn't worth fighting over. At least not right now. In time, you'll understand the need to protect your privacy and why I shield you from the press. I might be furious, but I understand why you did it."

"You do?"

"I do, even if I think it was the dumbest idea you've had to date," he scoffed. "You don't need to protect me. I'm just glad Hale got to you before you had the chance to talk with Mac Owens. He's ruthless and not someone you want to tango with."

My stiff body relaxed and I placed a gentle hand on his chest.

"I'm really sorry," I said again quietly.

He encircled my waist in his strong forearms and held me tight.

"I know you are, angel. And so am I. For all of this."

26

Alexander

Krystina and I climbed into the backseat of the BMW I recently acquired for Samuel to drive. Hale had the Cayenne and I didn't trust Samuel enough to put him behind the wheel of the Tesla. He needed his own set of wheels, not to mention the fact I'd been itching to add the coveted badge to my collection. Still, I had to give Samuel credit. He didn't even blink when I handed him the keys to the X6 M. If he was in awe, he didn't show it.

Krystina, however, was not impressed.

"Did you really need to buy *another* car?" she asked and rolled her eyes. I laughed and deliberately tossed her an arrogant grin.

"It was chump change, baby."

"Whatever," she said, seeming amused as she fastened her seat belt. "So, what time do we have to meet Hale in the morning?"

"We?"

"Well, yes. If it's okay, I just assumed I would go with you."

"I'm meeting him at nine. You don't really need to go. You can relax in the morning. I shouldn't be too long. I just want to make sure Hale's mother is getting more individualized attention going forward."

"Actually, I'd like to go. I feel like I should. It's hard to explain." She shrugged. "I only know that, as much as I joke about Hale being my shadow, he's become more than that to me. From what you said, he was pretty shaken up about his mother's fall. Hell, even if you didn't tell me, he took time off from work. That man never takes a minute for himself. That alone told me how upset he was. Plus, I know Hale means a lot to you. I want to be there for him."

I watched her intently for a moment before responding. I was always protective of what was mine. Hale was like family to me. The fact she cared enough to go tomorrow nearly shattered me.

"Alright. You can go with me. I think Hale would appreciate it as well."

She smiled, leaned her head against my shoulder, and we continued the drive in silence. We didn't need to talk, but I knew what she was feeling. I wanted to stay mad over her visit to the DA and the idea that she may have put herself at risk, but I couldn't because she only did it for me. I may have found her scheme to be outrageous, but I understood her desperation all too well. Now, there was an unspoken agreement between the two of us. There would be no more secrets. Not even the smallest of white lies. If there were any sort of walls left between us, they had effectively been destroyed.

Twenty minutes later, we pulled up in front of the Pavilion.

"A hotel?" Krystina asked in confusion.

"Not the hotel. The Marquee Nightclub is on the top floor. That's where we're headed."

"You've got to be kidding me! The Marquee? I heard that

place had a three-month waiting list just to get in. Ally is going to freak!"

"It looks like she already is," I said and pointed out the car window. Allyson and Matteo had just climbed out of the car in front of us. Allyson's face was lit up and she appeared to be talking animatedly, one hand waving up at the hotel while the other gripped Matteo's sleeve.

"Oh, yeah. She's freaking alright," Krystina laughed.

"Come on, angel. Let's go."

Samuel came around to open the door for us and we climbed out. As soon as Allyson spotted Krystina she squealed.

"Calm yourself, girl. I think you just shattered my eardrum," Krystina joked.

"It began as soon as she found out where we were going," Matteo said with a laugh. He slapped a hand on my shoulder. "Good to see you, my friend. And you too, Krystina. You're looking as lovely as ever."

Lovely was the understatement of the year. After taking two hours to dress for the evening, she came out of the bedroom looking like a goddamn sex goddess. Her eyes were shadowed dark and her lips painted a deep red. The makeup was heavier than what she normally wore, but I didn't mind it. Her makeup was the least of my concerns. I was too focused on her chosen attire. Decked out in a short black leather skirt and a burgundy silk tank with onyx straps, I was tempted to send her back to the bedroom to change. When she added five-inched black stiletto's, I did tell her to do exactly that. It didn't go well, her only compromise being a short jacket to ward off the cold.

Ignoring the exchange of pleasantries, Allyson continued to swoon.

"Krys, you do realize only A-list DJ's spin here, right? Celebrities come to this club! Oh my god! I remember reading Leonardo DiCaprio came here before. Oh, and Tina Fey, too! I would die if I saw her," Allyson said with wide eyes, still in awe and oblivious to anything else.

"Hello, Allyson," I said.

She glanced in my direction, almost as if noticing me for the first time.

"Hey, Alex," she greeted, then looked up the fifty-eight-story hotel in front of us. "I don't know how you did it, but this place is impossible to get in. Like, VIP if you're lucky."

I winked at her and wrapped my arm around Krystina's waist.

"I don't subscribe to luck. I make my own," I told her and glanced down at Krystina. Her breath was showing in white puffs in the cold night air. "Are we ready to go inside where it's warm? Or are we just going to look up and gawk from the street?"

Matteo laughed.

"I don't know. Allyson seems to be having a good enough time down here. I'm not sure if she'll be able to contain herself up there," Matteo goaded.

"Oh, stop it," she said and slapped him teasingly on the arm. "Let's go."

With that, Allyson walked up to us and lopped her arm through Krystina's. Krystina tossed me a helpless look but shrugged and took Allyson's lead. The two women walked ahead of Matteo and me. I took a moment to appreciate Krystina's long legs that disappeared under the leather skirt. I decided right then and there, she would need to dress in leather more often. Privately.

Perhaps a leather corset with a garter belt.

She was smoking hot. Unfortunately, every guy in the place would share my sentiments. That was why I wanted her to change her clothes. Because of her stubbornness, I'd have to be sure to keep her close tonight.

As Matteo and I began to follow the women toward the doors to the hotel lobby, I heard him chuckle beside me.

"Your eyes are glued to her, my friend. I know what you're thinking. And yes, many will stare at your woman tonight. Are you going to be able handle that?"

I tore my gaze from Krystina and glanced over at Matteo.

"Let them look. She knows she's mine and that's all that matters," I tried to shrug off nonchalantly.

"Whoa! Are you feeling all right?" Matteo laughed and I tossed him a knowing grin.

"Oh, trust me. She won't leave my sight, Matt. Sure, I don't like the idea of men checking her out, but I don't think she'd take kindly to me knocking out every guy who glances her way. But, if any man has the balls to go near her, I'll lay them flat."

"Ah, okay. I thought you had fallen ill for a minute there. Good to know you're still a jealous asshole," he kidded.

"Shut up, Matt," I said and shook my head.

Allyson and Krystina stood waiting for us near the bank of elevators.

"Hurry up, you two!" Allyson admonished.

"I'd like to gag her one of these days," I heard Matteo mutter under his breath.

I snorted out a laugh, knowing full well he'd have as much luck with gagging Allyson as I did with Krystina.

When we reached the top floor of the hotel, the elevator doors opened up to an opulent and sophisticated lobby. Security guards flanked the glass doors straight ahead. Behind the doors, a sea of bodies and neon lights could be seen. The concierge for the club waited at a podium to take our names.

"Alexander Stone, party of four," I told him.

He looked down at his list for a moment, then back up at me.

"Yes, Mr. Stone. Your VIP host has your table all set up. His name is Lance. He will assist you with your bottle service and

anything else you need this evening," he told me. I heard
Allyson give an audible gasp.

"Definitely not Murphy's Pub," she whispered to Krystina.

"No, it's not," Krystina agreed. She was trying to play it cool,
but I could sense the excitement in her voice too.

I smirked in amusement before directing my attention back
to the concierge.

"Thank you," I told him.

He gave a polite nod before turning to one of the guards.

"Please escort Mr. Stone and his guests to the Encore Bar
area and let Lance know his party has arrived."

We followed the guard through the mass of people and
stopped at a dimly lit corner booth draped in blue velvet. Once
we were seated, Lance came by to get our drink requests. I
ordered a bottle of Glenfiddich single malt Scotch for Matteo
and myself, and Dom Pérignon for the ladies. After our glasses
were filled, I raised a glass in a toast.

"To Matteo and the success of Krystina's Place."

"Ah, cut that out. Without your investment, there wouldn't
even be a restaurant. I should be toasting to you," Matteo said,
but still raised his glass.

"Maybe, but it was your food that sold it."

"Cheers to Matteo's cooking!" both Allyson and Krystina
said in unison.

Our glasses clinked and I sat back. It felt good to be out
with Krystina. With friends. It seemed like it had been ages
since I did anything like this. After joining Club O a couple of
years back, I tended to gravitate there rather than fall prey to
Stephen, Bryan, and Matteo's pleas to join them on their late-
night club crawls. I had nearly forgotten how much I enjoyed
this sort of setting. Yet, it felt foreign at the same time.

"I'd like to make another toast," Krystina began. "Not to
sound like I'm patting myself on the back, but it was a pretty
spectacular day for me at Turning Stone."

"Why? What happened?" Allyson inquired.

"Well, I landed an advertising contract with Sheldon Tremaine, the owner of Beaumont Jewelers."

"Holy crap, Krys! They're huge!"

"Hey, isn't that your guy Alex?" Matteo asked.

Shit!

I wanted to kick Matteo under the table, but the booth was too wide and he was out of reach.

"Your guy?" Krystina asked with her eyes narrowed.

"Yes," I confirmed, not skipping a beat. "Beaumont designed your necklace."

It wasn't a lie. Sheldon Tremaine did design her necklace and her engagement ring. There was no reason for her to know the rest – at least not for right now. I would tell her eventually, but not until after she used Beaumont's commission to strengthen Turning Stone's portfolio.

"I love this song!" Allyson suddenly exclaimed. Krystina turned her attention to Allyson and I've never felt more grateful for a distraction.

I recognized the DJ's transition as well. It sounded like a remix of Katy Perry's latest, a song Krystina often played when running on the treadmill in the home gym. Looking down, I noticed her foot tapping in time to the music and decided to capitalize on it.

"You're dying to get on the dance floor, aren't you?"

"I'm definitely ready, although I'm second guessing my choice in shoes. I don't know if I'll be able to dance in these things," she laughed, her bubbly laughter clear despite the loud noise of the club.

As much as I couldn't wait to feel Krystina's hips grinding against me in time to the music, I wasn't quite ready for dancing. She needed to get her focus off me and Beaumont first. Plus, I wanted to chat with Matteo about the restaurant ratings before I fully acclimated myself to the raucous crowd.

"Go with Allyson. I'll join you in a bit."

She smiled and leaned in to plant a chaste kiss on my cheek.

"Are you sure?"

"Absolutely. Just don't go far. I'll be watching," I warned.

She laughed again and shook her head.

"I'm sure you will be."

27

Krystina

Dancing never felt so good. It freed my mind and body of all my worries. All my troubles. I was lost in the beat, living only for the moment, and enjoying every bit of this unabashed fun with my closest friend. The last time Allyson and I hit the clubs, we were still in college. Being here with her tonight brought back a lot of fond memories, many of which were spent drinking our weight in wine.

After about thirty minutes of hard dancing, I motioned to Allyson that I was going back to the table to grab another drink. She responded with a shimmy and little spin. When I turned, I smacked right into a hard-bodied man behind me. I teetered on my stilettos and he caught my arm.

"Hey, there," he drawled and immediately began to grind against me. His face was slick with sweat causing his hair to plaster to his forehead.

Ugh, freaking gross!

There was nothing more annoying than an uninvited dance partner. I moved away quickly, but he grabbed me around the waist. His dark eyes leered at me, causing the hairs on the back of my neck to prickle. The guy was giving me a serious case of the creeps.

"No, I'm sorry," I said, but quickly realized my words were drowned out by the sudden uptick of music. I shook my head, but his grip tightened on me and he grinned. His hand moved down, precariously close to the curve of my ass. I tried to shrug away, flashing my left hand, hoping my engagement ring would hold meaning to this groping stranger.

If it did, I didn't get the chance to find out. Alexander was between us in an instant. It took me a few seconds to comprehend what was happening. Alexander looked ready to explode with anger, practically capable of murder, as he seized the man by the shirt front.

The man looked startled. I would have felt bad for him, but he made the mistake of throwing Alexander a challenging look. He reached up and gripped Alexander's wrist and attempted to loosen the hold. Alexander merely glanced down, as if there were nothing more than a fly on his arm. He pulled the man closer, their noses barely an inch apart.

"Keep your fucking hands to yourself!" he roared.

Alexander's other hand was balled into a fist. I thought he might hit the guy. I should have intervened, but it was like I was frozen, completely rooted to the spot as the scene rapidly unfolded. Thankfully, Matteo showed up behind Alexander and grabbed hold of his arm.

"Alex, not a good idea, my friend."

Alexander looked to Matteo, his eyes still flashing with anger, but he released his hold.

"What's going on?" Allyson yelled over the music, apparently not having seen my run in with the stranger.

"Nothing," I told her. As far as I was concerned, Alexander's rage was completely unjustified. I could have handled the guy just fine on my own. Now it appeared I would have to coddle Alexander's jealousies instead.

Stepping in between the two men, I planted a long and leisurely kiss on Alexander's lips. My hope was I could send a stronger message to the creep who grabbed me, as well as dispel some of Alexander's anger.

It seemed to have worked. Alexander pulled my body tight to his returned my kiss, his lips pressing passionately down on mine. When Matteo let out a loud wolf whistle, I felt Alexander's lips turn up in a smile against mine.

I pulled away and looked toward Matteo and Allyson. They were both dancing and smiling at us. After a quick glance around, I saw the man who grabbed me was nowhere in sight. I breathed a sigh of relief.

"You know, I could have handled that guy," I told Alexander.

"You also could have changed your clothes like I wanted you to," he countered. His eyes drilled holes into me and I could tell his anger was still simmering just below the surface. I tilted my chin up in defiance.

"Right. Like my clothes have anything to do with what happened."

Without warning, Alexander pulled me to him once more, hoisting me up just enough so my feet barely skimmed the floor.

"You will be the death of me, do you know that?" he growled into my ear. "Do you know what you look like out here on the dance floor? I've been watching your hips, your legs, your curves. And so has every other man in the place. You're so goddamn hot and you don't even know it."

To my surprise, I felt an undeniable hard rigidness begin to grow against my belly.

Holy shit. He's turned on.

Using the knowledge of his arousal to my advantage, I kissed him long and hard. The heat of his lips against mine spread like wildfire through my veins and my heart began to hammer an erratic beat in my ears. The music changed, spinning into a popular Ed Sheeran mix. After a moment, I pulled back to meet his gaze. His eyes were dark and hungry.

"Dance with me," I told him.

Alexander lowered me so my feet were firmly planted on the ground. Clasping my right hand, he flashed a wicked and melt-worthy smile, before sending me into a spin. He yanked me back into his arms, his chest hard against mine, and we began to move.

His motions were effortless, making me appear to be a much better dancer than I actually was. I had nearly forgotten how well Alexander could dance. He moved around me in a flawless rhythm, sexy and confident, before pulling my hips against him once more. He teased me with a slow circular grind.

"I know your grandmother taught you East Coast Swing, but please don't tell me she taught you these moves too."

He chuckled, the deep sound of his laughter carrying over the thumping music.

"No, baby. These are all mine."

In my semi-buzzed state, I found myself shamelessly gyrating against him as he lowered himself down my body. Grabbing my waist and pressing his face against my stomach, he ran his hands up and down my legs. All of his attention was on me, as if there wasn't another soul in the club.

"You're crazy, do you know that?" I teased.

His hips never stopped moving as he returned to a standing position.

"Not crazy. Just in love with the shape of you," he sang, mimicking the song lyrics. I threw my head back and laughed as he took hold of my hips again.

Feeling emboldened by his actions, I reached between us

and splayed my palm against the fly of his designer jeans. I felt him tremble before he pulled my hand away.

Gripping the back of my neck, he pulled my ear to his lips.

"I'm going to punish you for that, Miss Cole."

"Is that a promise?" I provoked. He groaned, the vibration against my ear followed by hot and heavy breaths.

"You really are trying to kill me, aren't you?"

I laughed and looked around to see where Allyson and Matteo had gone. They were still dancing, Matteo flinging Allyson's petite body around effortlessly. Matteo, like Alexander, had some pretty good dance moves as well.

The music began to fade out, transitioning into another track. I was panting and sweating from exertion.

"Why don't we go sit and have another drink," Alexander suggested. He too was sweating, his hair falling in damp waves over his brow.

"That sounds like a good idea," I agreed.

When we got back to the table, our server was there at the ready to pour us another round. While I was out dancing with Allyson, Alexander and Matteo must have added to our bottle collection. The Scotch and the Dom Pérignon was now joined by another brand of whiskey and a couple bottles of white wine. I eyed up the people who stood waiting in line for their drinks at the bar. I didn't envy them in the least.

I could get used to this bottle service thing.

Leaning back against Alexander, I took a sip of the chilled wine, feeling like a spoiled princess.

"We should go dancing more often," Alexander said as he trailed a finger up and down my arm. "Just do me a favor. Don't wear such a short skirt next time."

I rolled my eyes and ignored his comment.

"Yeah, we should do this again soon. It's a good time."

I pushed away the thought of what might be coming and

the possibility we wouldn't be able to do this again anytime soon. I didn't want to think about it. Not tonight.

"Oh, and another thing. Leather," he added.

I craned my neck up to look at him.

"Leather?" I asked in confusion.

He cupped my cheek and leaned in to kiss me. His tongue traced the seam of my lips, coaxing them open. Our tongues danced together for a brief moment before he pulled away.

"Yes, no more leather in public. It's too hard to keep my hands off you when you wear it."

I raised my eyebrows.

"Is that so?"

"Yes. But you will be wearing it more often for me. And only me. What color bra are you wearing?" he asked, his voice taking on a guttural sound.

I shivered.

"Black lace. Strapless."

He hissed out a breath.

"Fucking leather and lace. When we get home, I want you kneeling. Bra and skirt. No panties."

My insides burned, his command an inferno ripping through my body and settling at the apex of my thighs.

When I spoke, I said the words he always wanted to hear, but they were ones I often felt awkward saying. However, I couldn't think of a more appropriate and natural response to his current demand.

"Yes, sir," I whispered.

28

Krystina

"Y ou're beautiful."

My eyes fluttered open to the sound of Alexander's words. He said them so softly, I thought I was dreaming. In a daze, I rubbed my eyes and squinted from the light of the early morning sunrise flooding through the window. Giving in to a good body stretch, my eyes slowly came into focus and settled on a bare-chested Alexander. He was standing next to the bed looking down at me, his jeans unbuttoned and hanging loosely around his hips. His hair was damp from a recent shower.

"Morning," I said with a sleepy smile. "What time is it?"

He climbed on top of me, pinning me to the mattress, his hard and lean body spreading across the length of me. My nose filled with the heady scent of fresh water and body wash.

"It's almost seven-thirty," he told me as he brushed a few wisps of hair from my face.

I extended my arms over my head and stretched again, my body deliciously sore after the events of last night. And it wasn't from the dancing. Alexander had been on fire last night, coming at me hard and fast the minute he saw me kneeling in the bedroom. I didn't get to sleep until well after two in the morning, only to be woken up again at four-thirty for a round of slow and sleepy sex.

"I suppose I should get up and shower," I mused, not wanting to leave the comfort of the warm blankets or the weight of Alexander's body.

"Probably," he murmured, before leaning in to trail a line of kisses over my jaw. His tongue moved in slow circles down my throat.

He slid a hand down my arm, taking the sheet with him as he went, and uncovered my naked breasts. Using just a fingertip, he traced down the center of my breastbone and over the jut of my hip, before slowly moving back up to circle a nipple. He leaned in and captured it in his mouth, his hot and wet tongue doing a slow dance around the peak. I arched my chest against him and gave a soft sigh.

"You could join me in the shower," I breathed.

He groaned and shifted to the other breast, before moving back up my neck to claim my mouth.

"As enticing as that sounds, I don't want to be late. Hale is expecting me at nine. However, if you want to stay here, naked in our bed, I can promise you I'll hurry back."

I wanted to surrender and be the slave he made me; to stay naked in bed and wait for his return. But I knew I should be there for Hale. Moving my hands up, I rested my palms on either side of Alexander's handsome face. When I spoke, I tried to keep the regret from showing in my voice.

"I should go with you. The bed will still be here after we're through helping him with his mother. And, when we are done, we have all day," I added.

He took my wrists and pinned them to either side of my head.

"I could make you stay here."

As much as I didn't want to admit it, I knew he could.

"But you won't."

"You're right, angel. I won't," he chuckled and released my wrists. Leaning back to sit on his heels, the corner of his mouth lifted cheekily. "But I will hold you to the promise of being in bed all day. I plan on fucking you all the way through the night and into tomorrow."

I grinned.

"I may not put up a fight," I said with a suggestive wink.

Swinging his leg over me to get off the bed, he dragged me up to join him. He circled my waist and pulled my naked body against his. His hands reached around to cup my cheeks, drawing me tighter to him, as he leaned down to press his lips to my ear.

"Go shower and I'll get your caffeine brewing before you start jonsing for a fix," he teased before giving my rump a light smack. I sighed at the mention of coffee and used it as motivation to quickly shower and dress.

After throwing on a pair of jeans and a black top, I pulled my hair back into a loose ponytail and followed the aroma of freshly brewed Columbian beans into the kitchen. Alexander stood at the breakfast bar with a toasted bagel and a glass of orange juice. He pointed to the table where a steaming mug of coffee and a buttered bagel were set out for me.

"Eat," he ordered.

He didn't have to say it twice. My stomach was rumbling before I even came into the kitchen.

Once I downed two cups of coffee and we polished off our bagels, we were in the Tesla by eight-thirty and headed toward Brooklyn.

The Saturday morning traffic was light and we made good time. When we pulled into the parking garage, Alexander took the ticket from the machine at the gate and tossed it on the dash. After we pulled into the first available spot, he

244   DAKOTA WILLINK

picked up the ticket and studied it. A curious expression was on his face.

"What is it?" I asked.

"I found a parking receipt on the floor at Justine's place the other day. I had nearly forgotten about it until I saw this. I'm pretty sure the parking receipt I found matches this one."

"Perhaps she was here visiting Hale's mother?"

"I doubt it. Justine hates nursing homes. It would be out of character for her to be here, but I don't know why else she would be in Brooklyn," he murmured and shook his head. "I'll ask Hale about it after we get his mother settled."

Alexander looked worried, but I didn't pry as we made our way out of the parking garage. Once we got to the street, we hurried across to the other side. The cold New York winter winds whipped at the nape of my neck. I was wearing a warm coat but was wishing I had added a scarf. I shivered, feeling more than ready for the weather to break. I missed the smell of spring and the feel of the summer heat.

When we reached the entrance to the nursing facility, we had to be buzzed in. Once the door unlocked, Alexander placed his hand on the small of my back and led me into the main lobby. The lobby held several cream and blue cushioned high back chairs. The tabletops were filled with vases of fresh flowers, giving the atmosphere a homey sort of feel. A few residents moved about, talking with one another in hushed voices, almost as if they didn't want to disturb the quiet serenity of the home.

Hale strode across the lobby to meet us when he saw us come in. As he approached, I noticed how visibly tired he looked. His normally strong and alert demeanor looked deflated, almost as if he hadn't slept in days.

"How is she today?" Alexander asked Hale as we walked down the hallway toward Hale's mother's room.

"She's good actually. Her mind seems a bit clearer ever since

I got her back here. I think being back in her familiar surrounding helps."

When we walked into the room, Hale's mother was sitting in a rocking chair in the corner of the room. The creak of the wood floor was audible under the chair as she rocked back and forth. An afghan covered her lap and she was holding a picture frame in her hand.

"Mother, look who came to see you," Hale said.

She looked up at Hale's words and scanned us. She stared at us with indifference, almost as if she didn't see us, her gray eyes covered with a heavy fog.

"Mrs. Fulton, it's nice to see you," Alexander said.

She looked down at the picture in her lap and fingered the frame of the picture nervously.

"What picture do you have there, mother? Can I see it?" Hale asked and slid the picture from her hands. Looking up at Alexander, he said, "It's a picture of her and your grandmother. She always liked this one."

Hale set the picture down on the end table, next to a row of several other framed photos. I walked over to take a look at them while Hale and Alexander conversed about the care Mrs. Fulton would need in the coming weeks.

Hale's mother was beautiful in her youth, her eyes bright even in the old black and white photos. There was a picture from her wedding day and another with people who I assumed to be friends and family. My eyes rested on a colored photo of a younger Hale. The colors in the picture were faded, typical of technology for that time period. If I had to guess, Hale was probably in his early twenties when the photo was taken. He was in uniform and two children flanked either side of him. I leaned down to take a closer look. I smiled when I realized who the children were. There was no mistaking those intense blue eyes and nearly black hair. It was Alexander and Justine.

"Krystina," Alexander said. I stood and turned to face him.

"I'm going down to the nurse's station to see if I can speak to the head nurse. Will you be okay staying here to keep Hale and his mother company?"

"Sure, no problem."

When Alexander left, Hale walked over and picked up the picture I had just been looking at.

"They were so young," he said. "They both look like their mother, except Mr. Stone inherited some of his father's harder features."

"That's a great shot. I didn't realize your history with Alexander went so far back."

"My mother was best friends with his grandmother. After my father died, our families became very close. Mr. Stonewall stepped up and was like a father figure to me."

He seemed sad and I wasn't sure why. I wondered about their relationship and how it evolved. Hale always addressed Alexander so formally. I found it odd considering the family background.

"Hale, why do you address Alex as sir, or as Mr. Stone?" I asked, genuinely curious. He set the picture down afforded me a small smile.

"Because he expects it. Mr. Stone is very much like his grandfather in that regard."

"I wish I had the chance to know him. Alex speaks fondly of his grandparents. They seem like people I would like."

A loud tapping sound had Hale and I both turning in the direction of his mother. She had picked up the picture frame Hale just replaced and was tapping her finger hard against the glass. She was quite obviously agitated, mumbling words I couldn't understand.

"Mother, what's wrong?" Hale asked and rushed to her side. She continued to tap the picture. "The picture? Yes, I see the picture."

She shook her head, seeming to get more and more upset

by the second. Her finger tapped harder and her hands shook. She kept repeating something, but I couldn't make it out.

"What is she trying to say?" I asked, unsure if there was anything I could do to help calm her. Hale didn't respond but continued to address his mother.

"Mother, please don't be upset," he told her and took the picture from her hands before she could break it.

"Til em. Til em," Mrs. Fulton kept repeating.

Tiller? Until then? To them?

I couldn't figure it out, but it appeared as if Hale could.

"I know what you are trying to say. Don't worry. I will tell him," Hale soothed her.

She stopped the furious fidgeting and seemed to calm down somewhat. She resumed her rocking, her eyes taking on the vacant expression once more. It was completely heartbreaking. Her confusion and panic, disappearing into a blank nothingness, was such a sad sight to see.

"Tell him? Is that what she was trying to say?"

He bent to adjust the blanket around her, speaking to me in a low voice as he did so.

"She does this from time to time when she recalls a memory. When she can't find the words, she becomes agitated. It doesn't usually last long before her disease fogs her mind again and she calms down."

"You seem to have a way with her, which I'm sure helps. At the very least, you seemed to understand what she was trying to say."

"Yes, I did know what she was saying." He stood to his full height and turned to look at me. His normally emotionless eyes looked pained as he met my gaze. "Miss Cole, I have to tell Mr. Stone something today. It's something my mother wanted me to tell him for a very long time. It won't be easy for him to hear."

My brow furrowed in confusion.

"What do you mean?"

He glanced down at the picture of himself with Alexander and Justine.

"I've protected them for as long as I can remember. But I might not be able to anymore." He paused and took on a faraway look. After a moment, he continued. "I told you once before that he needs you. He'll be needing you now more than ever."

29

Alexander

When I returned to Mrs. Fulton's room, I found Hale and Krystina staring oddly at one another. Krystina looked concerned yet confused. Hale on the other hand, looked uncharacteristically troubled.

"What's wrong?" I asked. Hale looked at me with a pained expression. It was rather alarming. "Is it your mother?"

I looked past him and saw she was sitting peacefully in her chair, just as she was when I left the room.

"Mr. Stone, I need you and Miss Cole to come with me."

I stared at him in confusion.

"Hale, tell me now. What is going on?"

"Just please, follow me."

He walked out of the room, leaving Krystina and I little choice but to follow him. I was somewhat taken aback. Hale never ignored a direct question from me. I looked to Krystina.

"What happened when I was gone?" I asked her quietly as we walked.

"I don't know. Hale's mother had some kind of a panic

episode. He calmed her down, then told me he had to tell you something. I don't know what though, because you came back right after he said it."

"Something isn't right," I murmured, more to myself than her.

Hale came to a stop in front of a closed door. It appeared to lead to a room for another resident.

"She's sleeping, so please keep your voice down," Hale told us.

"Who's sleeping? For the second time, what the fuck is going on?" I asked, now feeling indisputably pissed off over the unexplained secrecy.

He didn't answer but turned the knob and pushed the door open. A sinking feeling began to form in my gut, yet I didn't know why. I only knew I had never once seen Hale behave the way he was.

I stepped into the room and was momentarily stunned by who I saw. Justine sat in a chair in front of a bed. I saw the outline of a person under the bedsheets, someone who I could only assume to be a patient. However, I could care less about who it was, as I was too shocked to see my sister.

"Justine! Where the hell have you been?"

She held a finger to her lips to quiet me and motioned to the person in the bed.

"I...I've been here," she said softly.

"Here? In a goddamn nursing home?" I shook my head in confusion. "Why haven't you returned any of my calls?"

She looked at Hale, and her eyes welled up with tears.

"I'm so sorry, Alex."

I looked back and forth between the two of them.

"Sorry for what? What in holy hell is going on?"

She stood up, stepped to the side, and looked down at the person in the bed. My gaze followed hers, still not understanding why Justine was even here.

My eyes landed on an older woman, her dark hair was streaked with gray and fanned out over the pillow. She was sleeping, her pale lidded eyes fluttering as if she were experiencing a dream. She looked frail, but...familiar.

No. It can't be.

My heart began to beat rapidly in my chest. Justine began to speak, and I snapped my head up to look at her.

"She usually takes a nap around this time of day. The medication she's on makes her a bit sleepy, but she'll probably wake up soon."

As if they had a mind of their own, my legs began to move. I kept my gaze fixed on Justine, putting one foot in front of the other, until I was directly beside the bed. I stared at my sister for a moment longer before slowly turning my head to look at the woman in the bed.

She had a narrow nose and defined cheekbones. Just like mine and Justine's. Age lines marred her face, the faint indents of crow's feet extending to her temples. There was a horrific scar spreading from the right side of her forehead to the middle, outlining a slightly caved in depression. It was in the shape of an elongated U, its deep purplish-gray color revealing how bad the original wound must have been.

As I stared at the scar, a vision flashed before my eyes. It nearly blinded me and I staggered back. I knew that scar. I had seen the wound that caused it. My eyes burned from the pain that began to build behind them, a migraine of the sorts I had never before experienced.

Abruptly, it was as if I was thrown back in time, the hazy details of the day Hale showed up and found Justine and me with my father's body suddenly becoming clear.

SOMEONE IS KNOCKING on the door. I'm afraid to answer, but I hear Hale's voice.

Hale is a soldier and it's dumb to be afraid of a soldier. I should answer it. He could help me and Justine. She's still acting funny and won't eat all her food. Grandma would say it's wasteful.

I open the door.

"Hey, champ," Hale says to me and messes my hair. "Where's your mom? Your gran made banana bread, your mom's favorite."

"Mommy's not here," I lie. *I don't want him to see her. He'll tell grandpa about her face, then grandpa will call Mommy a fool. That makes her cry.*

"Oh," Hale says. He sounds surprised. "Do you know where she is?"

I shake my head and look behind me. I see Justine down the hall going into her room. She's humming again.

"Something happened to Justine, Hale. Can you talk to her for me?"

He looks past me. He's too tall, and I can't block his view. I don't want him to look into the living room. He'll see him if he does.

"Champ, what's wrong? Where's your mom?"

He sounds afraid. Like me.

Hale walks around me and comes into the house. My heart begins to pound.

"Wait, no! Not in here. Justine's room is this way," *I say and pull at his sleeve.*

"Jesus fucking Christ!" he swears. *Grandma won't like his language.*

Hale starts running through the house. He's calling for Mommy. I shake my head. I want to tell him she can't answer, but decide I want to eat grandma's treat instead. It's better than following Hale and seeing her again.

"Justine," *I call out.* "Hale is here. Grandma made banana bread. Come have some."

Justine comes out of her room, and we sit on the sofa. She hums and rocks back and forth as I unwrap the foil. We each share a piece.

I can hear Hale in the kitchen. He's talking to someone. I think he's on the phone.

I wonder who he's talking to, but I try not to listen. I don't want to listen.

He comes back to the living room. He's carrying a person. I know who it is, but I don't look. I don't want to see her face. It's not pretty anymore.

"Alexander, I need you to do exactly as I say," Hale says to me. "I'm going to take your mother to get help. I'll be right back. Grandpa will be here soon too."

I look down at the floor. I see him still laying there and I feel angry. I look up at Hale, careful not to look at Mommy's face when I do. I take another bite of bread.

"Grandpa will be happy the lazy bastard is dead," I say in between bites.

"Dammit! Alexander, I don't want to leave you, but everything will be okay. Just stay with your sister. Don't leave the house. In fact, don't even leave the couch."

He seems upset. I don't want to make him more upset, so I nod.

"Okay," I agree and go back to eating.

MY MOTHER. She was there the whole time, yet I didn't remember it until now. I remembered her body on the kitchen floor. Her lips were pale, and she was unresponsive to anything I tried to do. Her skull was pushed in, a shallow crater oozing with blood and gray matter, causing her hair to mat to her face. I recalled it being sticky. My stomach rolled from the recollection of the terribly gruesome sight.

Is that why I blocked it out? And what about Hale? Where did he bring her?

I couldn't think, my vision flooding with a rush of more suppressed memories. This time, I recalled a conversation I overheard my grandfather having with Hale and my grandmother.

GRANDPA WILL GET *mad if he catches me out of bed, but I can't sleep. I don't want to have another bad dream. I need to ask Grandma for my sleep medicine.*

I go downstairs but stop when I hear Grandpa talking. He sounds angry.

"No, I don't care what your mother thinks, Hale. We can't tell them. Not now. It's been over a month. Justine still hasn't spoken a word, and Alexander can barely get through the night."

"These children have been through too much. They can't see her like this," *Grandma says. She sounds like she's crying. Grandma cries a lot now. I wish I could make her feel better.*

"Any improvement?" *Hale asks.*

"No. The doctors are not optimistic. It's most likely permanent," *Grandpa says.*

Grandma cries again.

"Lucille, get it together. You need to be strong for Alexander and Justine. Crying isn't going to bring her back."

"That's not why I'm crying. I'm crying because I feel guilty. Right now, we have her hidden away. She's stable, even if her mind is gone. I just feel awful for keeping the children in the dark. Will we ever be able to tell them? Bring them to see her?"

"Lucille, she won't even know who they are. You said it yourself. These children have been through enough. We have to protect them. Can you imagine what else they'd have to endure if it came out that their mother murdered their father?"

"He deserved it if you ask me," *Hale says.*

"Any news on the police investigation?" *Grandpa asks.*

"Nothing. They haven't even found the gun that shot him."

I begin to get nervous. They think Mommy killed the lazy bastard. What if they find out what I did?

"For the sake of Alexander and Justine, it's better Helena remains a missing person. Hale, are you sure you can keep her identity a secret?"

"Yes, sir. As far as anyone knows, Helena Russo is really Lena Silvestri."

My hands feel sweaty. I take a step back. The stair creaks.

"Alexander? Is that you?" I hear Grandma call out.

If they see me, they'll know what I did. I don't need my medicine anymore. I just need to get back to my room.

I TURNED TO HALE.

"You knew where my mother was this whole time."

I phrased it as a statement of accusation, not a question. Hale simply nodded and stared at some invisible speck on the floor.

"Alex, wait," Justine interjected. "You don't understand."

She spoke, but I wasn't hearing her. I was too busy watching my security detail, the man whom I had come to consider a friend and the man I had trusted longer than anyone else. For years, I sent him off to chase Jane Doe's, only to now learn he was simply placating me. A part of me wanted to deny he knew my mother was alive all this time, but my newfound memories told me that wasn't the case.

Heat rose to my face, and I felt my fists clench. I couldn't think. I couldn't speak.

So, I acted.

I lunged at Hale, landing a well-aimed punch to the center of his face. I heard a crack of cartilage. Whether it was from my knuckles or his nose, it didn't matter. Blood spurted immediately from his face, but I didn't pause. I hit him again. He staggered back a step but didn't offer me a return blow.

"Fight back, you bastard!"

I felt something, or perhaps someone, on my back.

Krystina. Justine. My subconscious knew it was them pulling at my arms, but I just kept swinging.

Then I heard her voice. A voice I haven't heard in over twenty years. It sounded exactly as I remembered, yet...different.

I stopped moving. My chest heaved and caused my breath to come out in rapid successions as I turned around.

"Mom," I whispered.

She sat up in the bed and clutched her blanket to her chest.

"Do I know you?" she asked.

"Alex!" Justine hissed. I slowly turned to look at her. "There are things you don't know. Please, just play along or you'll upset her."

Confused, I looked back at my mother. She stared at me with a curious expression. I wanted to go to her. I wanted to tell her I had somehow known she was alive and I had never stopped looking for her. However, there was something about her gaze that made me pause.

It had been decades since she last saw me. She wouldn't be able to recognize the man I had become. So instead of saying all the things I wanted to, I stepped up to her and extended my hand.

"I'm Alexander."

I waited to see if she would remember, but she simply stared at my hand. It was as if she didn't know what to do with it. To my astonishment, she didn't shake it, but took hold of it and turned it around in hers.

"I thought you had a sweet treat for me," she pouted. She pushed my hand away, pulled a stuffed rabbit out from under her pillow, and began fiddling with its floppy ears.

My eyes widened in horror. A wave of nausea hit me and I wanted to vomit. Swallowing the bile in my throat, I turned to Justine. Tears were falling down her cheeks.

"What's wrong with her?" I asked so quietly, I may as well have mouthed the words.

I heard Krystina clear her throat. I had almost forgotten she was there. When I looked at her, her face showed almost as much shock as I felt.

"Alex, why don't you, Justine, and Hale go find a quiet place to talk. I can stay here with, um...with her," she offered and pointed to where my mother sat in her bed.

I looked over at Hale who was standing quietly in the corner. His nose was bleeding and it appeared I split open his bottom lip. However, he made no attempt to wipe the blood away. Instead, he stood there like a statue, his expression stoic.

Fucking lying bastard!

I tore my gaze from him and looked back at Krystina.

"No. I can't..." I trailed off. I glanced at Justine, then down at my mother.

How long has Justine known she was here?

Anger and betrayal, painful levels I never knew to be humanly possible, sliced through me. It was a burning pain shredding through every inch of my body.

Then... I felt nothing.

I recalled reading a study about how the human mind could effortlessly construct the feeling of being out of body, as if you were experiencing a scene from the outside looking in. I saw myself standing in a comfortable and tranquil room. My mother sat on the bed pretending to walk her stuffed rabbit back and forth on her lap, almost like a small child would. She was humming, as if she too were in another world. Other people stood around me – Justine, Hale, Krystina. All were staring at me in expectation, but I was unable to find the words to describe what I was thinking.

"Alex," I heard Krystina say. She sounded far away.

Her hand touched my arm, pulling me back from the floating abyss and back into my body. I looked down at her hand, hoping to feel the familiar warmth I always felt when she touched me. However, I was numb. Then it occurred to me, I couldn't find the words I needed because there were no words to be said. I only knew I couldn't stay in the room any longer.

"I have to go."

I shrugged out of her reach and turned toward the door. Krystina called after me. So did Justine. But I just kept walking. It was all too much. My pace increased until I was in a full out run. I needed to get as far away from here as I possibly could.

30

Krystina

"Let him go, Krystina" Justine told me when I started to follow Alexander. I looked back at her.

"I can't just let him go! He's probably in shock."

"Yes, which is why you need to give him space to process. Alex has a temper. You'd be better off letting him alone so he can think."

I paused at the door when she said that. Alexander did have a temper, but he was usually careful to control it. However, having been on the receiving end of that temper once before caused me to hesitate. I was torn.

I glanced over at Hale, hoping he would give me some sort of guidance. His nose was badly bleeding, a sight that should have kept me rooted to the spot, as it was proof Alexander wasn't in the right frame of mind. Yet, I still wanted to chase after him.

"I don't know what to do," I said to him. He didn't respond, but the way his gaze held steadily to mine made me think he wanted to say something.

"Let's go to the lounge," Justine suggested. "Hale, go get cleaned up, then meet Krystina and me there. Maybe if we explain things to her first, she'll be able to get through to Alexander better than either one of us can."

Hale nodded and Justine stood. Turning to her mother, she said, "Lena, I'll be back in a little bit, okay?"

Once Justine seemed satisfied her mother would be okay, she led me to a quiet lounge area of the nursing home. She refused to speak until Hale joined us. It made me extremely anxious. The more time that lapsed, the more nervous I became. I needed to be with Alexander. I never should have let him go off alone.

When Hale finally entered the lounge a few minutes later, I rounded on Justine.

"I want answers. Now. And make it fast," I demanded.

Justine flinched from my harsh tone, but to her credit, her voice didn't waver when she spoke.

"I'm the one who shot our father," she announced, like it was some sort of grand statement. I didn't particularly care who killed him. I was more concerned over the fact Alexander's mother was very much alive, something that had been kept from him for over two decades.

"I don't give a flying shit about that!" I snapped. "Charlie already said as much in an interview to some sleazy reporter. I meant I want answers about your mother. I want to know why you and Hale hid the fact she was alive."

"I didn't know she was until a week ago," she explained, then darted her eyes in Hale's direction. "But Hale knew. He never told us because he was honoring a promise he made to my grandfather. Until recently, Hale believed my mom killed my father. Now he knows that's not the case, he had to come out with the truth."

"I don't understand," I stated testily, shaking my head back and forth in confusion.

"With your permission, I can explain, Miss Cole," Hale said quietly from his corner of the room.

"You don't need my damn permission, Hale," I bit out. "Just get it out already so I can get to Alex."

"I had just come off a stint in Japan. I was home on leave and decided to visit Lucille, Alexander and Justine's grandmother. Before I left her house, she asked me to stop over to the Russo's on my way home and drop off a loaf of banana bread."

It was strange to hear Hale refer to Alexander's family as the Russo's, but I didn't comment on it. I was too anxious to hear their explanation.

"I still don't recall you being there that day," Justine murmured. "I don't remember the weeks after either. I only remember..."

Justine trailed off, and Hale continued.

"When I got there, I found their father. He had been shot and had quite obviously been laying there for some time."

"Three days to be exact," I filled in.

"So Mr. Stone told you then?" he asked.

"Only what he could remember. He said the details were hazy."

"I bet they were," he said regretfully. "When I got there, both kids were like zombies. Their eyes were all glazed over, as if they were in an alternate reality."

"They had been living with a dead body for days, Hale. They had to have been traumatized," I said, annoyed I had to point out the obvious.

Hale shook his head, as if trying to clear his mind from the vision of two emotionally distraught children.

"Anyway, I found Helena, their mother, in the kitchen. It was evident from the state of the place that there had been a struggle. Chairs were toppled over. Dishes were broken. But...it was the blood. It was everywhere. The first thing I did was call their grandfather. I don't know why I didn't call the police first. Perhaps it was because of the dead man in the living room. I'm not sure. Either way, Helena was alive, but barely. Mr. Stonewall said ambulances took too long to respond to that area of the city, so he instructed me to take her to the hospital myself. He said he would meet me there."

"Then what happened?"

"Miss Cole, you have to understand. I didn't know what Mr. Stonewall's intentions were when I brought Helena to the hospital. He assumed, as did I, that his daughter shot her husband. Had I known what Mr. Stonewall was planning to do, I may have tried to talk him out of it before everything was set in motion. After all, it would have been easy for Helena to claim self-defense."

"I'm still not understanding. What did Alex and Justine's grandfather do?"

"When I arrived at the hospital, Mr. Stonewall was already there. He told the hospital staff his name was Ethan Stone, not Edward Stonewall. I was surprised by that at first, but then he registered Helena as Lena Silvestri. Lena was her nickname and Silvestri was Lucille's maiden name," Hale explained. "He also lied and said she was his wife's niece. Back then, hospitals didn't track patients by social security number and records were still all on paper. It was easy to give fake names. I knew what he was doing immediately. He was trying to protect her from a murder rap."

"That's ridiculous," I scoffed. "You said it yourself – it would have been easy for her to claim self-defense."

"I know that, but you didn't see him that day. He was so distraught. Worried. Furious. I can't explain it. He asked me a lot of questions about what I saw at the house. He wanted specific details. After I explained what I found there, he told me to go to the house and clean up any evidence of a struggle in the kitchen. He then instructed me to clean up when I could ascertain as Helena's blood only and find the gun but told me not to touch her husband's body. I didn't argue with him. That was my mistake. He was obviously grief stricken, not knowing whether or not his daughter would live or die. He wasn't thinking clearly. I just..." He paused, his voice cracking with emotion. "He was like a father to me. I couldn't say no to his requests."

I thought back to what Alexander told me about the gun. I probably shouldn't voice what I knew to Hale and Justine but, at this point, it didn't really matter anymore.

"You didn't find the gun, did you?" I asked.

"No, actually. I didn't."

"That's because Alexander thought Justine shot their father. She did, but he never knew for sure. In order to protect her, he threw the gun in the East River."

Hale shook his head again, but Justine remained silent after my revelation.

"The police came. They conducted their investigation, but with Helena missing and no murder weapon to be found, it went unsolved. If what you say is true, and Alexander threw the gun in the river, that's the piece of the puzzle I could never find," Hale said, seeming lost in thought. I shook my head, still trying to piece it all together myself.

"Alright, back to the story," I said, hoping to get more clarity. "None of this explains why Helena's whereabouts were kept from Alexander and Justine all these years."

Justine answered this time.

"My mother pulled through, but the damage to her brain was severe. I read through her medical records. Blunt force trauma, which I assume was the result of one of my father's drunken episodes. She wasn't right when she woke up. It was like she was a toddler and had to learn basic things all over again. Even her motor skills were nearly non-existent. After the first year of re-learning basic functionality, she stopped progressing. Now, she has the mind of a four-year-old, trapped in an adult body. She has no memory of me or Alexander at all."

A loose curl fell free of my ponytail and I hastily pushed it away. What Hale and Justine were saying was hard to process. However, I had a feeling we had just begun to scratch the surface.

"Justine, how do you tie into this?" I asked. "How long have you known it was actually you who killed your father?"

"I recalled what happened a couple of years ago. I was seeing my therapist, still trying to find ways to cope with issues I developed from childhood. However, I didn't remember a lot of specifics, and it made it hard to find an area of focus. My therapist suggested hypnosis. I wish he hadn't. There's a reason I blocked out the memories..." she trailed off and her gaze took on a haunted look.

I recalled Charlie's interview. In not so many words, he suggested Justine had been molested. As I stared at her tormented expression, I wondered if it was true and if that's what she was thinking about. I shuddered. Just the thought of a grown man touching a six-year-old girl was repulsive. Perhaps, in time, I would talk to Justine about it. The project I wanted to take on at Stone's Hope to help rape victims might help her cope with her past.

However, I was too angry at that moment to feel any sort of sympathy towards her. Needing to maintain focus, I stood and began to pace the room.

"You're selfish, Justine. After everything he's done to protect you. He's been second guessing every decision he's made over the years ever since he read Charlie's interview. How could you keep this from him? You knew he was looking for answers to the murder. Why didn't you tell Alex as soon as you remembered?"

"Why would I? You didn't know Alex back then," she said and began to sob. "He was obsessed with finding our mother for years. He had finally seemed to let it go around the time I realized I was the one who killed our father. Why would I dredge up a past both Alex and I wanted to forget?"

I lifted my arms in exasperation.

"Oh, I don't know. Maybe if you did, Alex wouldn't be dealing with Mac Owens right now. Or Charlie. Or any of it!" I exclaimed. My voice was growing louder by the minute. "He would have had answers! Did you know he planned to go to the DA on Monday? Can you imagine what could have happened if he did?"

"Nothing would have happened," Justine stated flatly. "Alex only had pieces of information. Most of his knowledge was circumstantial. The minute Hale told me about the article, I gave Hale the truth about what I did. I may have only been six years old, but I couldn't hide from it anymore. Once Hale found out it was me who shot my father, there was no need to keep my mother hidden. That's when he told me she was alive. Together, we decided to talk to the DA. We went last week Monday."

I stopped pacing and looked at Hale in surprise.

"Monday?" I asked him.

"Yes," Hale confirmed. "That's why I was really there that day, Miss Cole. I was meeting Justine. Running into you at the DA's office was a strange coincidence. I didn't track your phone. Samuel did tell me you went to a doctor appointment, but he had nothing to do with me finding you there. And, if you recall, I also told you that day to trust me. I said I was handling it."

"Handling it? You should have told Alex about his mother years ago," I said, my tone sounding more accusatory than I meant it to be.

"I know I should have," Hale admitted sadly. "My only defense is that I made a promise to Mr. and Mrs. Stonewall. They wanted their grandchildren to move on from the horrors of their past. They wanted them to be happy, living full and successful lives, just as Helena always dreamed they would have. They were heartbroken, but since they couldn't have their daughter, they were willing to sacrifice everything to make her wishes come true. I've never seen such devotion. Because of that, I vowed to watch over Helena and keep their secret safe, even if it meant never telling the truth to her children."

I shook my head, feeling like I was living a soap opera. It was all so surreal.

"I don't know what to think about any of this. I only know I have to get to Alex to make sure he's okay. He will be okay, right Hale? I mean, he's not at fault for anything."

"Alex will be fine," Justine assured. "There are still some things to sort out. Thomas Green said there isn't a case against me or Alex. However, we know there will be a lot of follow up questions for Hale. We don't know what will happen, but there will be an investigation. Hale understands his role in all of it and the possible consequences."

I didn't want to think about the amount of trouble Hale might be in. I didn't like the fact he kept Alexander's mother hidden for all of these years, but I understood it. He was only trying to protect the ones he loved. I could only hope the justice system would show some leniency.

"Hale, I'm assuming Alex left with the car. I need to get back to the penthouse. Can you drive me?"

"Of course, Miss Cole."

"Justine, don't disappear again. When I talk to Alex, I'll try to explain everything the best I can, but he's bound to have questions I didn't think to ask. If he does, you better be around to answer them."

"I will. I promise. And Krystina, please be careful," she warned.

"What do you mean?"

"I don't know what frame of mind Alex is in right now. I don't want him to push you away, or worse. Be careful with him. You might be the only one who has a shot at helping him through this."

31

Krystina

When I got back to the penthouse, I found it empty. Alexander was nowhere to be found. I tried calling his cell, but it went straight to voicemail. The same thing happened when I dialed the direct line to his office at Stone Enterprise. I sent several text messages to him as well. All went unanswered.

Time ticked by, the eerie silence in the penthouse almost scary. It gave me too much time to think. I tried turning on the stereo, but music only seems to make it worse. I shut it off after only having it on for ten minutes.

As the hours passed, I managed to completely psych myself out. I kept thinking of Justine's warnings about Alexander's temper. In my heart, I knew Alexander wouldn't hurt me. I wasn't afraid for myself, but afraid for him. Too much about his recent behavior was unsettling.

There were times when he acted like his typical controlling and assuming self. There were also moments when he showed me love and tenderness. All of those things I had come to know and understand. I could even empathize with the pain he felt from his past. My concern was about how tightly wound he had been recently. I knew the emotional strain from his nightmares had already taken their toll on him, but it was more than that. It was his constant mention of who he really was inside, like he truly believed there was a cynical monster just waiting to come out.

I didn't like it when he said things like that. If he was in that frame of mind, I didn't know what to expect when he returned. This latest development had to have made things worse. I was strong minded and determined but seeing him broken shattered me. I was terrified I wouldn't be able to put the pieces of him back together on my own. I didn't know if I was strong enough.

Until I could get a grasp on the situation and his mental state, I thought it best someone be with me while I awaited his return.

I picked up my cell and called Allyson. It rang five times before going to voicemail.

"Hey, it's me," I said. "Just wondering if you wanted to pop by for a bit. I could use some company. Call me when you get this."

I ended the call and silence fell around me once more. Never before had I felt so alone, even though I wasn't. Samuel was standing guard in the penthouse foyer. I wasn't sure why he was there, as he always left once I was safely inside. I suspected Hale told him to keep an eye on me. Whatever the reason was, I didn't want him there. He was a stranger to me and I wanted the company of someone familiar.

By six o'clock that evening, I still hadn't heard a word from Alexander. Pure panic began to set in, so I called Hale. As it turned out, he was just down one floor in his apartment. I asked him to come up.

When he got there, he sent Samuel away and we sat down

at the dining room table. He told me he had spent the afternoon trying to discover Alexander's whereabouts.

"What did you find?" I asked.

"Nothing. The GPS for his phone is off, so I can't track him," Hale said in a somber and regretful voice.

It was almost like Alexander didn't want to be found. I drummed my fingers on the tabletop and stared at my cell phone sitting on the table in front of me.

Ring. Please ring.

Feeling desperate, I decided to call Matteo. Perhaps he might have been in touch with Alexander. I snatched up the phone and pulled up his contact information. I waited impatiently for him to answer. After the fourth ring, he finally picked up.

"Hi, Matt. It's Krystina."

"Hello, my dear! I didn't expect to hear from you again so soon. What can I do for you?"

"Actually, I'm trying to locate Alex. Have you heard from him at all today?"

"No, I haven't heard from him since we left the club last night. Is everything alright?"

"Actually, it's not. I'm worried, Matt," I said, trying hard to control the anguish from showing in my voice.

"I'm assuming you tried his cell?"

"I did. It's off. He's not answering at the office either," I told him.

"What about Hale? He's almost always with Alex."

"Hale is with me. He can't track Alex either. He turned off the location services for his phone."

"Oh, that's really strange. It's unlike him to go off the grid like that. The only other time he did that was when..." Matteo trailed off and hesitated before speaking again. "What happened, Krystina?"

I blew out a frustrated breath. I didn't know how to explain it to Matteo without telling him everything. Alexander might not like it.

Oh, fuck it.

Finding him was more important, not to mention the fact everything would be all public knowledge soon enough. I quickly gave Matteo a brief rundown of what was going on. It was hard to explain it all without skipping too many important details, but I managed to get the gist of it to him in under five minutes.

"Shit. This isn't good," Matteo said when I finished.

"Don't you think I know that? That's why I have to find him. Do you have any idea where he might have gone?"

Matteo blew out a breath and was quiet for a moment, like he was trying to think.

"Actually, I think I have a pretty good idea."

I clutched the phone in my hand, desperate to hear his suggestion.

"Where?" I asked in a rush.

"Have you looked at Club O?"

My stomach dropped.

"No, I haven't looked there. Alex isn't a member there anymore," I replied, trying to keep the shakiness out of my voice.

"Go there, Krystina. I think you'll find what you're looking for."

Surely Alexander would not have gone there.

Or would he?

The panic I was feeling multiplied tenfold. It was suffocating and I almost couldn't breathe. Tears threatened and I forced myself to blink them back.

"I'll try, Matt. Thanks."

I ended the call and looked to Hale.

"What did Matteo say?" he asked.

"He said we should look at Club O."

Hale's eyes widened, as if he were comprehending something I didn't fully understand. He didn't say a word, but simply took his keys from his pocket and motioned for me to follow him. I didn't ask where we were going.

I already knew.

———————

THE DRIVE TO CLUB O, while it only took twenty-five minutes, seemed to be impossibly long. When we finally arrived and I stepped up to the large double wooden doors, I held my breath. I never thought I'd step foot in this place again.

"Is it safe to assume you're not a member?" Hale asked.

I blinked, momentarily confused.

"What?"

"If you're not a member, you won't be able to get in by yourself. I'm on the list here as being security for Mr. Stone. I can get you in if you need me to."

"Oh, of course," I said nervously and shook my head. "No, I'm not a member."

He nodded and opened the door for me. Once inside, we entered the main vestibule and Hale showed the doorman his credentials. After we were cleared, we continued on through, passed by the rock garden, waterfall, and marble statue of Venus. Goosebumps prickled at my nape as a feeling of déjà vu settled over me.

I struggled to relax, my nervous jitters heightening when the vestibule opened up to the cocktail lounge. The setting was just as I remembered it. People were milling about and chatting quietly. Some congregated near the expansive polished mahogany bar. Others relaxed casually on plush chaise lounges. I didn't see Alexander anywhere.

"He's not here," I said to Hale.

Hale's eyes continued to scan the room before coming to rest on me. He pressed his lips into a tight line.

"You're right. He's not."

"He might be downstairs in the club," I suggested.

"Perhaps. I'll take you down and we can check there."

I followed Hale down the long corridor that led to The Dungeon. The hallway split, revealing a wide staircase to my left. A chill raced down my spine as I looked up the stairs. Alexander had told me the common room and some of the private suites were up there. My heart began to pound wildly. The first time I came here, I was naïve and inexperienced. Now I knew enough about the lifestyle to know *exactly* what went on up there. I couldn't even begin to imagine the possibility of him being in any of those rooms. Watching. Or worse.

Please don't let me find him there.

I began to feel physically ill as I repeated the silent prayer over and over again. To whom I was praying to, I didn't know, as I was fairly certain no god ever set foot into this place. My stomach pitched and I shook my head to clear it. Refusing to believe Alexander would do anything that remotely stupid, I continued to follow Hale until we reached the massive stone gargoyle with the words "The Dungeon" written above it.

Hale pushed open the door and motioned for me to go on ahead of him. The loud drum of house music bombarded my ears from all directions. As I began to descend the stairs, I paused. I didn't know what I would find in the club, I only knew if Alexander was down there, I would need to talk to him alone.

I turned around to look at Hale and tried to drum up enough courage to display a confidence I didn't really feel.

"Actually, I've got this. You don't have to come with me," I told him.

"Are you sure, Miss?"

"Yes. If he's down there, I need to convince him to leave so I can speak to him alone, preferably someplace quieter than here. I'm afraid he won't listen to me if you're around."

He stared at me, seeming torn about whether or not to leave me alone in this place, but then eventually nodded.

"That's a fair assumption. I can wait in the car. Just...be careful down there."

Apprehension sent a hot flush over my skin. The thought of going downstairs alone caused me to break out in a nervous sweat. Suddenly feeling like I was suffocating in stifling heat, I shrugged out of my jacket and handed it to Hale.

"Thanks, Hale. I will."

After he was gone, I turned back to look down the long staircase in front of me. A lump formed in my throat as I put one foot in front of the other. My heart continued to hammer loudly in my ears, roaring over the thumping music.

What if he's not even here?

When I reached the base of the steps, I scanned the sea of dancing bodies. If Alexander was down here, I doubted he would be among them. More than likely, he'd be near one of the bars on the other side of the room. My palms pooled with sweat as I thought about navigating through the leather clad crowd. I glanced down at my own attire. I was wearing jeans and a black fitted cotton shirt. It wasn't leather, but at least I happened to be wearing black.

As I began to move through the crowd, I sent another prayer to whatever god might be listening. This time, I prayed for homogeneity.

32

Alexander

I didn't think about my mother, sister, and Hale. I wouldn't allow myself to think about any of them. I blocked it all out, including any thoughts of Krystina. She was too normal in a world that was incredibly fucked up. I never knew normal. It was foolish for me to believe I could have it with her. I was only lying to myself. I couldn't pretend anymore. This is where I belonged. It was what I knew best, and it was the only place I had complete control.

The waitress came by with another round of bourbon. She kept her eyes averted, never once meeting mine as she set the glass down. After she walked away, I picked up the glass and slowly sipped the aged liquor. Alone in my own corner of the club, I surveyed the people in Club O.

As always, the place was full of beautiful women, all exotic and different in their own way. I didn't know their names, but I didn't need to know. None of them knew my past and that's all that mattered. They would never ask questions about my life or try to get to know me. I wouldn't permit them too. The only thing I would allow them to ask for was my dominance.

My gaze continued to scan the room until I locked eyes with a curvy brunette nearby. I glanced down at her wrist. She was wearing a green bracelet. That meant she was free for any Dom who wanted to have her. She smiled and cast her eyes down, her way of inviting me to choose her. I expected to feel the familiar twitch of my cock that always happened when I was ready to move in for the kill. However, I felt nothing. I didn't want that woman. In fact, I didn't want any woman in here.

Annoyed, I tossed back the contents of my drink and signaled the waitress for another. Too focused on getting absolutely blitzed, I didn't notice the black-haired woman approaching my table until she was right in front of me. My eyes traveled up the length of her fishnet stockinged legs and curvaceous body. My buzzed mind barely registered her bracelet color before my gaze settled on the face of my very first submissive.

"Sasha," I said. I spoke her name in acknowledgment, but by no means was it a greeting or an invitation. I wasn't in the mood to deal with her tonight.

"Alex, it's good to see you." Her voice grated on my nerves and I looked past her dismissively. "Where's your pretty girlfriend tonight? What was her name again? Krystina?"

My head snapped to look at her. Her dyed hair fell in thin loose strands over her shoulders, and her face was painted with dark makeup. She was once beautiful, but her beauty had faded over time. Now, she looked haggard. My guess was too many Doms and possibly too many drugs had hardened her once perfect face.

"You don't get to speak her name. I will never hear it come from your lips again. Do you understand me?" There was an over-amplified edge of dominance to my tone, one that I knew came from being here. In this place.

She fixed her gaze on the floor, embodying the perfect submissive response. I raised my eyebrows when she took a step forward and lowered to her knees.

"Yes, sir," she said.

I rolled my eyes.

Oh, what the fucking hell.

"Get off the floor, Sasha. I'm not your damn master."

Her hand moved to my thigh and she chanced a glance up at me. Her eyes burned with need. I recognized the look. She was hungry, desperate to be dominated. However, I also knew her. She didn't crave me, but craved brutality. If she didn't get it from me, she would just move on to the next available Dom.

She shifted closer to me, her fingers coming dangerously close to my groin.

"Alex, we were good together. We could be again."

I looked away, not feeling a thing for the woman at my feet. She was pathetic and I wondered how I could have ever been with someone as spineless as her.

"That was a long time ago, Sasha. A very long time ago."

"I know what you like. Let me be the one to give it to you," she persisted.

I glanced down at the hand still resting on my lap. Even in my semi-drunk state, I knew I didn't want her. Not at all. But I did want to forget. To escape. She moved to slide into the booth next to me, her leather corset feeling hard and cold against my side.

"You're in my seat," said a familiar voice.

I looked up and saw Krystina hovering over the booth. A feeling of disbelief crashed over me, wondering how she tracked me here or how she managed to get through security. She looked beautiful standing there, with her hands on her hips and her eyes flashing. For a moment, it was as if everyone in the club had disappeared. All I could see was Krystina.

My angel.

That thought brought my reality to the forefront. I was the devil and I didn't deserve an angel. I scanned her up and down. Her casual attire was a stark contrast to Sasha's, as well as to every other woman in the place. It was another reminder of how good Krystina was. Too good for someone like me. She didn't belong here.

I saw her eyes dart down to Sasha's hand. It was still on my lap. Instinctively, I wanted to explain it wasn't what it looked like. I wanted to tell her I hadn't touched Sasha, nor did I even want her. My heart constricted from the accusation written plainly on her face. However, I didn't have the energy to explain anything to anyone. Even to her.

Don't feel. Just let her go.

It would be best if I let her make assumptions about the scene before her. It would give her an out from my fucked-up life. Krystina deserved better than me. The sooner she realized it, the better off she'd be.

"What are you doing here?" I asked coolly, leaning back and draping my arm casually across the back of the booth.

"I could ask you the same thing!" she lashed out, her eyes flashing angrily.

I looked over at Sasha. She sat in silence, waiting to for my response. She almost looked smug, as if she thought I would choose her over Krystina. The idea was almost laughable. She repulsed me.

"Get lost, Sasha," I told her. A pang of hurt momentarily shadowed her face, but she quickly recovered and got to her feet.

Walking over to Krystina, she leaned in and whispered something to her. I didn't know what she said, but Krystina's eyes widened until her expression became murderous. Her hands balled into fists as she pulled back to meet Sasha's gaze. For a moment, I thought Krystina might actually slap her. She didn't, but she did give her the iciest glare I'd ever seen her give anyone.

"You are nothing to him," Krystina hissed and jabbed a finger hard into Sasha's shoulder. Then she pivoted and slid into the space next to me where Sasha had vacated. Krystina stared hard at Sasha, almost challenging, yet clearly staking her claim. Sasha glared back at her momentarily, before laughing cruelly at her own private joke. She sauntered away with her hips swaying melodramatically in her wake.

"Well, now that was amusing. I thought I was about to have a cat fight on my hands. It could have been fun," I said. My tone was aloof yet mocking of the situation.

"Stop being a bastard and come home, Alex."

"I'm not going home," I told her and took a swig from my glass.

"You're not yourself and it's understandable after the day you had. However, I didn't just spend the last fifteen minutes being groped and molested for nothing. Come home where it's quiet and we'll talk."

My fingers clenched around my glass at her statement, tightening so much I thought it might shatter in my hands.

What does she mean by groped and molested? To think that some asshole in here thought he had the right to...

I looked at her wrist.

"Fuck, Krystina! You came in here without a bracelet? Are you stupid?"

She tilted her chin in defiance and I could almost visualize the steel rod running down her back.

"Not stupid. Worried. About you, dammit! I just forgot about the bracelet thing. It doesn't matter. I'm fine. You, on the other hand, are not. We can either go home and work through this, or we can talk it out right here in this..." she paused and waved her arm around angrily, her face grimacing in disgust as she motioned to the surrounding area. "In this fucking club. Take your pick, but I'd prefer to talk anywhere but here."

"I already told you. I'm not leaving."

She narrowed her eyes and glowered at me. I could almost see the steam furiously billowing from her ears.

"Fine," she bit out. "Have it your way. We'll talk here."

Krystina began to speak, her voice droning on and on amidst the loud music of the club, explaining everything Justine and Hale had told her. I was listening, but yet I wasn't. Her words seemed to fade in and out. Whether it was because my mind was clouded from drink or because I was in denial, I couldn't be sure.

Hale was only protecting us.

Following my grandfather's wishes.

Justine killed my father.

My mother was alive.

I didn't know if I was happy or sad about having the answers I had been in search of for so long. I didn't know what to feel at all about it. I didn't even care that Krystina was talking about it so openly and publicly. Rather than respond to anything she was saying, I swallowed the last of my drink and signaled the waitress for another.

When she brought it, Krystina snatched it from my hand.

"No," she snapped.

"Give that to me," I ordered harshly.

"You're not getting drunk, Alex. I won't let you."

"Too late, baby. I'm well on my way."

Her chocolate eyes gleamed with unshed tears, but I ignored them and wrestled the drink back from her. Amber liquid sloshed over the side of the glass, coating my hand and dripping onto the table. I looked at her as I slowly licked my fingers clean, eyeing her frostily as I did it.

"Why are you doing this?" she whispered.

"Because I can. It's who I am."

"You really do think you're just like him, don't you? Look at you, trying to prove a point by fulfilling some stupid destiny you conjured up. Sitting here in this club, getting drunk, acting like you're some big bad Dominant. Well, I've got news for you. Your behavior right now is anything but dominant. It's weak, Stone."

"The name's Russo. And it is high time I accept who and what I am."

"You're talking nonsense because you had too much to drink. This isn't you," she denied, shaking her head.

"It's not nonsense. It's the truth. You know it as well as I do," I spat out bitterly. "It's time for you to leave. I came here tonight to move on, and there's a whole slew of women out there ready to make me forget."

I said it deliberately to hurt her. To make her leave this place. However, I didn't anticipate the rage that boiled up in her, so hot and fast, I didn't even see it coming. In one swift motion, she slapped me square across the face. My cheek stung from where her palm connected with my face, leaving me momentarily stunned. However, I recovered quickly when I saw her hand rise again. I caught her wrist in the air and gripped it tight.

"Don't," I growled.

"You asked for it!"

"Do you really think you know me, Krystina? You want to go to a quiet place to talk," I said mockingly. "You don't want me alone in a quiet room. You don't know what I'm capable of. What's inside me, just waiting to come out. Keep pushing me and I will break you."

Her obstinate chin tilted upward again. Her eyes were still glazed with tears, but her expression was full of defiance as she stared me down.

"I dare you to try."

33

Krystina

Alexander led me down a dark corridor and shoved me roughly through a door near the end. After a quick glance around, my eyes widened in horror. A bed covered in black sheets sat ominously in the middle of the shadowed room, with a wooden grate of sorts hanging above it from the ceiling. Restraints lined the walls, along with a slew of other BDSM paraphernalia I only vaguely had time to process before I heard the door slam behind me.

I snapped to attention when I heard the click of a lock. I spun around to face Alexander, feeling beyond infuriated for the way he manhandled me. I was about to go off but stopped when I saw his face. It was dark. Menacing.

"You wanted someplace private? Someplace quiet? Well, here you have it," he growled as he moved toward me.

Before I could process what he was doing, he rushed at me. I went to take a step back, but he grabbed both of my wrists and pinned them behind me with one hand. With his other, he gripped my neck, spun me around, and shoved my chest hard against the concrete wall. I could feel his erection pressed up against my ass. I probably should have been afraid, but I wasn't. I was just royally pissed. This wasn't him. This wasn't *my* Alexander. And if he thought I would allow him to treat me like this, he had another thing coming.

With my face was pressed against the wall, I tried to wiggle free. I couldn't budge in his hold.

"Get off me," I hissed.

"No," he said into my ear, pushing his groin harder against me.

"Is this what it's come to, Alex? Am I just another random whore from your club? If that's how you want to treat me, then have at it!" I yelled.

His hold on me slackened at my words. Taking advantage of the opportunity, I pulled my wrists free and spun back around to face him. His face was only inches away from mine as I stared up at him. The smell of liquor was hot and pungent on his breath. His eyes were hollowed and dark, his chest rising and falling at an erratic pace.

I pushed against his chest, needing to find space, but I may have been trying to move a brick wall. He laughed at my feeble attempt but took a small step back. Grasping my upper arms, he looked me up and down, like he was trying to decide on what he wanted to do with me.

"Get undressed," he finally ordered.

Oh, hell no! Drunk or not, he's out of his fucking mind!

But I didn't voice the words, as I didn't want to provoke him further. His fury was of the likes I had never seen before. I knew why he wanted me to undress. He wanted to fuck away his anger. I even briefly contemplated doing as he wanted, knowing a quick roll might simmer his temper down a bit. However, as fast as it passed through my head, I quickly dismissed it. Sex wouldn't fix our problems – not this time. Giving in would be a mistake.

Instead, I tilted my chin up stubbornly to show my refusal. He was trying to prove a point by scaring me. It stung that he would stoop so low but, little did he know, I wasn't afraid. I knew the man beyond the façade. He would not hurt me.

"No, Alex. If you want me shackled to a wall, I'll be more than happy to oblige another day. I'll even help you secure the goddamn chains. But it definitely won't be happening today. Not like this."

He didn't respond but wrapped his hand around my ponytail and tugged. Hard. He brought his lips to the shell of my ear and whispered, his voice sounding broken and raspy.

"Why did you come here? You saw my mother's scar. He did that. I am capable of doing the same. Why are you tempting me?"

All my anger fell away at his words. The man I had fallen in love with, this powerful, physical, and captivating man, was allowing himself to be made small by things he had no control over. I knew in my heart he was wrong, but I just didn't know how to convince him otherwise. All my efforts to try to be there for him, to be his safe place, seemed to be in vain. Tears rushed to my eyes, falling in hot streaks down my cheeks.

"Alexander. Please," I sobbed. "This isn't you. I know it isn't."

He pulled back and stared at me long and hard, before eventually releasing his hold on me completely. His arms dropped to his sides and he took a few steps back.

"Go, Krystina. Get out of here. You don't belong here. In this place. In my fucked-up world. With me."

"I'm not going anywhere."

He staggered and, for the first time, I realized exactly how drunk he was.

"I said get out. Don't make this harder than it has to be. This is never going to work. I was foolish to believe I could have anything normal with you. Just go. Find another man to give you what you deserve."

Moving to the corner of the room, he collapsed down into a plush black velvet armchair. Bracing his elbows on his knees, he held his head between his hands. He looked defeated, but I refused to let him go down this easily.

I looked around the strange and foreign room, located in a place all too familiar. It was here, at Club O, where Alexander and I experienced the beginning of the end. While we eventually made our way back to each other, I had pushed him to his hard limit that night.

"Sapphire," I said quietly.

Alexander slowly raised his head to meet my gaze.

"What?"

"You heard me. I said sapphire."

"I know what you said. Why did you say it?"

"Because being without you is my hard limit – my only hard limit. You don't get to walk away from me, Alexander Stone."

He shook his head but didn't speak. I moved toward him, squatted down in front of him, and took hold of his hand. Raising it to my chest, I pressed his palm against my breast so he could feel the beat of my heart.

"Angel, what are you doing?"

"I left you once before. Here. In this place. But you eventually came after me. I won't leave you again, Alex. Not now, not ever. That day on the side of the road when my car broke down, we stood in the rain and you placed your hand over my heart. Do you remember?"

He blinked, as if trying to clear the fog in his brain.

"Yes."

"You forced me to acknowledge my feelings for you. My heart beat for you then, but it beats even stronger for you now. Please, let me take you home."

He searched my face through glazed eyes. I wasn't sure what

he saw, but he eventually nodded. When he stood, he wobbled. I took his arm and put it over my shoulder, barely able to support his heavy weight. Reaching into my back pocket, I pulled out my cell and dialed Hale.

"He's here, but in rough shape. I need you to help me get him home."

34

Krystina

"Are you sure you'll be okay? I'll just call off. I don't want to leave you," Allyson said. She sat across from me at the kitchen table of the apartment we once shared together.

"You already called in to work yesterday. I don't want you to get into trouble on my account. I'll be fine," I assured her. I picked absently at the buttered wheat toast Allyson had made me for breakfast. She insisted I eat, but I had zero appetite.

It had been over two days since I'd seen or spoken to Alexander – two days of agony, worry, and crying. After Hale and I got Alexander to bed on Saturday night, all the strength I displayed at the club left me and I completely broke down. The man I loved, the self-assured, confident, and beautiful man I knew, had been reduced to a hurtful drunk person I didn't recognize.

The fact he went to the club to forget about everything, even me, was almost too much to bear. But the idea of him turning to *her* ripped my heart into a million tiny pieces.

Sasha's words had been on repeat in my mind since that night.

"It's too bad you interrupted us so soon. He would have been fucking me in a matter of minutes. But he'll be back. They always come back. You'll never be enough for him."

Deep down, I knew I got there before anything happened between the two of them. However, I couldn't help but wonder about what she said and about what would have happened if I didn't arrive in time. I also worried her words about me not being enough for him rang true. Alexander said he didn't need the club as an outlet anymore, but what if he did?

Because of that, and because of the way he had deliberately tried to hurt and frighten me, I needed time to think. Hale understood this and offered to keep watch over him on Saturday night. He suggested I go to Allyson's for the night, so I did. Although, one night ended up turning into three. Now, it was Tuesday morning, and I had yet to hear from Alexander. There had been no phone calls from him. No texts. No emails. Just nothing.

"Anything new from Hale or Justine?" Allyson asked.

"Not yet today," I responded. "The last text from Hale came last night. He said Alex was okay and was still sorting things out."

"Yeah, well he'd better sort out some kind of apology to you soon before I get my hands on him. I still can't believe he hasn't returned your calls."

"Me either, Ally," I said sadly.

My eyes burned, threatening a new wave of tears. I didn't want to worry Allyson anymore, so I blinked them back, surprised I even had any tears left.

"I'm going to stay home today," Allyson insisted again.

"Ally, don't be ridiculous. I feel guilty enough over the fact I've called in to work two days in a row. Don't add to it. I'll be okay, really. In fact, I'm going to shower and try to get some work done from home today."

I didn't add the reason I wasn't going into the office was because I couldn't risk running into Alexander. She already knew that. I wasn't avoiding him, but simply doing as requested. According to Hale and Justine, Alexander needed space. If that's what he needed, I could give it – even if it killed me in the process. I just hoped he didn't need space for too much longer. As upset as I had been, I missed him so much. Every time my eyes closed, he was there. I felt empty without him, lost in a black hole of misery. I wasn't sure if I could go on living this way for much longer.

"Promise to call if you need me? Even if you just have to cry it out for a minute, I'll listen," Allyson said, her expression full of worry.

"I promise. Now get out of here before you're late," I scolded.

"Love you, doll," she said, her voice full of compassion. Coming around to my side of the table, she gave me a fierce hug. Once she broke away, she walked to the front door and grabbed her coat off the wall hook. "He'll come around. I know he will. He loves you too much not to."

I smiled weakly at her.

"I know."

After she left, I sluggishly made my way back to my old bedroom. I glanced at the foot of the bed and saw my laptop sitting open. Waiting. Just waiting for Alexander to respond to my email. While he hadn't responded to any of my texts, maybe he had too much to say and replied to my email instead. Hoping for a response, I sat on the edge of the bed and opened my inbox.

Nothing.

What if he misunderstood what I said? Had I said the wrong things? Should I have said more?

I knew I should have followed him when he left the nursing home. I never should have let him go off alone, but I didn't know if he understood my regret. Feeling unsure about the words I had written, I clicked on the email I sent to him on Sunday night.

To: Alexander Stone
From: Krystina Cole
SUBJECT: I'm sorry

Alex,
Hale and Justine said you needed time. I don't like having to go through them to find out how you are. I want to talk to you. I don't know why you need time away from me, but I will respect your wishes until you sort things out.
I know I screwed up. I never should have let you walk away from me. You shouldn't have been alone after the shock you received and I'm sorry for that. Perhaps if I followed you, we wouldn't be here right now. My only excuse is I was torn. I wanted answers for you, yet I was scared at the same time. I was scared for you. And if I'm being perfectly honest, I was scared for me too.
I don't want to be afraid. I love you and I miss you so much. Please call me when you're ready.

All My Love,
Your Angel
XOXO

I meant what I said in the email, even if I did sound like I was close to begging. However, I didn't particularly care. I knew we both screwed up Saturday night, but this time I was willing to shoulder all the blame. It was as if he were my air, and I felt like I was suffocating without him.

Closing the laptop, I stood and went into the bathroom. I turned on the faucet in the shower, barely registering what I was doing. Everything I did over the past two and half days seemed to be in slow motion, like nothing more than a measured blur.

The bathroom mirror began to cloud with steam as I stripped out of my sweats and t-shirt. Climbing into the shower, I pressed my forehead to the tiled wall and allowed the piping hot water to flow over my back. I imagined it was rinsing away all the pain and agony I felt during Alexander's absence.

I washed my hair and body methodically until eventually the water began to run cold. Stepping out of the shower, I dried my body and wrapped my hair up in a separate towel on top of my head. Moving over to the sink, I watched the clouded mirror begin to clear and my gaze fell on my reflection. There were dark shadows under my eyes brought on by lack of sleep. But they also had a hollow look I didn't recognize. My cheeks were flushed from the heat of the shower, a sharp contrast to the rest of my pale, almost ashen colored skin. Dropping the towel, I looked at my naked body in the mirror.

I recalled a time when I would critique my reflection, judging all the flaws and imperfections. I wasn't overweight by any means, but I would still feel self-conscious about my behind that I thought was just a little too big, or my breasts that were slightly too voluptuous. I didn't do that anymore, as Alexander taught me how to appreciate my body. He made me feel beautiful. Treasured.

I ran my hands slowly up my hips, past my breasts, until my arms crossed my chest and a hand rested on each shoulder. I stared back into my own eyes through the mirror. They looked tired, devoid of the spark and fire Alexander always said I had.

This isn't me.

I was not the type to just sit and wallow and wait. I wasn't pitiful. I was strong. I was a fighter. And it was high time I fight for Alexander. For us. Letting him walk away was a mistake and I knew it. Now, he had taken enough time.

What if he doesn't want to see me? What if it's all too much and he doesn't want me anymore?

I pushed the thoughts aside, not wanting to think about the what-ifs. I needed to take back what was mine. Resting my palms against the edge of the counter, I leaned in toward the mirror.

"You can do this," I said to my reflection.

Feeling suddenly reenergized with a sense of purpose, I quickly bent to scoop up my towel from the floor. Wrapping it around my body, I made a dash for the bathroom door. I didn't know where Alexander was at that exact moment, but I was confident Hale did. The faster I got dressed, the faster I would be able to get to him.

I threw open the bathroom door in a rush, only to smack hard into the chest of someone on the other side. I staggered and they grabbed my arm to steady me. I looked down at the hand gripping my arm and froze, unable to look up. I didn't have to. I knew who it was. I would recognize the strong lines of those fingers anywhere. I closed my eyes and breathed deep, knowing I would inhale that familiar sandalwood and all male scent that never failed to make me weak in the knees.

I slowly lifted my head and ran my eyes over the features of the man who held me in his grasp. Two days' worth of stubble marred his skin, but he was still raw, potent, and gorgeous as ever. My gaze settled on the hypnotizing sapphire blue eyes I adored so much. The vulnerability revealed in them was laced with just enough ruthlessness to let me know he was back. Gone was the man I found in the club. Standing before me was the man I fell in love with.

"Alex," I whispered.

35

Alexander

My words, everything I'd practiced that morning, got caught in my throat as I stared down at Krystina. She looked exhausted, as if she hadn't slept in days, but she was still stunning and beautiful. I reached up and pulled the towel from her head. Rich, brown curls tumbled free, damp from her recent shower. I ran my fingers through them, trying to remember the many things I wanted to say to her.

"Angel, I..."

I wanted to pull her close to me. To hold her. To kiss it all away. But I hesitated. After the way I treated her, she may not want me to touch her. I wouldn't blame her if that were the case. I was a complete asshole. She should make me beg for her forgiveness.

Trying to get a read on what she was thinking, I carefully studied her face. Her eyes were moist with unshed tears. She looked confused, yet relieved at the same time. My hands still held her arms, but she didn't try to shrug me off. I took that as a good sign at the very least.

"How are you?" she whispered.

I had a thousand answers for her question, but I didn't voice any of them. Instead, I walked over to retrieve the overnight bag sitting on the floor in front of her old dresser. Seeing it there pained me, as I didn't want to acknowledge that I'd allowed us to spend the last three nights apart. I didn't dare glance down at her bed, as images of her being alone under the lily comforter was almost unbearable. I had slept on the couch in my office, unable to even look at the bed we shared, knowing she wouldn't be in it.

I unzipped the bag and began to rifle through it in search of clothes for her. Pulling out what I needed, I returned to her. She watched me curiously but didn't speak.

"I don't want you to catch a chill while we talk," I explained. Kneeling in front of her with a pair of lace panties, I tapped her leg. "Step in."

Still silent, she did as I told her to. I slowly pulled the undergarment up her legs until it was in place. Turning her so her back was to me, I pulled the towel from her body. As I stared at her naked back, my dick throbbed. Dressing her was extremely odd. I was accustomed to taking her clothes off, not putting them on. It killed me not to touch her, to keep my hands from running over her smooth curves and tight ass, but it was not the right time. She didn't need seduction or dominance. She needed my humility.

Reaching around her torso, I slipped each of her arms through the straps of her bra and secured the hooks at the back. After sliding a cream-colored wool sweater over her head, I turned her to face me once more so she could step into a pair of jeans. Once I fastened the button at the waist, I bent to scoop her up behind the knees. Cradling her in my arms, I carried her out to the living room. I set her down on the sofa and went back into the bedroom to get a hairbrush.

When I sat down beside her and began to brush out her hair, she finally spoke.

"Alex, what are you doing?"

"Taking care of you and treating you like the angel you are to me. It's how I should have been with you the other night when you came to me at the club."

"You were upset. I understand," she said, although not very convincingly.

"No. There is no excuse for the way I behaved. I can't begin to explain how sorry I am, angel. Everything you said to me that night was correct. My behavior was weak."

She looked down at her hands. She was fidgeting. As if noticing her nervous habit, she clamped her palms together and turned to look at me.

"Why haven't you returned my calls?" she asked quietly.

I set the brush down on the coffee table and tried to formulate the words that would make her understand.

"You don't know how bad I wanted to call you. To hear your voice. I took that time away to figure some things out. Dragging you through the gauntlet of hellish emotions I went through just wouldn't have been fair to you, especially after the way I acted on Saturday night."

"I could have helped you through it, Alex. I can't help if you push me away. You don't have to do this alone."

"Perhaps, but I felt like it was more important for me to get my head screwed on straight first. I didn't want to risk hurting you again. It was like something dark triggered inside me. I can't explain it, but it was very disturbing. The things I said to you..." I trailed off momentarily as a wave of shame and regret rolled through me. "I didn't mean them. I can't stand the thought of you not being mine."

Taking a chance, I wrapped my arms around her and pressed my lips lightly to her forehead. She didn't push me away but closed her eyes and seemed to melt into me. Leaning back, we both settled into the deep cushions of the couch.

"I didn't recognize who you were that night, Alex. It was like a stranger was saying those things to me. You did hurt me, but I know you were hurting more. I know why you went to the club and why you tried to push me away. Everything in your life is out of balance, and that's the one place where you feel you can have total control. Yet, you failed to recognize one thing – me. All you had to do was talk to me."

There was something in the tone of her voice. I couldn't place it, but it made my heart hammer in my chest.

"What are you thinking?"

"I'm thinking you feel like you have to deal with this mess all by yourself. You never let me in. In fact, you never really have. It makes me wonder if we can be a real husband and wife someday. It's more than sex. Obsession. Desire. We have to be able to be friends too."

It would have hurt less if she stabbed me in the chest with a knife. The pain on her face damn near destroyed me. I reached up to cup her cheek, my chest so tight it was hard to breathe.

"I know that and I'm sorry, angel – so very sorry. I don't know how to make this right. I love you and I need you. In fact, that's the only thing I've been sure of these past few days. I'm nothing without you."

She stared back at me for a long while, her expression distant and untouchable, as if she were trying to hide the feelings she was trying to sort out.

"Where have you been for the past two and a half days?" she finally asked.

I exhaled the breath I hadn't realized I was holding.

"A lot of the time was spent with my mother and her doctors. I wanted to learn more about her and her condition, the prognosis and long-term care options. The rest of the time was spent with Hale and Justine. I'm pissed about what Hale did, about what Justine did. But I can understand it to an extent. This is my grandfather's doing more than anything. Hale was stuck. His only mistake was he didn't tell me after my grandfather passed."

"So, are you and Hale okay then?"

"Samuel is going to be picking up some of Hale's duties for a while. I need some distance from Hale right now. My relationship with him needs time to heal, angel. It's not going to happen overnight and he understands that. At the very least, I didn't fire him completely. He's still in my employment. In fact, the ribbon cutting for Stone Arena is tomorrow. Hale and Justine are going to handle it. I'm not going to it."

"Why not?"

"I don't know how to explain it, but I'm having a hard time with the idea of celebrating an arena I only pushed for because of my grandfather. I don't know what I think about him at the moment. It's going to take a while to sort out my feelings about what he did."

She nodded her understanding.

"What about any legal trouble for Hale?"

"I've spoken with Thomas Green. The situation is sticky. He needs to look more into the statute of limitations, but even if it falls within, any investigation is going to be tough. As of right now, it's basically just a story. There's little to no evidence to support it. I suspect it will be dismissed and the case will finally be closed after more than twenty years. Only time will tell. And, as a result, Mac Owens no longer has an article to publish."

She sat up straight and turned to face me.

"Really? No PR mess? How did you manage that?"

"I spoke to Owens, too. Off the record, of course. You can imagine his surprise when I called," I smirked. "I gave him the truth, or at least a very loose variation of it. Once I did that, there were too many holes in Charlie's interview. I suspect Mac

Owens will be back eventually once he looks into the info I gave him, but it is what it is. He knows publishing Charlie's version would be career suicide for him. Plus, there's no proof or anyone to corroborate it."

"Not even Suzanne?"

"Justine assured me she doesn't know anything of real importance. The only thing she knows is that our name used to be Russo. I'm not too worried about it anymore."

"What about Justine? How are things with you and her?"

I felt my jaw clench and had to force myself to relax.

"They're okay," I offered as a response.

"Okay? She makes me so angry," Krystina spat out and her eyes flashed. "I'm not happy about what Hale did, but she knew she was the one who killed your father for years and she never said a word. It was selfish and cowardly."

I sighed, knowing every word Krystina spoke was the truth. But Justine was still my sister. And just like Hale, I could never turn my back on her completely. My relationship with her also needed time to heal.

"She did act selfish, but there's no changing it. I suspect things might never be the same between us again. I don't know. Only time will tell. Hanging on to anger in the meantime won't help matters."

Krystina softened at my words and settled back into the crook of my arm.

"You're right, Alex. It's time to let go of the anger. All the hurt," she murmured. "Considering the chaos of the past week, it now looks like everything is all tied up in a neat and tidy bow."

While she had openly participated in the conversation and asked questions, she now seemed far away in thought. So far away. I worried I wouldn't be able to reach her. My gut knotted, knowing what she was thinking. She had been through so much because of me. I was afraid she was questioning whether or not it was all worth it.

"Not everything is all tied up neat and tidy, angel."

She looked up at me, her eyes wide and full of so many emotions. Anger. Sadness. Confusion. And love. I still saw love.

"What about us, Alex? Where do we go from here?"

36

Krystina

My gaze held steady to Alexander's.

"Where do we go from here?" he repeated. "Well, I was hoping you'd still like to take that walk down the aisle."

That fact he would even question it astounded me. I was resolute in my decision to marry him, but I did think it was safe to assume he would want to wait until the dust settled before we tied the knot.

"Alex, of cour –."

"Wait," he said and help up a hand to silence me. "Before you say yes, I need you to listen. I love you so much it hurts. But there are few things that are going to change – things I didn't plan for that I need you to be on board with. If you can't be, I'll understand."

My heart began to pound rapidly, wondering why he would think I wouldn't support what he needed. I loved him irrevocably, without any sort of stipulations. Yet, it seemed as if he was going to give conditions to me. Apprehension crept into my bones.

My brow furrowed in confusion for a moment before the realization dawned. I nearly stopped breathing as a shiver raced down my spine.

"A playroom. You're making us a playroom," I stated, my voice coming out in almost a whisper. My pulse began to race as he gripped the nape of my neck and leaned in to whisper in my ear.

"On Friday night, I saw your body wrapped in leather and lace. On Saturday night, despite the terrible circumstances, I got to see you in a shadowy setting surrounded by whips and chains. Just the idea of combining the two makes me inexplicably hard. And, if I recall correctly, you did say something about helping me secure the chains that would bind you to the wall."

"Shackled. I said shackled," I breathed the correction.

His fingers began to trace small circles near the hairline of my neck.

"As twisted as it sounds, I can't seem to get that image out of my head. I don't plan on ever stepping foot inside Club O again, but I did realize something as a result of that night. You were right when you said I needed that outlet. But it was never to release violence like I once thought. It's for my pleasure. It's what I enjoy. And with you, I can't ignore it. I can't explain how much I get off on seeing your strong spirit willingly submit to me. So, I'm creating a playroom of our own. That is, of course, if you still want me," he added and pulled away to look at me. His eyes were intense when he met my gaze. "Do you still want me, Krystina?"

The tone of his question was low and husky. Goosebumps pebbled over my skin. I wasn't sure if it was from the idea of a playroom or from the potent way he was looking at me. There was no doubt I still wanted him. However, his gaze was so penetrating, the words got caught in my throat.

Tears began to well hot in my eyes and threatened to fall. It didn't matter what his past was. He was still Alexander. He was still mine. He would always be mine. I reached up and cupped the side of his beautiful face.

"Yes, I still want you. I want forever with you," I whispered.

Alexander grasped my shoulders, his sapphire eyes blazing fiercely with love and possessiveness, before tugging me into his embrace. I clung to him, absorbing the moment for a long while. When he pulled away, he leveled his gaze to mine. His expression was serious.

"Pick a date," he said.

"A date?"

"Yes, for our wedding. I *want this set in stone today*. Right now."

God, he's always so demanding.

I contemplated toying with him over it and tossed him a cheeky grin.

"Oh, well...I don't know," I said slowly.

"So help me, Krystina," he began in warning. I laughed and swatted at his arm. It felt so good to be here with him. In this moment. It was where I belonged and where I planned to stay for a very long time.

"You make it too easy," I kidded. "But, if you insist on picking a date today, I was thinking about sometime in the summer. I kind of fancy a certain boat docked at Montauk Marina."

"You want to get married on *The Lucy*?" he asked, almost sounding incredulous.

"Only if you want to. It was just an idea," I shrugged and looked down at my lap, trying to sound indifferent. The fact of the matter was, I had been thinking about getting married on his boat for a while now and couldn't get the images of a sunset wedding out of my head. But, if Alexander had a different idea, I'd be open to it. I didn't want to fight anymore, especially about the most important day of our lives.

Alexander reached up and took my chin in between his fingers. Lifting my face to meet his gaze, I found his blue eyes alight with happiness.

"Miss Cole, I can't wait to call you Mrs. Stone and I think getting married on *The Lucy* is an absolutely perfect idea."

37

Krystina

The summer had been exceptionally warm and humid, even by New York standards. However, today was comfortable with temperatures in the mid-seventies. A gentle breeze danced off the waves of Lake Montauk, causing water to lap against the docks and boats at the marina. I closed my eyes and listened to the soothing sound coming in through the porthole of *The Lucy*. It was rhythmic and relaxing, and worked wonders to soothe my tremulous nerves.

After a few minutes, I opened them and stepped up to the full-length mirror in the master suite of the boat. Running my hands down the sides of my wedding dress, I took in the exquisite satin. My stomach was a ball of nerves, but not so much I couldn't appreciate how incredible the gown felt on me. Inspired by Inbal Dror, my dress designer created a backless satin bridal gown with hints of lace. Of course, her creation didn't go without input from my mother, Justine, and Allyson. They suggested embellishments be added to the plunging V-shaped backline. It was now scattered with clear sequin beading set on lace, giving the gown that hint of simple elegance I was looking for.

I fingered the pearl spaghetti straps as I took in my reflection. The straps dipped into a sweetheart neckline, accentuating the curve of my breasts without revealing too much. Not wanting to bother with my unruly mass of curls, a stylist came on board that morning to do my hair. She styled it half up and half down, leaving most of it to cascade down my back with just a few curls left free to frame my face. My veil wasn't overly long, the pearl edges stopping just below the tips of my hair.

"Oh, love! You look stunning!" my mother gushed as she entered the suite. I smiled at her through my reflection as she stepped up behind me.

"You don't think my makeup is too much?" I asked.

"Absolutely not. It's delicate and natural. It's just perfect!"

We stood together in the full-length mirror, a million unspoken words passing between us, before I turned to face her.

"Thank you, Mom."

"For what?"

"For helping me plan all of this. I never thought you would do it, but when you jumped right in, it meant the world to me. I know you've had your reservations about me and Alex, but –," I stopped, my eyes welling up with tears. I was suddenly feeling overly emotional, all of my childhood memories coming to the forefront of my mind.

"Now, now. Don't do that. You'll mess up your makeup," she chided.

"No, really. I know the sacrifices you made for me years ago after my father took off. Then, when I was ten years old and you got together with Frank..." I trailed off, unsure of how to explain what I thought about her marriage to my stepfather.

"Krystina, I know what you think about my marriage. You

think I didn't marry Frank for love. In some respect, you are correct. Frank offered a means to an end at a time when I could barely afford to put food on our table. But I knew he was a good man and I cared deeply for him. Eventually, I did fall in love with him. He was very persuasive," she added with a light laugh. "Perhaps I didn't fall for him in the conventional way, but it did happen."

"Does Frank know? I mean, that you didn't love him in the beginning?"

"Oh, I suspect he might. That could be why he's always spoiled me so much. You know how he dotes on me and likes to take care of me. That's why, when I saw you and Alex together, I got scared."

"Scared? What do you mean?"

"Alex has a possessive way about him. He looks at you like there's not another soul on the planet, like he would move mountains for you. I've only seen one other man look at a woman the way."

"Frank," I said immediately. "He looks at you like that."

She smiled softly and nodded.

"I knew it wouldn't be long before Alex staked his forever claim on you, and I was right. But," she added.

"There's always a 'but'," I laughed.

"But, don't go having babies right away. You have years to do that. Take some time to get to know each other first," she advised.

My mother reached down to squeeze my hand just as the door to the suite burst open. Allyson came hurrying in, her arms laden with flowers, boxes, and who knew what else. I could barely see her burgundy maid of honor dress behind all the things she was carrying.

"Delivery!" she sang.

"Ally, what is all that?" I asked as she placed everything down on the settee. She picked up a huge bouquet of cream-colored lily's and handed them to me.

"These are from Alex, along with this," she said and handed me a small gift box with a note card attached. I set the items aside with the intent of opening the card and gift box in private.

"What's the rest of the stuff, Ally?"

"Something borrowed and something blue," she stated matter-of-factly. I had nearly forgotten the tradition. "We talked about you borrowing my pearl necklace, so this works perfectly for your something borrowed."

She pulled the necklace out of its case and held it out to me. Moving in, she reached around my neck and secured the clasp. I smiled my thanks as I touched the pearls resting near my collarbone.

"I know my dress is the something new, but what about the something blue?" I asked. "To be honest, I never even thought about it."

"Oh, don't you worry about that. Your mom has you covered there," Allyson assured.

I turned toward my mother. Tears shone in her eyes as she picked up a shallow rectangular box Allyson brought in. She opened it up and pulled out a white scrap of material with blue embroidery.

"Your grandmother, although you don't remember her, was a hopeless romantic," my mother explained. "On the day you were born, she had this made for you. It's a handkerchief with your name embroidered on it in light blue. Of course, naturally I asked her why she chose blue instead of pink. She told me I was to give this to you on your wedding day so you would have your something blue."

I smiled.

"And you kept it all this time?"

"Of course, I did! She'd come back to haunt me if I didn't!" my mother laughed.

"I guess that just leaves my something old," I murmured,

glancing over to Allyson's pile. There didn't appear to be anything of use, as our flower bouquets were the only things left sitting there.

"Open your gift from Alex," Allyson suggested. Her eyes were sparkling with mischief. I narrowed my gaze at her.

"Have you been scheming?"

"Obviously," she said with feigned exasperation. "I am the maid of honor after all. It's my job to think of the things you forget."

Curious about the tiny box from Alexander, I picked up the note card that came with it and slid my fingernail under the envelope seal.

"In the flush of love's light, we dare be brave. And suddenly we see that love costs all we are and will ever be. Yet it is only love which sets us free." ~ Maya Angelou
I love you, angel.
Alex

For Alexander and me, our love did dare us to be brave. Together, we beat the odds, and now we were free. Tears prickled at the corners of my eyes. It was a real struggle to keep them from falling, but my mother was right. I had spent an hour perfecting my makeup and I didn't want to mess it up.

I blinked rapidly and took a deep breath. Once I was more composed, I picked up the box and tore the seam of the gift wrap. Inside was a small jewelry box with an emblem on top. It was one I recognized well, as I had been running their ad campaigns for months.

Beaumont Jewelers.

I shook my head. Although he never admitted to it, I had a sneaky suspicion Alexander had something to do with me landing that contract. With everything else happening, I realized I didn't have the time to worry or care about it.

Alex will be Alex.

I smiled to myself. Cracking the lid, I slowly opened the jewelry box until a stunning pair of triskelion earrings came into view.

"Oh, wow!" I breathed.

"This is your something old because the center diamonds belonged to Alexander's grandmother," Allyson told me and pointed to the sparkling gems in the middle of the triskelion's. "They used to be stud earrings. She wore them on her wedding day. He had them removed from the setting and placed into these earrings for you."

I stared down at the pair of intricate spirals. Round diamonds and tiny pearls dotted and sparkled throughout the design, but not so much as to take away from the fire and beauty of the center stones. The tears I blinked back earlier began to well up again and I heard my mother sniffle. I looked up only to find her and Allyson both crying. The sight of them opened the floodgates.

They hurried to my side and wrapped me in a fierce group hug.

"My baby is getting married," my mother sobbed.

"I am," I choked out, hardly believing it myself.

A knock at the door interrupted us.

"Who is it?" we all yelled in unison.

"It's Matteo," said the familiar male voice from behind the door.

"Is it bad luck for the best man to see the bride before the wedding?" Allyson asked. She dabbed the corners of her eyes with a tissue before passing a separate one to me.

"No, I don't think so," I said with a shrug. "But who cares? It's Matteo."

When my mother opened the door, Matteo took one look at the three of us blubbering and shook his head.

"It's not a funeral! Why are you all crying?"

"Alex gave Krys earrings," Allyson explained.

"Ah, say no more. But, as much as I hate to break this up, it's almost time. Besides, Alex has been pacing like a crazy man all morning. I've never seen him in such a state. If you don't get down that aisle soon, I wouldn't put it past him to come in here and haul you down the aisle himself."

"He totally would, too," I laughed.

Matteo and my mother went on ahead and left Allyson and me alone. She picked up her small bouquet and handed me the larger one.

"Are you ready, doll?" she asked.

"As I'll ever be." I smiled at my best friend, suddenly feeling overwhelmed with nostalgia. She was always there for me, and now here she was, with me again, on the most important day of my life.

We walked out of the master suite and stopped when we reached the bottom of the glass staircase. I gave her arm a light squeeze before she could head up.

"Thank you, Ally."

"For what?"

"For pushing me to take a chance with Alex."

She grinned and winked.

"I believe I told you to have a little fun. I never said anything about marriage," she laughed and tossed me a wink. "Come now. Your husband-to-be is waiting."

The climb up the glass staircase seemed to take forever. With every step I took, warm memories of Alexander and I came flooding back. From our chance meeting at Wally's, to the day Alexander proposed, to the endless nights entwined in passion – images of it all consumed me.

I also remembered the heartache. I recalled how empty I was when I left him. I could envision his face twisted with worry over my abduction and car accident. Then there was his controlling nature and my own stubbornness to give in, inevitably resulting in numerous fights and arguments. His nightmares, although now coming less and less frequently, would not be something I'd soon forget either.

However, Charlie's trial was now behind us. Our relief finally came when he received a twenty-year sentence. It meant we didn't have to worry for a long time to come. Our home was near completion and all the arrangements had been made to move Alexander's mother. It still pained him to see her mental state, but it wasn't enough to keep him away. After regular visits, she now recognized both of us, even if she doesn't know who Alexander truly is to her. Justine and Hale's relationship with Alexander was still slightly strained but improving. Only time would heal the wounds enough so they could move past everything that had happened.

Despite it all, the heartache and stress paled in comparison to all the good Alexander and I shared. Even his possessive and domineering side was overshadowed by his moments of love and tenderness. I knew we were stronger together than we were apart and I welcomed a lifetime of accepting the good with the bad.

Until death do us part...

I could barely believe it was happening – we had finally made it to this day, withstanding it all. I almost wanted to pinch my arm to convince myself I wasn't dreaming.

When I reached the top of the stairs, a white runner lined with chairs and guests came into view on the expansive open deck. I did a brief scan of the crowd, hoping the distraction would calm my nerves.

I saw Mr. and Mrs. Roberts and a few others from Wally's. The staff from Turning Stone sat near the back with Laura Kaufman and Gavin Alden. Angelo and Maria Gianfranco were also there with their children, surprising me by closing La Biga so they could all come. Stephen, Brian, Samuel, and Justine sat in the row behind my Mom, Hale, and Vivian. There were also others that I didn't recognize, presumably business associates of Alexander's. Everyone stood when they saw me and my heart began to pound in my chest.

The pianist began to play "Can't Help Falling in Love", the song we chose for me to walk down the aisle to. We opted to skip the traditional wedding march since Alexander and I were anything but traditional. However, as my vision blurred with tears, I wondered if we should have stuck with the traditional and mundane. The song, while there were no vocals to accompany the piano, didn't stop me from singing every lyric in my head.

"...Take my hand. Take my whole life, too. For I can't help falling in love with you."

I closed my eyes to blink the threatening tears. When I opened them again, my gaze settled on Alexander. He was standing on the far side of the deck under a trellis covered in thick ivy and white lilies.

My breathing hitched and I faltered. It was as if I were seeing him for the first time all over again. He stood still with his hands clasped in front of him, his stance slightly parted, accentuating the broad span of his shoulders. His white tuxedo highlighted the golden tan of his face and near black hair. Even from where I stood, his blue gaze was piercing, devastating, just as it was on the day we first met. The man was a force of nature and he was waiting for *me*.

He stared down the aisle and our eyes locked. Gone were the people, the boat, the pianist. All I could see was him. His smile shown bright, beckoning me to make my way toward him.

I don't remember Frank taking my arm and I don't remember walking down the aisle. Yet, I must have because, before I knew it, Alexander was directly in front of me and reaching for my hand. The way he looked at me caused me to tremble. I may have been covered in satin and lace, but his eyes burned so deeply, one could swear I was stripped bare.

"Angel," he said in a husky voice.

That one word made my heart swell until it was near bursting, effectively banishing the nervous jitters plaguing me. Alexander was about to become mine, and I was about to become his.

The celebrant began the ceremony, but Alexander's gaze never left mine. The only time we looked away from each other was when the celebrant cued us to collect our wedding bands from Allyson and Matteo.

"A wedding ring is a symbol of unity. It's an unbroken circle that embodies a promise. Wherever life leads them, they will always come back to each other. As Krystina and Alexander exchange their rings, they have opted to recite their own vows they wrote for each other," the celebrant announced. Turning to me he asked, "Krystina, are you ready?"

"Yes," I whispered, nearly sobbing tears of joy on the word. I stared into the eyes of the man I loved and began reciting the vows I had written from my heart. "I take you, Alexander, to be my partner for life. I promise, above all else, to live in truth with you and to communicate completely and fearlessly. I vow to have the patience love demands, to speak when words are needed and to share in the silence when they are not. I give you my heart as a sanctuary of warmth. You will always find home within my embrace. As I join my life to yours, I vow to love you with all my body, mind, heart, and soul."

My hands shook as I slipped the platinum band onto his finger, but I never once pulled my eyes from his. When he began to speak, his voice was thick with emotion and it was as if the world stood still. All I could hear were his words.

Alexander

I LOOKED DOWN at the most beautiful woman I ever laid eyes on. I was about to make her my wife. My throat clogged as a surge of emotion welled up in me. I almost couldn't speak. But then she smiled softly, her chocolate brown eyes so full of love, and my voice returned.

"Krystina, I love the spark that's inside you," I told her. I reached up to touch her face with the hand she had just placed my wedding band on. "Your eternal glowing flame is my light in the darkness. You've taught me how to feel. Your mind stirs my soul, your touch soothes me, and your devotion gives me strength. My vows to you are not only my promises, but my privileges because you have chosen to give yourself to me. I enter into this life with you without reservation, without fear or confusion, but with a clear heart and sound mind. You are my past, present, and my future. When you accepted my engagement ring, it was more than just a diamond to me. For diamonds, like angels, are unique. They cannot be made, but only found. You are *my* angel, my diamond in the rough, and I found you. I promise to cherish our love as a love everlasting."

I vaguely remember the celebrant telling me to kiss her, but neither of us needed his encouragement. When we leaned into one another and pressed our lips together, we sealed our love with a fierceness only Krystina and I could understand.

It was a kiss I'd never forget for as long as I lived. The Fates had tested us and brought us both humbly to our knees. But with our mouths molded as one, we proved we could overcome their odds and create something truly magical.

Together.

After the ceremony drew to a close, we posed for pictures and went through the traditional cake cutting. Before long, the reception on *The Lucy* was in full swing. Krystina and I opened up the dance floor to everyone in attendance after our first dance, but that first dance ended up turning into many. We probably should have been mingling with our guests, but I couldn't bring myself to break away from her. I wanted her to stay wrapped in my embrace, swaying to the music, all night long.

As we danced, I leaned down to place a gentle kiss on her lips. I absorbed the moment, adding her kiss to a mental box of memories from the day.

When I eventually pulled my lips from hers, I smiled down at her. However, she didn't return my smile. Instead, she suddenly looked frantic.

"Angel, what's wrong?" I asked in alarm.

"I was just thinking I don't want to forget one second of today. And about how – how," she faltered. "And about how our wedding story will be one we tell our children and grandchildren."

"Yes?" I prompted, completely bewildered about why she seemed so panicked.

"Babies. I want them," she blurted out.

I felt a slow smile began to spread over my features, as images of a beautiful little girl with wide brown eyes and curly hair formed in my mind.

"I think we might be able to arrange that, Mrs. Stone."

"Really?" she asked, as if surprised I was so quick to agree.

"Yes, really," I chuckled and tossed her a mischievous wink. "As soon as we kick everyone off this boat and set sail for the Caribbean, I think we should get straight to work on making them."

"Oh, I..." she faltered again. "I don't know if I want them right now. I only meant..."

I laughed again, the sound coming deep from within my chest. She was just too damn adorable. I spun her around, twirling her on my finger, before bringing her back to me. I placed my hand against the warm skin of her spine, appreciating the open back of her wedding dress as I drew her close.

"How about we just practice while on our honeymoon? We'll have plenty of time to talk about when we should have children later."

She relaxed then and met my gaze, her eyes twinkling under the lights of *The Lucy*.

"We do, Alex. In fact, we have a lifetime."

"Look at you two!" I heard Allyson chime from behind us.

My brow furrowed in aggravation over the interruption as Krystina turned to look at her friend.

"What about us?" she asked.

"I remember telling you a while back that I would have an I-told-you-so moment. Well, here it is. The two of you literally melt my heart. I need to take a picture of you."

She whipped out her phone and snapped a photo before either of us could even react. I shook my head and held out my hand.

"Give me that phone, Allyson."

She arched a confused brow but handed over her phone.

"What are you doing?" Krystina asked me.

"I'm taking a selfie," I announced matter-of-factly.

I held out the phone in front of us, but Krystina wouldn't stay still long enough for me to snap the picture. She was too busy laughing hysterically.

"Taking a selfie? Now that, Alexander Stone, is the one phrase I never thought I'd hear from your mouth."

"Calm yourself," I scolded, but there was no heat to my words. I, too, was grinning just as broadly as she was. "Say cheese."

Instead of doing as I asked, she turned and planted a kiss on my cheek just as I took the picture.

"Sorry, I couldn't help myself," she laughed and I frowned at her.

"You know, I noticed you never mentioned honor or obey in your wedding vows," I pointed out.

She tossed me a sassy grin.

"Did you honestly expect me to?"

I shook my head.

"Oh, you really are glutton for punishment. Will you ever be able to follow my directions?"

Her smile broadened.

"Probably not."

The right side of my mouth quirked up in amusement.

"Angel, that's exactly what I'm counting on."

To be continued...

WISHING STONE

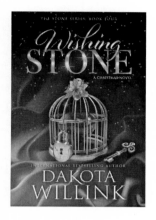

Thank you for reading *Set In Stone*! Want to see where Alexander &
Krystina go next? Check out *Wishing Stone*, a Christmas novel that
sets the stage for the final installment of Alexander and Krystina's
epic love story.

Grab your copy of Wishing Stone today!

**He could give her anything her heart longed for—except one
thing.**

Alexander

I refused to be trapped in hell ever again.

But even devils have dreams.

If I had one wish this Christmas, it would be to give Krystina what she
desperately wanted more than anything—a baby.

I would do anything for my wife, but that was before the world fell into chaos. Too much had changed and fear of the madness surrounding us was all-consuming.

I had to protect the woman I loved above all else—even if it meant keeping her locked in a gilded cage.

Krystina

Alexander promised to love me forever, but just like all great loves, we had our challenges.

My husband was provocative and commanding, but we'd found our groove. Our connection was fierce and the attraction unending. There were no more secrets and no more lies.

At least, that was what I told myself.

But some secrets were meant to be kept hidden—even if only for a little while. After all, the best gifts weren't always found under the tree.

If you loved *The Stone Series*, check out a some of the other books in my catalog!

The Sound of Silence

Meet Gianna and Derek in this an emotionally gripping, dark romantic thriller that is guaranteed to keep you on the edge of your seat! This book is not for the faint-hearted. Plus, Krystina Cole has a cameo appearance!

Fade Into You Series

What's your favorite trope? Second chance, secret baby, suspense, enemies to lovers, sports romance? *Untouched, Defined, Endurance* will give you all that and more! Prepare to be left breathless!

MUSIC PLAYLIST

Thank you to the musical talents who influenced and inspired *Set In Stone*. Their creativity helped me bring Krystina and Alexander to life.

Playlist now available on Spotify!

"Walk" by Foo Fighters *(Wasting Light)*
"The Way I Do" by Bishop Briggs *(The Way I Do - Single)*
"Blame" by Bastille *(Wild World)*
"Alive" by Sia *(This Is Acting)*
"La Vie En Rose" by Louis Armstrong *(Louis Armstrong's All-Time Greatest Hits)*
"So Cold" by Breaking Benjamin *(We Are Not Alone)*
"Drive" by Glades *(Drive - Single)*
"Falling Short" by Lapsley *(Understdy - EP)*
"Listen" by Claire Guerreso *(Listen - Single)*
"Roadside" by Rise Against *(The Sufferer & The Witness)*
"Chained to the Rhythm" by Katy Perry feat. Skip Marley *(Chained to the Rhythm)*
"Shape of You" by Ed Sheeran *(Ed Sheeran - ÷ Deluxe)*
"Can't Help Falling in Love" by Haley Reinhart *(Can't Help Falling In Love - Single)*
"Feeling Good" by Muse *(Origin of Symmetry)*
"Firestone" by Kygo feat. Conrad Sewell *(Cloud Nine)*

BOOKS & BOXED WINE CONFESSIONS

Want fun stuff and sneak peek excerpts from Dakota? Join Books & Boxed Wine Confessions and get the inside scoop! Fans in this interactive reader Facebook group are the first to know the latest news! JOIN HERE: https://www.facebook.com/groups/1635080436793794

OFFICIAL WEBSITE
www.dakotawillink.com

NEWSLETTER
Never miss a new release, update, or sale!
Subscribe to Dakota's newsletter!

SOCIALS

ABOUT THE AUTHOR

Dakota Willink is an Award-Winning and International Bestselling Author. She loves writing about damaged heroes who fall in love with sassy and independent females. Her books are character-driven, emotional, and sexy, yet written with a flare that keeps them real. With a wide range of published books, a magazine publication, and the *Leave Me Breathless World* under her belt, Dakota's imagination is constantly spinning new ideas.

The Stone Series is Dakota's first published book series. It has been recognized for various awards, including the *Readers' Favorite* 2017 Gold Medal in Romance, and has since been translated into multiple languages internationally. The *Fade Into You* series (formally known as the *Cadence* duet) was a finalist in the *HEAR Now Festival Independent Audiobook Awards*. In addition, Dakota has written under the alternate pen name, Marie Christy. Under this name, she has written and published a children's book for charity titled, *And I Smile*. Also writing as Marie Christy, she was a contributor to the Blunder Woman Productions project, *Nevertheless We Persisted: Me Too*, a 2019 *Audie Award* Finalist and *Earphones Awards* Winner. This project inspired Dakota to write *The Sound of Silence*, a dark romantic suspense novel that tackles the realities of domestic abuse.

Dakota often says she survived her first publishing with coffee and wine. She's an unabashed *Star Wars* fanatic and still dreams of one day getting her letter from Hogwarts. She enjoys traveling and spending time with her husband, her two witty kids, and her spoiled rotten cavaliers. During the summer months, she can often be found taking pictures of random things or soaking up the sun on the Great Lakes with her family.

ACKNOWLEDGMENTS

This past year has given me a lot to be thankful for. There are so many individuals who have helped me on this journey. When people say it takes a village, it is a complete understatement.

To the ladies of Team Dakota - I cannot express how much I appreciate your hard work. I also want to thank you for your patience, as I'll probably need another Google Spreadsheet made before you finish reading this (shhh...no eye-rolling allowed). Without your amazing talents, Krystina and Alexander's story would not have reached the audience that it did. You are simply the best!

To the beta team – as always, your feedback is immeasurable. A lot of time and effort goes into the beta process and I don't know if I'll ever be able to thank you enough! A special shout out goes to Amanda - thank you for making me "feel" the music again.

To Lacy and Jeffrey - for bringing Krystina and Alexander to life. Lacy, you believed in this story so much. Your words of wisdom and friendship will always be treasured. Thank you for being you.

To my mom, the strongest woman I know – you are the woman who defines the full circle. You create, nurture and transform. Thank you for your acceptance and unending support.

To my charming and witty teenagers – thank you for understanding the many late nights I spent tapping away on the computer. But, mom is now back from the writing cave. Your rooms better be clean.

To my husband...my best friend, my rock, and my number one fan. You made me believe the sky was the limit. It was a roller coaster of a year, but your support for my writing career never wavered. I love you so much, babe.

And finally, I'd like to thank the readers. This book is dedicated to you, as words cannot define how grateful I am for the many relationships I've made with readers from around the globe. I wouldn't be able to write full-time without your continued love and dedication to my stories. Whether you picked up a copy, shared with a friend, or are one of my beloved Diva's in my Facebook reader group - you have helped me chip away at my goals one page at a time. You believed in Krystina and Alexander as much as I did and I can only hope I did their conclusion justice. Love you all!

Made in United States
North Haven, CT
20 July 2022

21594591R00205